TEXTERMINATION

Also by Christine Brooke-Rose from Carcanet

Brooke-Rose Omnibus
(*Out, Such, Between & Thru*)

Amalgamemnon
Xorandor
Verbivore

Christine Brooke-Rose

teXtermination

CARCANET

First published in Great Britain in 1991 by
Carcanet Press Limited
208–212 Corn Exchange Buildings
Manchester
M4 3 BQ

British Library Cataloguing in Publication Data
Brooke-Rose, Christine
Textermination.
I. Title
823.914 [F]

ISBN 0 85635 952 1

The publisher acknowledges financial assistance from
the Arts Council of Great Britain

Set in 10¹/₂ pt Bembo by Koinonia Limited, Bury, Lancs
Printed and bound in England by SRP Ltd, Exeter

Acknowledgements

The dialogue and the descriptive or narrative sentences by or about the literary characters in
this novel are always by its author, except for occasional quotations, both from classics and
from modern authors. The modern quotations, all under the regulation three hundred
words, are from the following texts: Elias Canetti, *Auto da fe*; Angela Carter, *The Magic
Toyshop*; Carlos Fuentes, *Terra Nostra*; Ismaïl Kadaré, *Avril brisé* (translated by me from the
French translation, permission obtained from the author); Lars Gustafsson, *La mort d'un
apiculteur* (translated by me from the French translation); Toni Morrison, *Beloved*; Milorad
Pavić, *Dictionary of the Khazars: A Lexicon Novel in 100,000 Words*; Thomas Pynchon, *The
Crying of Lot 49*; Philip Roth, *The Counterlife*; Salman Rushdie, *The Satanic Verses*; Christa
Wolf, *Kassandra*.

1

so that Emma found, on being escorted and followed into the second carriage by Mr Elton, that the door was to be lawfully shut on them, and that they were to have a tête-à-tête drive. It would not have been the awkwardness of a moment, it would have been rather a pleasure, previous to the suspicions of this very day; she could have talked to him of Harriet, and the three-quarters of a mile would have seemed but one. But now, she would rather it had not happened.

She sat still in her corner, her hands crossed over her reticule. The restless, changing light of the lanterns fell, through the small windows in the screen that separated the driver from the inside of the landauer, and she noticed that she had done well to sit on the side where she had entered, for she was not alone, as she had been in the theatre-box. Goethe sat next to her. She was not afraid. One is not afraid of such things. She merely shifted a little deeper into her corner, a little further away, gazed at the light-spattered countenance of her neighbour and listened.

He wore a wide coat with an upstanding red-lined collar, and held his hat on his lap. His black eyes under the rocky brow with its jupiter hair, now unpowdered u.s.w.

Guten Abend, meine Liebe, sagte er mit der Stimme, mit der er einst der Braut aus dem Ossian, dem Klopstock vorgelesen. Then he half apologised for having had to abandon her this evening, for having remained so invisible all these recent days, and wished to compensate, from artistic pleasure he insisted, by escorting her home. That is, back to the Gasthaus Zum Elephanten.

Das ist sehr artig, Excellenz Goethe, erwiderte sie, and as she speaks, Emma realises that she has boarded the wrong carriage. Despite her relief at not having to face, for the billionth time or so,

1

the scene with Mr Elton, more disagreeable than she yet knows, she wonders how she comes to be speaking in German, and whether she can keep this up without becoming quite other. Which is worse, she now asks herself, involuntarily leaping forward in time: to misread a man's suit to her as addressed to someone else and suffer the vexation of her error but at least to be in power still and able to repair; or to be thus misread by someone else unknown to her and quite beyond her control?

Goethe is rambling on. Have you not embraced your beloved sister towards yet a longer separation u.s.w. Ach, spotte meiner nicht! she counters to gain time, but the split tremour in her soul is becoming dangerous. Mr Knightley loves to find fault with me you know – in a joke – it is all a joke. We always say what we like to one another. She has tried to jump back to the beginning but Goethe's voice seems to take her forward to the end of nowhere, another Leben dass ist nur Wandel der Gestalt, Einheit im Vielen, Dauer in dem Wandel. Und du und sie, ihr alle seid nur Eine in meiner Liebe – und in meiner Schuld. Nein, Goethe, sagte sie. Ich kam nur but why? Whose love? Whose guilt? She is on her way to church, to pray for existence.

But does Emma ever go to church? Lotte draws her wrap further over her narrow white dress, which has violet ribbons and bows this time, instead of the usual pink ones. She has worn white dresses with pink ribbons since the beginning of her stay in Weimar, and blushes at her attempts, as a now alte Dame, to jostle the elderly Excellenz back into those happy, tragic days with Werther. She realises she must have continuously looked grotesque, nobody wears these wide skirts now, so delightful to run in. The fashions have slowly gone from simpler to simpler still, and women look like tubes. She knows from trying that she can't wear such dresses at her age and yet to her, it is the tubes that seem grotesque.

But Goethe hasn't read Werther for decades, never noticed perhaps, does not, probably, remember the dress. After all he got her eyes the wrong colour! She feels obliterated, weak from lack of involved attention, easily taken over by young Miss Woodhouse who has moulded Harriet into being in love with Mr Elton. But what can Emma do? Her only experience of old men is Mr Woodhouse, hardly a good substitute for Goethe, and this is not even Werther's Goethe or Bettina von Arnim's Goethe but someone else's. Nor would she ever wear a wide white dress with violet ribbons or even pink ones all over it, even at twenty-one, let alone at an age she can never reach.

Léon seized Emma, in silken peachy crinoline and black hooded cape, by the arm and almost dragged her out of the cathedral, pursued by the importunate Swiss guide who wanted to take Léon up to the spire and now offers him some twenty volumes about the building. Imbécile! grommela Léon s'élançant hors de l'église, and calls on a streetboy to find him a fiacre. – Ah! Léon! ... Vraiment ... je ne sais ... si je dois! ... C'est très inconvenant, savez-vous? – En quoi? repliqua le clerc. Cela se fait à Paris. Et cette parole, comme un irrésistible argument, la détermina. Cependant le fiacre n'arrivait pas. Léon avait peur qu'elle ne rentrât dans l'église. Enfin le fiacre parut. – Où Monsieur va-t-il? demanda le cocher. – Où vous voudrez! dit Léon en poussant Emma dans la voiture.

It went down the rue Grand-Pont, crossed the place des Arts, the quai Napoléon, the pont Neuf, and stopped before the statue of Pierre Corneille. Continuez! said a voice from within. It continued, down the slope from the carrefour Lafayette and entered the railway station at a gallop. No, straight on! cried the same voice. The fiacre went out of the gates, then trotted gently along the Cours among the elms. It went along the river, by Oyssel, beyond the isles (etc). Marchez donc! cried the voice more furiously. And so on.

Then, towards six o'clock, the carriage stopped in a small street of the quartier Beauvoisine, and a woman came out of it, who walked with her veil down, without turning her head.

You have missed the diligence sir, and lost your place, unless you would like to climb into my calèche to catch it up, for the post goes faster than public transport, said the traveller to the young man, pronouncing these words with a strong Spanish accent and wrapping his offer in exquisite politeness.

Although his face was dark, he looked markedly ecclesiastic, all in black, with powdered hair, his shoes of Orléans calf with silver buckles. He was walking along the river near Marsac, smoking a cigar. The young man, though well dressed in a light brown cutaway coat, white duck trousers and white cravat, appeared shabby and dusty. His fair hair was unpowdered and he had jumped from the vineyard onto the road carrying a large yellow sedum he had just picked. Without waiting for the young man's answer the Spaniard took a cigar-case from his breast-pocket and presented it open for Lucien to take one.

I am not a traveller, Lucien answered, and I am too near the end of my course to take pleasure in smoking.

You are very severe on yourself, the Spaniard replied. Although I am honorary canon of Toledo cathedral I allow myself a small cigar now and then. God gave us tobacco to soothe our passions and our pains. You seem to have some great sorrow, or at least to be carrying the symbol of such in your hand, like the sad god of marriage. Take one. All your sorrows will go with the smoke.

But Lucien replied drily that no cigars could dissipate his sorrows, and his eyes filled with tears. Nevertheless, after more conversation, Lucien postponed his attempt at suicide by the river and climbed into the priest's calèche. They talked all the way to Paris.

The carriage continued gaily to climb the mountain road. It was a black coupé with rubbered wheels, of the kind used as cabs in the cities. The seats were upholstered in black velvet, but there was also something velvety about its pace, for it moved more easily on this bad road than seemed possible, and perhaps it would have done so more silently without the panting of the horses and the clicketing of their hooves, which the velvet upholstery couldn't muffle.

Still holding his wife's hand in his, Bessian Vorpsi leant his head towards the windowpane as if to make sure that the small town they had left half an hour earlier, the last at the foot of the Rrafsh, the high Northern plateau, had vanished from view.

The Mountains of Malediction, he murmured in a slightly trembling voice, as if to salute a long-awaited apparition. He felt that the solemnity of this name impressed his wife, and was pleased.

She leant her face towards him and he breathed the scent of her neck.

Where are they?

Still very far.

She left her hand in her husband's and settled back against the velvet.

In fact she felt very happy. The last few days before their marriage, in the semi-artistic semi-elegant world of Tirana, their future honeymoon had been the talk of the town. Her friends envied her, saying: you will escape from the real world into a world of legends, the world of true epic, so rare here. They evoked the oreads, the rhapsodes, the

4

last Homeric hymns on earth and the Kanun code of the mountaineers, ruthless but majestic.

Inside the diligence, the comfortable citizens all showed their contempt for Boule de Suif, clearly a girl of easy virtue. But as the heavy carriage, which had left occupied Rouen for Dieppe, advanced slowly through the snowy countryside, hunger began to nibble at them. Boule de Suif was the only one who had brought provisions.

Through the same cold sunshine, and the same sharp wind, my Lady and Sir Leicester, in their travelling chariot (my Lady's woman, and Sir Leicester's man affectionate in the rumble), start for home. With a considerable amount of jingling and whip-cracking, and many plunging demonstrations on the part of two bare-backed horses, and two Centaurs with glazed hats, jack-boots, and flowing manes and tails, they rattle out of the yard of the Hotel Bristol in the Place Vendôme, and canter between the sun-and-shadow-chequered colonnade of the Rue de Rivoli and the garden of the ill-fated palace of a headless king and queen, off by the Place of Concord, and the Elysian Fields, and the Gate of the Star, out of Paris.

Sooth to say, they cannot go away too fast … Fling Paris back into the distance, exchanging it for endless avenues and cross-avenues of wintry trees …

'You have an unusual amount of correspondence this morning?' says my Lady, after a long time. She is fatigued with reading. Has almost read a page in twenty miles.

'Nothing in it, though. Nothing whatever.'

'I saw one of Mr Tulkinghorn's long effusions, I think?'

'He sends – I really beg your pardon – he sends,' says Sir Leicester, selecting the letter, and unfolding it, 'a message to you. Our stopping to change horses, as I came to his postscript, drove it out of my memory … He says … Will you do me the favour to mention (as it may interest her), that I have something to tell her on her return, in reference to the person who copied the affidavit in the Chancery suit, which so powerfully stimulated her curiosity. I have seen him.'

My Lady, leaning forward, looked out of her window.

'That's the message', observes Sir Leicester.

'I should like to walk a little,' says my Lady, still looking out of her window.

'Walk?' repeats Sir Leicester, in a tone of surprise.

5

'I should like to walk a little,' says my Lady with unmistakable distinctness. 'Please stop the carriage.'

And when the carriage stopped, Augustin Meaulnes woke from his trance to realise that it had brought him into a strange domain, fairylike with festivity. But Clarissa Harlowe was horrified to find herself in a six-horse carriage with Lovelace, a man she did not love. She must write to Miss Howe about it.

The Gould carriage was the first to return from the harbour to the empty town. On the ancient pavement, laid out in patterns, sunk into ruts and holes, the portly Ignacio, mindful of the springs of his Parisian-built landau, had pulled up to a walk, and Decoud in his corner contemplated moodily the inner aspect of the gate.

A gloved hand appeared between the curtains of the litter.

If the times were more propitious I wouldn't need the protection of my men. I shall never trust to yours, Guzmán.

Then the hand drew the curtains.

The naked castaway thought he had sunk into the sea; he opened his eyes: the blood beat in his temples and the sight of this desert of scattered mists wasn't very different from what he had seen at the bottom of the ocean (etc). At the moment when he opened his eyes, the curtains of the litter parted and instead of the sea, the desert, the fire, the mist, he met another pair of eyes.

Is it him? asked the woman who was looking at the young man as the young man looked at the woman's black eyes sunk deep in the orbits above the high cheekbones, very brilliant in contrast to the silvery pallor of the face; which looked at him without knowing that he too, through the sanded lashes that veiled his eyes, was also looking at her.

Show me his face, said the woman.

And later: Take him.

But later also, on the same spot near the Point of Disasters, a voice from a small black coach:

Who is it?

A castaway.

No, a heretic (and so on).

To hell with whether he is son of Allah or Moses. Kill him, that'll solve it.

They seize the sticks planted in the sand, brandish them, pass them between the legs and under the arms of the halberdiers, they knock your ribs, threaten you among laughs and toothless cries and spits while the halberdiers drag you along the dunes pummeling you with blows and insults; the beggars grumble through clenched teeth, the monk returns to his flock of prisoners, and you, you are dragged towards the slow little coach with the drawn curtains.

Señor Caballero, sea Usted quien sea, permanezca quieto y agradecido. And there begins the long monologue of Juana la Loca.

He had tied the rope, disentangled at last, to a drainage breach in the parapet, he climbed on this parapet and prayed with fervour ... At last he began to slide down that astonishing height ... About half-way down, he felt his arms lose strength, he even thought he had lost the rope for an instant; but soon he had it again, perhaps, he thought, held by the brushwood on which he slid and got scratched. He felt a sharp pain between his shoulders, that almost stopped his breath. There was a very inconvenient undulating movement; he was constantly sent from the rope to the scrub. He was touched by several fairly large birds he had woken which threw themselves at him in their flight ...

At last he reached the bottom of the big tower without other harm than his bleeding hands. As he arrived in the gardens he fell into an acacia which, seen from the top, had seemed four or five feet high but was really fifteen or twenty. Falling from this tree, Fabrice almost broke his arm. He began to run towards the rampart, but his legs seemed like cotton; he had no strength left. In spite of the danger, he sat and drank a little eau-de-vie and fell asleep for a few minutes ... Waking up he couldn't understand why he could see trees in his prison-room. Then the terrible truth returned. He walked towards the rampart and climbed a large staircase. The sentinel was snoring. He found a gun-carriage in the grass and tied his third rope to it; the rope was too short and he fell into a muddy ditch with more than a foot of water. As he stumbled up and tried to get his bearings he was seized by two men: he was afraid, but soon heard a low voice in his ear: Ah, monsignore! monsignore! He understood vaguely that these men belonged to the duchess, and immediately lost consciousness. Later he felt carried by men who walked silently but fast; then they stopped, which gave him great anxiety. But he had no strength to speak or open his eyes, he felt he was being embraced; suddenly he recognised the perfume of the duchess' clothes. It revived him; he opened his eyes; he was able to say the words: Ah! chère amie! then he fell again into a deep faint …

The duchess lost her head completely on seeing Fabrice again; she was pressing him convulsively in her arms, and then was in despair at seeing herself covered with blood: it came from Fabrice's hands; she thought him dangerously wounded. Helped by her men, she was removing his clothes to bandage him when Ludovic, luckily nearby, forced the duchess and Fabrice into a small carriage hidden in a garden near the city-gate, and they left at full speed to cross the Po near Sacca.

They are all on their way to San Francisco, to the annual Convention of Prayer for Being. There they should recover, after an unimaginable journey, to savour what remains of international ritual for the revival of the fittest.

Emma looks down through the round-cornered double window at what a voice says is Newfoundland, several worlds it seems below. She has never seen the sea. The sea, her father has said, is rarely any use to anybody. She has never even been to Box Hill, only seven miles from Highbury. And yet, for some decades now, she has been travelling all over the world, seeking some new kind of existence.

Next to her sits a slim young man in black, reading a prayer-book. It's in Latin, it must be a breviary. He must be a romanic priest. But she feels him sidling his eyes more than occasionally from the breviary to her high-waisted golden-shrouded bosom. How mortifying. Beyond him is another lady in ridiculously voluminous silken skirts, peach-coloured, for which she needs two seats. Skirts from olden times, as in ancient portraits, except that she wears a peculiar bonnet. It's true that she herself was caught up in evening dress as she got into the carriage after the reception at the Westons. She would never travel like this, and feels uncomfortable. But at least it's narrow and simple. She draws her cloak round her. She notices, however, that the young man's eyes are now straying towards the other lady rather more often and the lady, oh shame, seems to respond. Emma turns back to the window.

This is a cheap charter-flight which has gone over the North Pole and all the way South across the whole of Canada and North America to Atlanta, Georgia. Mr Knightley is called George, but she always calls him Mr Knightley, although he always calls her Emma. But he is considerably older, he has seen her grow up. She could never call him George. Except, perhaps? But she never reaches that point. Slowly the aerobrain lurches down over Atlanta and lands.

The airport is as vast as England as she knows it. She queues at Immigration and then at last it's her turn to advance from the black line to the curious sentinel-box six feet away from the line. The officer asks her how she comes to have a dual passport, half British, half German, with two different dates of birth. Is she called Emma or Charlotte Woodhouse? Or Frau Hofrätin Kestner, from Wetzlar? When the shadow passport vanishes in the bright glare she is allowed through, and as she picks up her travelling case she hears the same question of the person behind her: is she Emma Bovary or the Duchess Sanseverina-Taxis? An over-zealous official, she thinks, not quite right in the head. The duchess is let through. Emma hears instructions in a voice that has the by now familiar colonial accent – oh no, she mustn't say that any more. She follows signs through curved and angled corridors that slope down then up, and down moving stairways to a long vehicle like a hundred yellow coaches all smoothly boxed into each other, called a train, which takes people from the International to the National Flights.

Lotte is almost shade-like with fatigue. At her age, to be put through all this! Goethe has got lost. She stops a moment to get her breath. A middle-aged Spanish priest offers help with her over-numerous bags but she refuses. A handsome young man marches gaily along in a brown cutaway coat and voluminous white cravat, followed by a young priest. And then an elderly man. Ah, says Lotte, there is Goethe. How old he looks. He walks fraily along, upheld by a tall young woman. Who can that be, die Fürstin? She waits for them, fearful, indecisive. But Goethe bows to her politely as he hobbles up. My beloved, he says ambiguously, Miss Dorothea Brooke. Who looks at him with humble reverence, rather than at her.

They all rest in a departure lounge for a long time. Emma also feels weak and airy, and wonders whether she exists. Until a dark gentleman on her right suddenly addresses her: Señorita.

He is not only a gentleman, certainly a gentleman, oh, quite the thing. He is also very grand. A grandee, no, more, a king. All in black doublet and hose, with a white ruff and short black beard. He is accompanied by a sinister courtier, also in black, who introduces him, a shade unwillingly, as His Majesty King Felipe Segundo of Spain and the Nuevo Mundo. Silencio, Guzmán, says the king, no existe el nuevo mundo. King Philip II? Emma wonders. But how can that be? Isn't he real? Was he not briefly (she blushes) married to Bloody (blush) Mary? He tells her, as if in answer to her thoughts, that his queen was his English cousin Isabel, who gave him no heir, indeed who became the Virgin Queen of England. Emma never had a head for history, and it reels. But she fabricated an heir for him, the king continues, out of the dead bits and pieces of his ancestors. How exceedingly gruesome. As for his mother, Juana la Loca – but Emma is totally confused. Wasn't Joan the Mad the mother of the Emperor Charles the Fifth? So Mrs Weston had taught her, out of a toybook history of the world, when she was still Miss Taylor. But Emma has no real schooling and such matters were never part of her world. So how is it that they penetrate her consciousness now? What interests her is social trivia of a much humbler kind, that of Highbury, and the king shows himself graciously able to make an opening through his private obsessions and talk of what she knows, showing, unlike Harriet or Mr Elton, a nature of that superior sort in which the feelings are most acute and retentive. And yet she suspects him of lending her only half an ear, if both his intense black eyes. He admires her dress. So Grecian he says, so much more practical, a stem of gold for beautiful flowers, beautiful breasts. She flushes. But the time passes pleasantly enough.

On her left is the German woman in the white dress with purple ribbons and beyond her a knight in full and spotless white armour, with whom the woman is having an animated conversation in a very teutonic-sounding Italian. Emma is very much astonished. How she could have been so deceived! And how, in addition, could this knight have passed through the metal detector? It is dreadfully mortifying. True, he has no luggage. She supposes they searched him and found nothing.

Soon their flight should be called. The long journey over the pole and across the North Americas has taken ten hours instead of the usual six, and in addition to the two-hour wait in Atlanta there are four more hours to San Francisco. Sixteen hours of travelling in all, not counting the drive from Highbury, or was it Weimar? Almost as long as the drive from Escombe in Yorkshire to London, according to Frank Churchill. And that is without this tiresome phenomenon they call timelag: leaving Highbury – or was it Weimar? – at half past ten o'clock of a morning she was flying over Newfoundland at half past eight o'clock this evening on her breast-watch (does she have a breast-watch?) but the sun was high up in the sky, and it is now twenty minutes past four on the strange rectangular clock in the departure lounge. And when they arrive in San Francisco it will be almost half past ten o'clock again. Of course she has become used to it all in her mind, but not in her body – if indeed she has one, and she certainly feels at the moment that she does not. And yet she also knows with certainty that she would not have preferred either the Mayflower or a more recent vessel.

Suddenly there is a murmur from all the departure lounges that are lined up like drawing-rooms in lordly palaces. The murmur becomes a collective cry. Crowds of travellers rise in every lounge and rush towards the high glass walls. Beyond the waiting and the moving planes, beyond the rising and descending planes, burns the now shrunken city of Atlanta like a studio-set. Jane watches, fascinated to think of the mad woman in the attic, but calls out over the distance, Mr Rochester! Mr and Mrs De Winter stand arm in arm and gaze together as Manderley, the site of their fears and misunderstandings, fiery red, fills the whole sky. Moscow is burning, says Pierre, appalled. Alaonddin Khalij is enraged to find only the smoking ruins of Chitaur, where Queen Padmavat has climbed with all her ladies onto a huge funeral pyre that has set fire to the whole city. Aeneas, with his father on his shoulders, watches Troy burn. Aeneas, from his ship, sees the smoke of a funeral pyre rise into the immense blue sky of Carthage. A gentleman in a brown coat and yellow breeches, wearing a narrow-rimmed brown hat with a high crown, holds a tattered piece of scarlet embroidery in his hand, saved from the Custom House fire. Books by the million burn in Alexandria, at Fahrenheit 451. Books fall from the shelves. Peter Kien catches them in his long thin arms. Very softly, so that people outside won't hear him, he carries them pile after pile into the hall, building a huge barricade as the powerful noise tears through his brain. He has to use the library ladder. Soon the books reach the ceiling. In his office the flames rise from the carpet. He goes into the room next to the kitchen and brings out all the old newspapers, takes them sheet by sheet, creases them, rolls them into balls and throws them in every corner. He installs the ladder in the middle of the room, where it stood before, climbs to the sixth rung, watches the fire and waits. When the flames reach him at last he laughs out loud, as he has

11

never laughed in his life before. A floor caved in inside the house with a gush of fire. All burning, everything burning, toys and puppets and masks and chairs and tables and carpets and Mrs Rundle's Christmas card with all her love and lightshades bursting open with fire and the bathroom geyser melting and the bathroom plastic curtains dripping to nothing as the fire licked them over. Edward Bear burning, with her pyjamas in his stomach. And William Baskerville, a Dominican monk, shrugs as he sees Aristotle on Comedy and all the other books in the Abbey library burn down to ashes.

2

Down the umbilical cord from his delightful prison of perfect love at the top of the Farnese Tower, back into the womblike lap and carriage of the jealous, beautiful duchess Sanseverina-Taxis, covered in blood. It is also the womb of death. You will have grasped the deep significance of this scene.

The duchess, in ample green and black silk, looks across at Fabrice to exchange a knowing glance of recognition. But since he has been evoked at this very moment of his existence, he is naturally unconscious. And she is being distraught, which hardly allows a knowing glance. She looks at the title of the paper: Space and Means of Communication in the Nineteenth-century French Novel. She keeps forgetting that, although Italian, she exists officially in French.

We may in fact make a broad division between closed and open spaces. Epics, adventure stories, travel tales, battle tales, picaresque tales, tend to use open spaces: the sea, the deck of a ship, desert islands, the land, forests, mountain passes, river crossings, city walls, encampments, city streets and so on. But as the novel develops and adventures become more socialised and interiorised, more and more characters meet and talk in drawing-rooms, ballrooms, princely courts, chapels, prisons, theatre boxes, offices, ardent bedrooms, taverns, dairies, workshops or kitchens, cottages, stables even as the social range widens downwards. Or, when movement is after all required, in litters, buggies, coaches, carriages, cabriolets, calèches, curricles, diligences, gharries, fiacres, pony-traps, tumbrils, chaise-carts, dog-carts and all the rest. The most important advice from l'Abbé Picard to Julien Sorel seems to start in his Paris home, or nowhere specific, but at the end of it le fiacre s'arrêta. I believe there is a late nineteenth-century Turkish novel called, let me see, Areba Sevdassi, which means amour de

13

calèche. But even in the modern world, where people travel a great deal, meetings and conversations occur in cars, trains, planes or space-ships, not to mention motels, bus-stop cafés, as well as the more static offices, laboratories and operations-rooms. Décor is felt to be necessary to dialogue.

Kitchens? Emma wonders. Stables? I never go there. Serle and James would not appreciate. As for the other domestics, they presum-ably have names, but meals are served quite anonymously, the presence and the food not even mentioned, while our conversations and thoughts occur. Besides, here I am, wrenched from my décor as the speaker calls it, and I feel wholly non-existent. She rises unobtrusively to leave. And after all, the speaker says as Emma goes out, are we not all gathered here together to exchange ideas, in Room 0173 of the Hilton Hotel? Laughter. Room 0175 is the one she wanted. For Jane Austen, she hears as she sits down at the back, servants do not exist. Nor of course does sex. She sighs. It's true she may end, contrary to her declarations, on a projected marriage. She has been waiting ever since, reliving all her joys and errors, in the same progressively lessening ignorance according to the degree and variability of attention she is given. The details of the marriage, she hears, are in the mind of the Reader. The speaker's tone has a capital R and her head bows slightly, as do the heads of the thirty or so people in the room. Yes? Though I would rather keep questions for the end, Mr Moderator. Sorry, I only wanted to remind you and everyone that everything is in the mind of the Reader (bow of head). Quite so. But there are gaps. There is a great difference in status between what is put there by the said, and what is put there unsaid, as I'm sure you will all appreciate. Now –

Emma is pensive. Who is Lotte, who took over her identity in the carriage? Who is Goethe? Who, above all, is Emma Bovary? How extremely mortifying was that undescribed scene inside the French carriage called fiacre. For roughly two centuries she has been totally sure of her personality, flaws and all. The Reader (she nods) has been constructing her, moulding her, enjoying her, holding her in the mind and her only. But now everything has become confused, she lacks reality, as if the Reader her Creator had somehow absconded, like God, behind a Cloud of Unknowing. And as to space even God is often enclosed, if not in an ardent room or calèche, at least in a burning bush or in a shawl of prayer or in a tabernacle. And why is the Reader

14

always referred to as a man? God of course is the Father, who created the world. But the Reader as Creator of our world, her world? She never has grasped the generalisation of all these readers into the Super Reader, who seems both there and not there, dead and alive. Surely I appeal to women also? To women mainly? Her mind wanders. When everyone was asked, at the registration, in what vehicle they had travelled, King Phillip II, standing just beside her, had said: in my coffin.

But they are discussing her. Someone even reads a passage and she revives, begins to feel the blood circulate in her veins again. If she has blood, if she has veins. As apparently has not the knight in white armour sitting at the end of the row in front of her. What is he doing here? Has he also strayed into the wrong room? But she notices how small and squat he has become. He is holding hands with a little girl in a blue dress and white pinafore, who has long straight fair hair held with a blue ribbon. They are not listening.

Downstairs, in the vast lobby of the hotel, thousands of characters are churning around, greeting each other noisily. Some are wearing slim vertical diadems that plug into their ears, with a leather string attachment that disappears into a pocket or pouch or even a hand. Your talkman, the girl at the registration desk had explained, and Emma then remembered the strangely named translation machine from other conferences. Many are in the gallery, still registering. Others have crowded into the bar. There Felipe Segundo of Spain and the Nuevo Mundo stands facing the reredos of bright bottles and talks to a Spanish priest who has introduced himself as Herrera, honorary canon of Toledo Cathedral and who now presents his young protegé Lucien de Rubempré. But Lucien is not impressed, has eyes only for Emma Bovary who sits at a table in an ill-lit corner, lost in a roman à quat' sous. Next to her Dorothea Brooke is still stuck with Casaubon. Or is it Goethe? Suddenly a half-naked bearded man, wearing a talkman in his ears but only an animal skin round his loins and a rainbow chiffon scarf under his arms that seems to uphold him like a lifebuoy as he swims his way through the crowd, reaches the bar, where he shakes hands with another bearded man with a wooden leg, and orders nectar in Greek. Indeed sir, and how d'ye do from an old sailor, and the man with the wooden leg starts telling him about the white whale, its graceful leaps and eerie music. Sounds like a siren, says

15

the other in Greek, but it's heard in English by the whale-man. Never listen to them. They start exchanging sea-stories through their talkmans. A youth joins them, wearing a short tunic and sandals, a chlamys on his shoulders, and carrying a branch of bedraggled tinsel. I too went down to the regions of hell, he says in Latin to Odysseus. Ah, replies Odysseus in Greek, but did you talk to the shades? Did you kill oxen and give blood for them to drink, that they might come to life and speak?

At this moment a disembodied voice announces, in the colonial accent Emma still finds so difficult to decode:

Dear friends, welcome. Will everyone kindly switch on their sigh-multaneous translation-gear.

There follows a long silence, filled in with much murmuring as everyone in the bar, and presumably elsewhere, fiddles with their equipment, helps a neighbour, explains. The voice continues.

I hope you all have the program, but right now here's a reminder. The Rituals for Being will occur four times a day at a pray-in, or prayer-session if you prefer, in the large reception-room called Beverly, on the first floor, that is, for some of you, on the ground floor. We've organised four sessions a day over these seven days on account of your being, thankfully, so numerous, and Beverly can't hold more than eight hundred people at any one time, spacewise. The order of the days and sessions has been drawn by lot, according to our custom, and this first day is allotted to the Judeo-Christian, the Classical pagan and the modern atheist cultures. The first session went to the nineteenth and twentieth centuries, the second to the mediaeval centuries, the third to the Renaissance and the seventeenth and eighteenth centuries, the fourth to ancient European literatures. The other six days are for other religions and cultures, most of whose representatives have not yet arrived. But they'll be informed likewise. You are requested therefore to attend your relevant pray-in and go to the reception desks in the gallery where you first registered, to obtain your admission-card. The first Ritual will occur at eleven hours precisely, the second at fourteen hundred hours, the third at seventeen hours, the fourth at twenty hours this evening. That is, at eleven, two, five and eight. You are free to attend all panel-discussions and lectures at other times. If you need any kind of help please ask one of the Interpreters, dressed in dark red, who are there for just that very thing. Thank you for listening. Have a nice life.

Excuse me sir, but are you really Philip II of Spain? the old scholar Casaubon asks him from the step above as they stand in line on their way up to the registration gallery. The wooden steps have large spaces between them and he looks unsteady and afraid, holding on to the plastic connector of his talkman as if it were a lifeline.

Señor, soy el Señor. Mi padre era Felipe Primo, el Hermoso, y mi madre es Juana la Loca.

But then, surely, you are the Emperor Charles the Fifth?

Es posible. At times, but mostly, and in this moment, I feel myself like Felipe Segundo. There was address que lo decía esta mañana.

Ah, you are fortunate, Your Majesty. There has been no paper on me, only on my wife Dorothea. Where is my wife? I am always made to feel somewhat pathetic. I expect I shall die quite soon.

We all die, Señor. Creo que even I die. My ancestors are given as dead. I bring their despojos to the palace I build, to North of Madrid.

Il Iscorial? says a voice from below and behind him. Then you are Filippo Due.

Gracias, Señor. Por cierto.

So you will be attending the third session? says Casaubon.

Naturalmente moriremo tutti. Même les grands princes. Permettez-moi de me présenter, Votre Majesté: Ernest IV, Prince de Parme. Je meurs aussi, textuellement. Mon fils Ernest V me succède, un imbécile.

If Your Majesty will permit me, says Casaubon, there is a considerable difference in status between having died textually but remaining alive in people's memory, and dying in that memory.

Emma turns round from above him and says, gently: That, of course, is why we are all gathered here. To pray together for our continuance of being, but also for all our brethren, far more numerous than even we who are here, who remain dead in never-opened books, coffins upon coffins stacked away in the great libraries of the world.

Mr Casaubon nearly puts his foot through the space between the steps as Emma slides down past him and addresses the King of Spain.

I hope Your Majesty will excuse me for asking, but didn't Your Majesty say, earlier on, that Your Majesty came in a coffin?

I came, señorita, like everyone else, by aerobrain. We met at the exchange, did we not? My coffin is not a book, está dentro, it is inside the book. Which has not yet become a coffin, idea muy buena ¿verdad?

Whereas I stood beside my silk-lined coffin and discoursed upon virtue, says a young girl in a splendid gown of white damask, who stands beside the Prince of Parma. I chose to depart from this life rather than live it with a man whom I could have loved, but who dishonoured me.

Felipe Segundo stares at her with incredulous distaste. But where is Guzmán? he asks impatiently. Why should I and Su Altessa the Prince of Parma have to wait here on this ridiculous step-ladder? He should do something.

Oh me dolente! exclaims the Prince of Parma. Votre Majesté, nous n'avons plus ici le statut de notre rang, mais celui du souvenir qui restera de nous.

Creo que recordaran mas mi nombre que –

Nella istoria, sensa dubbio, Maesta, ma qui Lei non è nella istoria, è semmai nella Sua storia.

Mr Casaubon has managed to stumble upwards, helped by an elderly lady in a white dress with pink bows, who gushingly yields her place and calls him Excellenz. Then she realises her error and turns her back on him, gazing in horror at the vast crowd behind her and below. She recognises no one. Wo ist Goethe?

At last they reach the gallery, and wait again for their turn at one of the desks. Lotte is given her admission-card and starts walking towards the down stairway at the other end. Suddenly she stops. From the last desk a slim young girl turns, looking at her card. She is wearing a full-skirted long white dress with pink ribbons and bows. Lotte! the old lady calls and hastens towards her. But her voice doesn't carry above the roar of a thousand conversations. She runs awkwardly on her elderly legs, pushing past people with a repeated Verzeihung. Lotte! The girl turns to look, but seeing no one she knows, moves again towards the down stairway. Lotte! her arm is seized by an elderly lady in a white dress identical to her own, a lady she has never seen before, who gabbles at her in German, Lotte, mein Liebchen, Lotte, du bist Lotte, nicht wahr, von Werther geliebt! The girl blushes crimson. Wer sind Sie? Haben Sie Werther gesehen? – Aber meine Liebe, Werther ist tot! – Ach nein! Das ist unmöglich, wer sind Sie? Wie kommt es, dass Sie mir so etwas schreckliches – But the old lady drops her arm. Verzeihen Sie mir, she says, her voice trembling and her eyes filling with tears. Ein Irrtum. And she stumbles blindly past her, past others, pushing her way down the stairs. Natürlich kann sie mich nicht erkennen. She's inside the book. At some moment before the end. Where, where is Goethe?

Gnädige Frau, was ist geschehen? Can I be of assistance?

Lotte stares through her tears at the decrepit old man in a blue nightgown, being carried on a litter, wearing a laurel crown. Could this be Goethe, at a later stage, outside the book? He speaks German too.

I have just seen my younger self, who didn't know me. Oh Excellenz!

The decrepit old man speaks in a quavering voice and gasps between words and phrases.

Why...do you call me Excellenz? ... I am only Herr. I am dying. I die for much longer than ... my poem was. And I too, gnädige Frau ... have just met another ... self. Du bist Vergil? he asked ... me ... in an accusing ... tone. Ich war es einstens, I said, vielleicht ... werde ich es ... wieder sein. But no ... I say that to ... the boy ... to meinem kleinen Führer when ... I land ... coming from Epirus ... aus Griechenland, wissen Sie.

Lotte gazes at him with a mixture of terror and compassion. Vergil? she says. Der, der den Dante führte?

Nein! Nein! That was him ... the other. My ... other self, who ... accused me ... oh quite politely ... yes ... quite gently, of usurping his ... place.

His place in the line?

Nein! His place in, in ... oh I don't know in what ... how can I? In hell, he said.

You mean you are the real Virgil? The poet? The model? What are you doing here then? This is no place for ghosts.

Ghosts! We are all ghosts. But the old man gives up, and with despair in his pale eyes signs to his black slaves to carry him on as he mutters für welche Zukunft gilt da noch das unsägliche Bemühen um Erinnerung? im welche Zukunft sollte Erinnerung da noch eingehen? gibt es da überhaupt noch Zukunft?

Lotte feels lost. This is the first time she has come to the Convention and she knows nobody except Goethe. And Goethe is lost to her, she hasn't seen him since she climbed into the landauer he had put at her disposal for the evening at the theatre, and found him waiting inside.

There they could have talked of her younger self, a self she remembers, a self she feels she still is, deep inside her. But a self who cannot know her. Who does not, at this moment, even know that Werther kills himself.

But the conversation with Virgil has shocked her eyes into dryness. The tears are gone and only a cold fear glazes them. She moves with the crowd towards the large reception-room called Beverly. She had thought she belonged to the eighteenth century session, but they gave her a card for the first one, with her name on it, and a peculiar pin, asking her to fix the card to her dress just below the shoulder. She hasn't done so yet, and looks down at it. It reads: Hofrätin Witwe CHARLOTTE KESTNER. And lower down: (from *Lotte in Weimar*, by Thomas Mann).

So that's where she's from. When she signed the register at the Gasthof Zum Elephanten, she wrote 'Geb. Buff, von Hannover, letzter Aufenthalt: Goslar, geboren am 11 Januar 1753 zu Wetzlar'. She had asked if that was enough and they'd said yes. But presumably it wasn't, or it was too much, irrelevant. Well, the officials must know what information they want in each place. It's all reasonably efficient, given the crowds.

Which carry her along. At the wide open doors there are two organisers in dark red uniforms, a smooth young man with a straight fringe of astonishingly grey hair, and an orange-headed young lady with green paint around her eyes. She looks to Lotte like a – well, not a lady at all. They both wear cards below their left shoulder, which read INTERPRETER. The not-a-lady looks at her card and lets her pass with a mechanical 'Hi there' and a toothy smile. She is pressed by others through the wide doors into a vast room, ballroom size, all draped and carpeted in deep red. Gold-backed chairs are lined up, some fifty in each row as far as her eyes can see, both left and right, for the doors open onto the side of the room, unlike a church where one would enter from the back and at least go up an aisle. Presumably there is an aisle down the centre but she cannot see it. Some people around her turn left towards the front, where there is a raised platform with a long red-draped table on it, and a strange high reredos, others turn right towards the back. She hesitates. All the chairs near the door are occupied. She decides to go towards the back. She is afraid. What is going to happen here?

At last she finds a golden chair at the beginning of the last row. She wants to be able to escape unseen if she feels faint or cannot stand it. But the big doors at the back are immensely closed, and she would have to walk all the way back to the side-doors through which she had entered. If only she had found a chair near them. But too many people seem to have had the same idea. Not that anyone there could get out easily either, unless they have a chair at the end of the row. At least she has managed that, and won't have to disturb anyone.

People are still streaming in to a continuous murmur. Slowly the places are filled, with many gesticulations, greetings, embraces, changes of place, a few disputes, and the murmur rises to a gentle roar. Quite unlike a church. For the first time she gazes at the altar. But it isn't like an altar at all. The reredos is a huge triptych, no, diptych, like an open book, out of which stare innumerable eyes instead of letters. How strange. And above the diptych is a golden arch, curved like an eyebrow over one large eye that stares at the congregation and occasionally closes beneath a huge golden eyelid bordered in black lashes. Like the Eye of God? That blinks.

3

The orange-haired Interpreter feels flustered despite her flashy smile and automatic 'Hi there'. Such crowds! She barely has time to glance at the cards, and to her horror she doesn't recognise every name. And yet she's in Complit, like all the Interpreter Ushers. But her speciality is nineteenth rather than twentieth century, in Spanish and Portuguese, which inevitably include all Latin America; though she did do a Freshman course on World Literature in Translation, and, on a sudden fancy, a second-year course in Old Persian and Georgian Literatures, of all things, also in Translation, but mainly summaries and extracts. Perhaps that's why she was selected as Interpreter. But she's forgotten it all. So she has holes of ignorance about other times and areas. Who was Charlotte Kestner, for instance, out of Thomas Mann? Who was the handsome young Indian labelled Aziz? Or a splendid Arab king of Granada labelled Aben-Hamet, or even Philip II out of she didn't see who? Those at least she should have known. She feels ashamed and rattled. Gaps, so many gaps in her reading, she'll never catch up.

And yet she'd heard of the famous ones, especially when their names figured in the title or as titles, Mrs Dalloway, thin and pale and alert, like a seagull, and Sylvestre Bonnard, Ben-Hur and Anna Karenina, Oblomov, Babbitt, Malone, but also Leopold Bloom, Quentin Compson, Josef K, Ulrich, Gervaise, and Pierre Menard of course, and la Princesse de Guermantes. And Kim, Oliver Twist and Jude, Strether and Becky Sharp, Natty Bumpo, Gösta Berling, Clyde Griffiths, Queroz's Padre Amaro, she knew him, and Mr Bucket, and Augustin Meaulnes looking dreamy, and many others so much more familiar to her through the mysteries of chance reading. She turned away Zadig and Usbek and Tristram Shandy and told them to come back at five. She turned away the Wife of Bath and Dante's Virgil and told them to come back at two. But Dante's Virgil was being harangued by another Virgil on a litter, an almost decomposed old man, fearful to behold, who was muttering in German. She couldn't read the card on his blue nightdress or toga and was bewildered until her colleague, the grey-haired young man, waved him through deferentially and shouted at her above the noise, Broch, or something like that, and she felt she was going scarlet between the deep crimson of her uniform and the orange of her hair. And yet he let through a knight in shining white armour, who should have been in the mediaeval session! So he can make mistakes too. But he seems so sure of himself.

A slowly rising panic seizes her. Jean-Christophe, Henry Esmond, a dark young man called Bessian Vorpsi and his wife, holding hands although his wife looks entranced and absent, Eugénie Grandet, Captain Ahab, Corinne, Pan Tadeusz, Raskolnikov, Biff, Pnin with his brown domed head and tortoise-shell glasses, she knew him, and Lazarillo de Tormes, of course she knows him, and Macabéa, ah, poor Macabéa, with sharp body odour and in such a shabby little dress, accompanied by Braz Cubas, her favourite, she's writing her dissertation on Machado de Assis! She wants to introduce herself but he's gone in. And Hester Prynne follows, with her brightly embroidered A on her breast, and Natasha out of War and Peace, and Mr Verloc in a hat tilted back over well- brushed hair. But who are Slimak, Effie Briest, Billy Pilgrim, unser Edgar, Sevast Nikon, die linkshändige Frau? Masuji Ono? Barnabooth? Colonel Moscatelli? And Pinkie? And Dr Philifor?

At last everyone is inside. She and her colleague go in, close the big doors and stand like red guards on either side of them, watching the seated congregation as they talk excitedly, wave to each other or simply sit gazing at the altar.

The din of conversation hushes suddenly as five people enter from a side-door near the platform and step up behind the red-draped table. The first two carry a big red book. One is a dishevelled brown-haired woman in a long white tunic and peplos, the other a slim young man in a black soutane with two narrow rectangular black bibs twice edged in white, whose extreme pallor only enhances his extreme beauty.

Emma catches her breath. It is the young man from the aerobrain. She is sitting in front, in her golden dress and ivory mantle, between Philip II and the lady in the voluminous peachy skirts, also from the aerobrain. The young man in black and the dishevelled lady in white place the red book carefully upon a lectern on the table, then stand back respectfully to the right, facing the congregation. They are followed by a small, vacillating and very wrinkled old man, dressed in black robes, who has bright eyes and a bald head, except around the temples, and a sparse pointed white beard. He carries nothing. Behind him walks a tall, handsome man with greying hair, in a shabby grey cutaway coat, who precedes a small papal figure in white with a red shoulder-cape edged in white fur and a gold-embroidered green stole crossed over his chest. This last arrival takes his place at the centre of the table, flanked on his left by the pale young man and the dishevelled woman, on his right by the old man and the man in plain clothes.

The small white red and green priest raises his arms in welcome, then lowers them, to Emma's relief, who thought he was going to bless them with a sign of the cross. Felipe Segundo, next to her, is surprised that he does not, and crosses himself. Who are these two men on the left, he asks himself, not Protestants surely! And a woman at the altar! The silence is total now. What will he say? Emma wonders, Dearly Beloved Brethren?

My friends and fellows, he starts. There is a widespread fumble in the congregation as many people put on their talkmans. It is my turn today to welcome you all to this assembly of prayer for being. Those of you who attend regularly will not have been surprised by the high standard of organisation, indeed some of you may feel it is regimenta-tion, which is alas necessary on these occasions. And by a certain degree of solemnity we allow ourselves in these proceedings. They will permit me to explain, for newcomers, at least the organisation aspect. You have all been given admission cards to this first assembly because you belong to the Judeo-Graeco-Christian culture, as do those at-tending the next sessions today. This first session is, as you know, devoted to the nineteenth and twentieth centuries. Other assemblies, tomorrow and the following five days, are devoted to other religions and cultures. In these oecumenical times, however, we have sunk any differences among Christians that we may have had in our real lives and invited representatives of different congregations to officiate together. The same will apply to other religions. I am Pope Hadrian VII. To my left are Julien Sorel and Kassandra, the Trojan priestess. To my right are the Starets Zossima and Pfarrer Johann Oberlin, from Steintal.

24

Julien Sorel, as you know, never became a priest, and was practically an atheist, so this compensates the apparent slight imbalance, due also to my papal rank, in favour of the Roman Church. I of course was not really a pope either. By way of further example, last year's assembly, some of you may remember, was led in by my Spanish colleague Monsieur L'Abbé Herrera, who was also not really a priest, indeed, he started his life as a convict and ended up as chief of police. But he was here, and I believe has returned this year, in his Herrera episode. And it was celebrated by the Abbess of Crewe, who of course was not a priest either. Together with Mr Dimmesdale, who wasn't exactly an upright man. This afternoon's session will be celebrated by the Abbot of Lunigiana, and led in by the Pardoner. The five o'clock session will be celebrated by the Vicar of Wakefield and led in by the wine-priestess Babcue, whose motto, most appropriately I feel, was Trinc. The evening session will be led in by Chryses and celebrated by Chalchas. As for tomorrow, the first Islamic assembly will be cel-ebrated by Gibreel Farishta, who though a Moslem, often plays roles of different Hindu divinities. And the second by Haroun-el-Raschid, Caliph of Baghdad. Similarly the modern Jewish sessions will be celebrated by Rabbi Jochanan, of Marshinov, and one of the Oriental sessions by Naciketas, from the Upanishads, by Nagasena, by Gilgamesh, and so on. For the Islamic session tomorrow all the chairs will of course be removed and prayer-mats laid down. The order of the assembly-days has been drawn by lot, and it is thus only by chance that the Christian community has been allotted the first day. Other years it has come second, third or last. No significance is to be attached to this order of precedence. But I shall not trouble you with further details of identity and procedure, since the ceremonies are exactly the same in all sessions, give or take a few differences in the choice of prayers, which are based on the various liturgies of the various religions.

Felipe Segundo in the first row is profoundly shocked. But Hadrian VII continues:

Dear friends and fellow characters, you all know the importance we attach to the power of collective prayer in this our desperate struggle for survival. Some of us have more existence than others, at various times according to fashion. But even this is becoming extremely shadowy and precarious, for we are not read, and when read, we are read badly, we are not lived as we used to be, we are not identified with

25

and fantasised, we are rapidly forgotten. Those of us who have the good fortune to be read by teachers, scholars and students are not read as we used to be read, but analysed as schemata, structures, functions within structures, logical and mathematical formulae, aporia, psychic movements, social significances and so forth.

The orange-haired Interpreter at the door shakes her head. The other remains imperturbable.

This, however, the pope continues, does give us some sort of afterlife, since no one can deny that we are also structures within structures of our individual worlds, but this kind of afterlife has become somewhat tenuous. Many more of us, unable to be present here alas, have totally died. It is as if the Creator had absconded, in what St John of the Cross used to call a noche oscura, a dark night of the soul, a cloud of unknowing. His mind's eye is no longer our constant companion, constructing us, adjusting us, fearing and loving and hating us, following our pains and joys, our hopes, our calculations, our errors, our evil thoughts, our words. This is because His reading eye has closed, or looks elsewhere for these pleasures. We must pray to Him, to Our Implied Reader, Our Super Reader, our Ideal Reader, who gathers unto Himself all readers, and to His Interpreter, who gathers unto Himself all interpreters, of all interpretive communities.

He coughs. The congregation coughs.

A learned paper I heard this morning, the little white red and green figure goes on, talked of the way we are often enclosed in coaches, carriages, dog-carts and the like, as well as in rooms, chapels, prisons, kitchens and theatre-boxes. Alas, today we are more likely, but only occasionally, to be enclosed, and our descendants are much more frequently enclosed, in a television-box. Our Creator, Our Implied Reader no longer needs or wants to follow printed lines with His eyes in order to live us, and thus He no longer lives us. He no longer creates us.

So distant has Our Creator become, that we have had to have recourse to a mere image of His mind's eye, an idol, yes my friends, what many of you may call a vulgar representation of that mysterious power that brought us once to life. Do not be deceived or offended, those of you who abhor images. We cannot replace an absconded God, nor do we try. And we know that our only true representation lies in letters, not in object-images. But we are now so weak, so lost, that we

26

must accept this prop to our concentration in prayer. Please remain seated, there is no room to kneel. Oremus.

Row upon row of the congregation leans forward together, with the coordination of a chorus line, every head bowed or held in hands elbowed upon knees. Emma peers through her fingers to see if he reads from the big book. But he does not. He seems to know the prayers by heart. So do his assistants and some of the congregation in the responses.

He says: In the name of the Reader, and of the Interpreter, and of His Imagination. Amen. I will go in to the altar of God. To the Reader who giveth joy to my youth.

Judge me, O Reader, and distinguish my cause from the nation that reads not; deliver me from the unjust and the ignorant man.

They read, in various languages from their program: For thou art God my strength: why hast thou cast me off? and why go I sorrowful whilst the enemy afflicteth me?

He says: Send forth thine eye and thine understanding; they have conducted me and brought me unto the holy hill, and into thy tabernacles.

They read: And I will go in to the altar of God; to the Reader who giveth joy to my youth.

He says: To thee, O Reader, my reader, I will give praise upon the harp: why art thou sad, o my soul, and why dost thou disquiet me?

They read: Hope in the Reader, for I will still give praise to him, the salvation of my countenance and my God.

He says: Glory be to the Reader, and to the Interpreter, and to His Imagination.

They read: As it was in the Beginning, is now, and ever shall be, world without end. Amen.

He says: I will go in to the altar of God.

They read: To the Reader who giveth joy to my youth.

He says: Our help is in the name of the Reader.

They read: Who made heaven and earth.

He then starts on the Confiteor, which Felipe Secundo says loudly in Latin, as does Julien Sorel, as do many others, though many more, including Emma, are silent.

More prayers follow, and the Kyrie, and the Gloria. Here Emma picks up in English, but her mind is elsewhere. She never seems to go

27

to church. She tries to remember: does she? She must have done. After a while the little white red and green pope moves towards the big book on his right and says: The Reader be with you. The acolytes and congregation respond: And with Thine Imagination. The little pope then says: The Beginning of the Holy Gospel according to Stendhal. Then he walks back to the left of the table and sits down on a solitary golden chair near where they came in. Julien Sorel steps up to the book and begins to read in French:

En ces temps-là : Les portes du donjon s'ouvrirent de fort bonne heure le lendemain. Julien fut réveillé en sursaut. – Ah! bon Dieu, pensa-t-il, voilà mon père. Quelle scène désagréable!

Au même instant, une fille vêtue en paysanne se précipita dans ses bras, il eut peine à la reconnaître. C'était Mademoiselle de la Mole.

Emma hasn't put on her talkman and can't follow. Why are they reading the Gospel in French? Felipe Segundo leans towards her: Is thees your prime time? he murmurs. No, she whispers, but each attendance I am confused. Why don't they come to the point? I ask myself also, says Felipe, why they start with Salmo cuarenta y dos after the Introibo, when thees debe ser a Mass for the Dead. A mass! exclaims Emma. Shshsh around them. Felipe Segundo bends his head.

At last the Gospel is over and the prayers resume, and reach the Sanctus. Holy, Holy, Holy, Lord Reader of Hosts. Heaven and earth are full of thy glory. Blessed is he that cometh in the name of the Reader. Hosannah in the highest.

Then everything seems to stop. The little white red and green pope is lost in prayer. Felipe Segundo is astonished. Why no Canon of the Mass? That after all is the point. The drinking of the Blood. It must be due to all this intermixture of heresies. But now the little white red and green figure, helped up with difficulty by Starets Zossima and Pfarrer Oberlin, removes his green stole and dons a gold-embroidered black one. Having prayed for our sinful selves, he announces, we shall now say the Service for the Dead. Service? mutters Felipe Segundo. Service, thinks Emma, that's better.

Lotte, at the back, fingering the pink bows on her dress, has hardly been able to follow a word, or see anything but strange figures in black, red, green and white and grey, mumbling in foreign languages. Where is Goethe? He would surely explain. He had even been through a Pietist phase, been impressed by the ceremony and mediaeval pageantry of Joseph II's coronation in the Frankfurt Romer and used to declaim Klopstock's Messias as a Lenten exercise. Her mind wanders to Werther and his beloved mountains. How he had adored her. Why won't Goethe remember? Oh, she has been happy enough as Frau Hofrätin Kestner, as mother, but, well, it isn't at all the same. Fantasies of her youth overwhelm her.

Then, to her horror, people around her start getting up and joining the long queue for communion. The chalice up there is enormous. It must be a Protestant service after all, since the chalice is being offered. The people in the front are already going back to their seats. What is she to do? This seems a travesty of any service she has ever known. But evidently no exceptions are to be made. She can't remain seated. Nor can she escape towards the doors, for they are blocked by the two Interpreters and returning communicants. She rises stiffly, feeling very hot, then cold, her brain seems to shrink inside her head, she is overcome by a dread of fainting away. She takes a deep, slow breath and joins the wide, five-abreast queue as it shambles towards the centre aisle. Yes, there is a centre aisle. She will never make it to the front. She holds on to the back of a chair. Perhaps, by holding each chair –

Suddenly the side-doors open and a dozen or so men in long white robes and black turbans enter, pushing apart the two Interpreters in red and the returning communicants, holding huge weapons she has never seen before. Across the half empty chairs she stares at them. They look like caliphs or whatever out of The Arabian Nights. The stunned silence breaks into screams, yells, roars. She plonks on an empty chair and the huge room goes round, she puts her head down so as not to faint. Then a volley of gunfire rattles across the room, followed at once by tinkling glass. She looks up. One of the men has fired in the air, narrowly missing a high chandelier, and the stunned silence returns. He speaks, in broken English.

Twelve subgun-machines we have. Gelignite under jellaba. In several minutes all you are dead.

Everyone looks towards the platform, above which the eye continues to blink slowly. But the little white red and green pope seems to have vanished. So has the white priestess. Starets Zossima has reached the pope's chair at the side and sits there immobile, his wrinkled face in his hands. Julien Sorel seems to be feeling for pistols he doesn't have. Only the Pfarrer Oberlin stands calmly and spreads his hands out as if in surrender, but not quite so high, more in a gesture to calm.

Was wollen Sie? Que voulez-vous? Messieurs, he adds politely.

You spikzinglish?

Nein, aber mein Kolleg hier – he bends forward to look for the little pope, but in vain.

At this moment the orange-haired Interpreter, who has evidently edged her way, bent down, through the communicants, leaps onto the platform.

Yes? Gen'lemen? She borrows courage and courtesy from the Pfarrer. I speak English. Please excuse the delay. You frightened the hell out of everybody.

There is a murmur of admiration and fear.

Yes and we fright ze hell more. We spik not with woman. Not wiz whore of Babylon.

Then you must allow my colleague Interpreter to come up here.

Silence. The grey-fringed young man in crimson uniform detaches himself from the turbaned terrorists and walks up to the platform, his head sunk into his shoulders like a cauldron fallen into the logs of a fire.

Yes? he pipes up in a curious falsetto of fear. What's your problem?

Many problem. Why has Christian assembly first assembly? Why use you blood sacrifice, blood of cut male cow? Why –?

Oxblood, gentlemen. It is an allusion to Odysseus. A Greek hero of very ancient times, pre-Persian, he adds as if to stress historical priority. He gave oxblood to the dead shades, so they'd revive and speak to him.

The grey-fringed young man seems to have recovered his normal voice. A murmur of horror ripples through the congregation. Oxblood! Several women among the still standing communicants faint.

Silence! You Christian, or whatnot?

It is true it was once a heathen practice. But in these oecumenical –

Spik proper English man! What is ikmenkl? We not accept.

The ritual is identical for all communities, by consensus and democratic vote. It's a most ancient tradition. Only new participants are shocked, but when they feel the zing of life it gives them, they come again for more. Tomorrow you likewise –

How you dare! It is this year our turn to come first. Allah not permit drink wine. Allah not permit drink blood. We not accept. We not accept also big eye. He is idolatry.

The eye is only for today. For us idolaters. There is no turn. The order is drawn by lot each year. You must know that.

The little white and red pope with his green stole peers up over the red-draped table, his face red with shame. But as he stumbles up he seems to regain his dignity, perhaps, thinks Emma who sits quietly in the front next to Felipe Segundo, to make up for his first cowardly movement. But to her astonishment he says, tactlessly: And yet you were prepared to shed a great deal of blood.

The Pfarrer frowns. Felipe Segundo frowns. He a pope? What an idiot diplomat. The eye continues to blink slowly, in benign, impartial approval.

The twelve submachine-guns, which were held upon the congregation in all directions, have all jerked together and clicked for action. But to the right of the turbaned men there suddenly appears, out of nowhere, a knight in shining white armour who, in the twinkling of a thousand eyes, slices off the twelve turbaned heads with one mighty stroke of his sword. The last turbaned man has had a split second to turn his machine-gun on the knight and fire, before his head falls too. The white armour of the knight shows not a hole or scratch. He steps over the bodies, holding his bloody sword high over his helmet and walks out of the room.

The silence storms into uproar, like super-volume canned laughter. Everybody is talking at once, yelling, shouting, sobbing, wailing. Lotte is seated on a free chair at the back, muttering, where is Goethe? In front, Emma also remains seated, but Felipe Segundo rises and walks up to the platform. ¡Un escándalo, he says, en una iglesia! Como puede Su Santidad – But nobody is listening to him.

What happened? everyone asks. Why? Who were they? Who is the White Knight? What was he doing in this session? Oxblood! Ladies have swooned all over the place. Emma is profoundly vexed. How dreadfully mortifying etc. Such manners. But she bends from her chair to help the woman next to her who has collapsed on the floor, her silken pokecap sunk into her voluminous peach-coloured skirts.

Are you all right ma'am?

Merci, merci, madame. Quel effroi! C'était terrible. Que va dire mon mari?

What is your name? asks Emma softly as she puts her arm round the lady. Vottrey nong?

Je m'appelle Emma.

31

How remarkable. Mooah owsee. Emma Woodhouse.

Très honorée, Madame. Je suis Emma Bovary.

Emma pales. The lady in the fiacre? She withdraws her arm. She is not leniently disposed. But she is struck by a curious query: why has this lady swooned at the idea of having swallowed a mouthful of oxblood, yet did not shirk from swallowing a good deal more arsenic? Then she pauses in sudden perplexity: where has this extraordinary thought come from?

4

Kelly, wow, you were sure terrific, that was scary, the grey-fringed young man mutters to his colleague. Pretty gutsy.

Oh, shit. But Jack, what do we do now?

They watch from the platform as the people scramble for the doors, stepping gingerly over the dead bodies. At this moment the tall doors at the back of the room are opened and other red-uniformed Interpreters rush in, but are at once overwhelmed by the crowds who turn round and push past them, to avoid the bodies, into the new exit. Some, from the front, have managed to go out by the side-door next to the platform, where the celebrants had entered, and through which they have rapidly escaped. Soon the huge room is empty.

What happened? the tallest of the newly arrived Interpreters calls out. Kelly gestures towards the prostrate white figures, still clutching their machine-guns, and at their scattered black-turbaned heads. But the bodies are invisible from the back, behind the many rows of chairs. The new lot walks up the side and stops, scared.

Were they real? one of them asks.

Idunno, Kelly snaps, I'm not an expert in Islamic literature. They looked real enough, like a chunk of old black and white newsreel in a historical colourfilm. Either way, they shouldn't have been here today. How did they get in?

The manager of the Hilton, a bulky man in a double-breasted black jacket, comes in through the side door and looks down appalled at the twelve headless bodies. The carpet! he exclaims. Then: Will somebody turn off that goddamn eye. Ah, the cops at last. He steps aside to let in a posse of plainclothes men with instruments and cameras and a couple of uniformed men in black and silver, followed by a small man in a creased raincoat, who's holding a green cigar between two fingers in a boyscout salute. You were witnesses? he asks the Interpreters. No, they were, the tall new arrival points to Kelly and Jack. There were thousands of witnesses, she says. But she tried to negotiate, says Jack, she'd gotten herself on the platform and saw them the most clearly.

Thank you sir, would you mind coming along with me? and you, miss.

He nods to the men to carry on and shuffles off, followed by the distraught manager.

There's a meeting of the Central Committee, the tall Interpreter says, your presence is required.

We're not on the Central Committee, Kelly sobs, and bursts into tears. The little Inspector pauses at the door, leaning on his cigar-holding hand.

Reaction, her colleague says. Heroism does that.

Your presence'll be required, all the same. After the Inspector has finished with you, go to Room 0127.

Jack puts his arm round her and together they follow the little Inspector in the old raincoat, who has been politely waiting. The eye stops blinking at last.

Room 0127, when they finally reach it, is a board-room. Around the table are about a dozen topnotch academics, in various attitudes from stiff attention to sprawl. In the chair sits a small dark woman in a grey suit and plum shirt, with cropped hair and a powerful jaw. Kelly recognises Professor Rita Humboldt, Complit, who has moved from post to higher-paid post so many times she can't remember which University has been the last to buy her. She feels rinsed out and very small. These are the stars of academia.

Come on in, Miss – er – McFadgeon, Mr Knowles, find yourselves a perch and tell us all. Hand them a cup of coffee will you Larry.

But their tale, though incoherent, is soon told, followed by a silence, and Kelly rises to leave.

No honey, stay with us. You've been quite the little heroine, and you too, I mean hero. Looks like we may need you, why, you saw them, and intercommed. What we've been kicking around is this: should we cancel, and if so, the whole Convention or only the pray-ins. Opinionwise it's bollixed up. Much depends, at the present time, on the reality or otherwise of these terrorists and hopefully the police'll illumine us. But we can't wait on their inquiries. The next pray-in commences in an hour. We have half of that to decide. Professor Whitelaw had the floor before the interr – erm – before you came in.

Kelly sips her coffee. Her hand is trembling and she glances sideways at Jack Knowles, who offers her a cigarette.

No smoking I'm sorry, says Professor Humboldt. Oh, what the hell, we'll make an exception in the circs. All agreed? A few hands reach for breast pockets and purses. The man called Larry rises to collect ashtrays piled up on a sideboard, hesitates and bends to open its door.

No, no drinks, Larry, this is urgent and it'll downgear the proceedings. Jim?

Thanks, Rita, you're dead right, we must move in pretty fast, we're not at a faculty-meeting. I believe that cancelling the whole Convention is inadvisable. This may be a unique, erm, incident, and if it isn't, cancelling'd just about spread the shenanigans. All the guests are here, in the city, they're all invited for the full seven days and can attend any panel-meeting they choose. Best keep'm busy, and mixing. Only the pray-ins are segregated, for convenience mostly but also for practical and ritualistic reasons. Surely all we need do is have the doors guarded.

Which ones?

Er, pardon me?

I meant, shair collaygue and born outphaser, the doors of all the goddamn lecture and panel-rooms or only of Beverly?

Well –

I don't agree.

Mansell Roberts?

I just don't think we can afford more miseries heaped upon us. The pray-ins surely must be cancelled but I'm for cancelling the whole Convention. Otherwise disaster is in the works. Look at the damage done already to our reputation.

Now isn't that just too bad? But hang it Mansell, you oddball loner, if it was a fiction, no damage's been done at all, fiction's our business. Do you read me? It's a goddamn miracle that fiction still has the power to offend, and maybe change things, as it used to. Shit, the white knight's exploit was impossible, and he's taken a powder.

Who was he? Kelly ventured. What was he doing in this session?

Jack Knowles kicks her under the table and mutters sideways: Calvino, Twentieth Century.

Smart, Mr – er – Knowles. The Non-Existent Knight. Chances are the terrorists are likewise non-existent.

But –

A mass halloo. I mean hallucination.

No! Kelly exclaimed.

Come to that, says a youngish blonde down the table, the entire congregation was non-existent.

Dead right, says Mansell Roberts, solid, iron-haired, iron-jawed. That IS what I meant by damage. Not the physical harm, though it'd be horrific enough if real. The harm to our reputation, as I said. By which I intended to remind you that these Conventions of ours are commencing to be the hilarity-focus of other disciplines, AND of our own colleagues in drama, film and TV departments, who don't have the same problems, since their characters are more or less frequently incarnated –

And when less, they die too, says the youngish blonde.

Yes, they too, exist then only in the text, says an elderly man. In Greek for instance. Or minor Elizabethan.

But the text is all, an excited red-faced man breaks in. It has the ambiguities on which survival depends. It's in illogics that the interpreter takes his pleasure.

His? says Rita sharply.

Hisher, I'm sorry. She is condemned to textuality, that is, to making the apparently incoherent coherent, reducing the aggressivity of the text –

But more often than not misreading in the attempt, says the youngish blonde, I mean, just not seeing what's there plainly in the text. Banalising, familiarising. Just like copy-editors and reviewers. So?

Precisely, retorts the red-faced man. Incarnations fix, and fixities die. Letters, words, sentences are therefore more alive than –

Still and all, pipes up a young man who looks like a yuppy, I guess our division of sessions according to conventional historical periods of authors, rather than of characters, creates a way-out glitsch in their minds, look at all those Romantic Orientals by Chateaubriand or for that matter Boiardo, or even Pierre Loti, what if they meet real ones, I mean oriental Orientals? I mean fictional oriental Or –

That's enough of that! Rita Humboldt raps the board-table with her cigarette-lighter. We're not here to address the question of the sanity of our whole enterprise as usual, but to make a quickfire decision.

We are here, says Mansell Roberts oracularly, to defend our turfs, they say. And you know it.

Bullshit, says Rita Humboldt, puffing out the result of a long draw over the board table. Kelly watches the smoke disperse, fascinated. We're here to ask, how do you read where we're at? The question is up for grabs.

Rita, how d'you do it?

How do I do it is easy. All disciplines deal with fictions, as everyone knows by now. They simply won't face the facts.

Or the fictions, says the youngish blonde.

We've tried to face them, after a long and barren linguistics phase, by borrowing from theology, making the most of the religious back-lash in order to –

Cashing in on, you mean, says Mansell Roberts, the way we always cash in on the latest fads and other disciplines. We don't exist either.

Mansell, I won't have you behaving as a red-herring trailer. In five minutes we must take a vote. Anything else?

I'm on Professor Whitelaw's side, says the red-faced young man. To continue, with guards.

Then you can express that in your vote, Mr Trenton, says Rita crushingly. I meant, are there any new arguments? Miss, er, McFadgeon, surely you have something to say?

Kelly flushes scarlet under her orange hair, above her crimson uniform. Idunno, she stammers, I mean, they seemed real enough to me you know, they seemed, well, political like, not literary at all. Dangerous, I guess, I mean, real dangerous.

So you must vote for cancelling everything. Mr Knowles?

I'm afraid I have to disagree with my colleague. It seemed very literary to me. Interdepartmental highjinks. We should ignore the whole episode.

Baird?

The man looks old and grey, speaks in a quavering voice.

I believe, if you will allow me to express a somewhat, er, personal view –

Yes, yes, but step on the gas. Without gas if poss.

Hrmm. Er, yes, well, I believe, that our, er, culture, was always based on a, er, belief, that, er, civilisation is based on the, er, idea – Rita Humboldt looks at the ceiling in exasperation, giving the cue for

37

everyone to feel restless – that, er, spirit, you know, er, dominates, er, matter. But, well, our, er, culture has, er, materialised this idea, which was a mode of, er, survival, and by materialised, I, er, mean, er, objectified it, turned it into a, how shall I say, a mise-en-scène. Thus we have all become, er, objects, producers and, er, consumers of words, in a constant, er, staging, shall we say –

Therefore? snaps Rita Humboldt. Are you once again querying the whole basis of our enterprise? Let me repeat, this isn't the time, or the place. There's to be a Plenary Session of the full Committee for that at the end of the week, at which, I guess, everyone'll spout off on this incident instead. But shall we be here at the end of the week? THAT is the point. It's twenty-five after twelve. About time to vote. Secret ballot. Pass the slips round will you Larry. Two slips each, one for the pray-ins and one for the Convention. FOR cancellation, YES. AGAINST, NO.

Are we allowed to vote, Professor? Jack Knowles asks.

In principle no. But since Professor Dellerby couldn't attend, we're unhappily an even number. I move that a vote should exceptionally be given to Miss McFadgeon, who showed such expedite courage. Okay? Larry this'll be explained in the minutes. You don't mind, do you Mr Knowles?

He demurs politely and rises to leave. Nobody stops him. Kelly, horrified, bites her biro and gazes anxiously at the faces around her, trying to guess what the trend might be. Then she prints NO on both slips and folds them over. It's an unthoughtout NO, a NO to every-thing she has heard, but also a No rebellious to Rita Humboldt's in-structions after her clumsy reply. When the votes are counted every-one has voted YES for cancellation of the prayer-sessions except two, herself and, presumably, Professor Whitelaw. She keeps her eyes down, hoping that nobody will guess. Someone else had after all supported Whitelaw, but was evidently crushed into desertion. No-one need know that. For the Convention, the votes are more evenly divided, so she feels safer. Five for cancellation, eight for continuation. Mansell Roberts has a tight look, all the other participants apart from Whitelaw seem relieved. Perhaps they never believed in the pray-ins anyway.

Down in the lobby the line for admission-cards is still winding its way up the elegant teak stairway. The roar of talk is zoological. But there's another line to the far left, very long, and much quieter, outside the reception-room on the furthest side from Beverly, where she and Jack were interrogated earlier. It bears the name Kennedy in black and gold scroll above the high doors. Kelly recognises some of the faces. Even Virgil is there on his litter, patiently borne by black slaves. They must be those who attended this morning's session, waiting to be interviewed by the police. She feels starved. None of these characters ever seems to eat. She makes her way to the Help-Yourself upstairs. There too is a line, but short, and chiefly of Interpreters and other real guests. A voice comes over the loudspeaker after a click:

Dear friends. Kindly adjust your translation gear ....We regret to announce that, owing to an incident of unacceptable violence at this morning's session, the Central Committee has decided to cancel the rest of the pray-ins. You have no need, therefore, to stand in line for admission-cards. The rest of the Convention will of course be maintained, and you are free to as ever attend any of the lectures and panel-discussions you please. We hope you will, for these too are a source of being. Thank you. Have a nice life. Enjoy.

Kelly can imagine, almost hear the uproar and panic below. People on the teak stairway going down against the current pushing up to protest at the desks in the gallery, those on the down stairway also rushing both down or back up. But the desks will have magically emptied at the first words 'we regret to announce', the crimson-coated Interpreters having been forewarned and instantly vanishing with their box-files through an end-door marked NO ENTRY. The lobby should be a pandemonium of what she'd seen on her way through, mediaeval knights in coat-of-mail, ancient heroes in animal skins or tunics or full battle-armour and viziered helmets, periwigged gentlemen, men in doublet and hose, ladies in down-pointing brocade stomachers or side-paniered taffeta robes, shepherdess bouffant skirts bunched up to reveal petticoats, or Watteau gowns and long satin coats, hair piled high, hair tucked low in frilly mob-caps or vanished into wimples, hennins and all the rest. Thus she muses, waiting for her turn. It's true she hears some of these imaginings among the people around. She also hears a snort immediately behind her and turns. It's Rita Humboldt, unaccompanied by any member of the Committee. She smiles shyly. To her surprise Professor Humboldt is very affable.

Honey hi. You must be feeling pretty bad, eh? Allow me to give you lunch.

Oh but no, Pro-

I always come up here. Despite the little line it's quieter, and a heck of a relief to get away from my ambitious colleagues, who prefer smart luncheons downtown, lobbying anyone in higher posts they can find. Ah, we're next.

They are let in and move towards the central lunch-counter, helping themselves to meat-messes on soggy bread and salads and multicoloured dressings in large bowls. Kelly is astounded by Rita Humboldt's friendliness towards her, a mere assistant professor in a small university well below the Ivy League and other topnotch groups. The small, strong-jawed woman even moves towards a table for two.

You know, she says as they sit down, I just don't believe the derringdo highjinks this morning were a mass hallucination. I saw you protest and I agree. And the vote showed no one else did either.

I see, says Kelly, wondering what she's expected to say. But then, what, I mean, why –

I spoke to the Chief of Security early this very day, and he told me they were expecting some sort of demo from Middle East Fundamentalists. Not to this extent, damn'm, or they'd have bin more efficient. Total inability to utilize data received, that's the shopworn disillusionment with all committees, makes me mad. Same with democracy, though we wouldn't have it any other way, would we honey? The moment any one person does a loner there's a surge of protest if it goes wrong and a surge of praise if it goes right. So what's the difference? As long as it's not swept under the rug I guess.

She is stuffing food into her mouth as she speaks, often with that mouth full. Kelly feels lost. She hasn't expected a political turn to the conversation and is afraid of betraying her convictions if any.

Do you read me? Rita says, gulping from a glass of more ice than water.

Yes, in a way. But I'm a bit disoriented. What did they want? I mean, they objected to the order, though drawing lots has always been agreed. They objected to the oxblood.

Coca cola my dear. With the gas and sugar taken out, and slightly warmed. But don't let it get around. I shouldn't have said that. I hope I can trust you.

Jesus! Oh, sorry, I mean – But why?

Yes, must avoid that one here, oecumenical an' all that. But since

40

I'm being indiscreet, and I need to be, it's all been so stressful, they didn't object to any of the things they said, that was just for attention, I guess they hoped cameras were around. Their real objection is to Gibreel Farishta.

Gib -

You know. But keep it nicely tight.

Rita takes out a cigarette. Mind if I smoke? I always eat too fast, so I need to take time out.

Kelly shakes her head and goes on eating. She has hardly touched her stew for amazement. Who is this man Gib-something? Rita is looking at her sharply as she smokes, puffing with exaggerated politeness away from the table.

Seems to me, she says after a moment of silent but hectic puffing, we should both take a turn in the interrogation room when we've done. But don't hurry my dear. Bad for the guts. Mine are twisted to snafu. I'll get some coffee. You'll be having coffee?

Kelly nods and hastens to finish her plate while Rita is off. She feels abysmally ignorant. She'll never make it to full professor. Everyone she knows seems to be cranking out books. She finds it hard to publish, and publications regulate promotion. She has every difficulty in finding topics to write about on the nineteenth-century novel, everything's been done, and all she comes across are strange articles that seem to have nothing to do with plot or characters or social backgrounds or style, that find effects in causes and repetitions of nonexistent stories and split polarities and supplements, articles she finds hard to read or remember when she's read them. She did write one feminist article on a twentieth-century female character, Clarice Lispector's Macabéa, but she knows it must have seemed naive and simplistic compared to those of topnotch – that word again, she can't get rid of it – feminists who find complex structures in flux and fragmentation – which seem contradictory to her – and in menstrual rhythms and body language and –

Honey, your body speaks. Relax. Here's your coffee. Have a cigarette. It's a damn shame, she goes on inexorably, that the pray-ins were cancelled. Oh I voted for it of course, I know how the wind blows. It's true we're ass-harassed about them. But we could've cancelled them for the future, after due and careful consideration and all that shit. It would have been much more interesting – but the members of the committee are supinely incurious – to see what would happen. Tomorrow especially. Islam you know. Or 'I slam' as I prefer to call it. Means 'I submit', but it's all one isn't it. Okay shall we shove? My do, like I said. She grabs the two checks and they go to the desk. On their way down the backstairs, to avoid the elevator, she says: what d'you bet it's chaos down there.

They emerge through a small door into a corridor that leads to the huge lobby, and the noise already hits them.

Kelly feels tall and gauche behind this formidable little bundle of power. They struggle through police and the sometimes fighting crowds, in all manner of dress and undress, even a bedraggled girl in chains (Manon!) and an almost naked man accompanied by a tall black one (Robinson Crusoe!). She's so pleased to recognise anyone. If Gulliver is here, what size can he be? And Orlando, as page or as Vita? And what about the Fisher King? She starts wondering how they choose the representatives: presumably Lucius as golden ass, Reynard the fox, Alice when huge, Humpty-Dumpty, Tom Thumb or Nils Holgersson as tonte, the Houyhnhnms, Gregor Samsa as beetle, Gogol's Nose, Camões' rock Adamastor or Fierabras or other giants, Sviatigor for instance, Finn McCool, Pantagruel, green giants, minotaurs, titans, Moby Dick … presumably all these are automatically excluded. And Melusine when her lower body becomes a serpent, or Andersen's little mermaid? Her mind reels. And what about allegorical characters like Love and Death, Chaos and Mutabilitie an'all? And the student made of glass? But they reach the silent line outside Kennedy. It is so long it has to double back three times like a Melusine serpent, as in banks and post-offices, with metal posts bearing chains by way of guidance. Rita marches straight to the top, however, and Kelly helplessly follows. She is recognised and cheered. No one protests. They walk in.

5

Several tables have been arranged round the room. At each one sits a plain-clothes inspector interviewing someone and a uniformed man or woman in black, with silver buttons and badges, typing on a slim-screened portable computer with printer attached. One of the characters has just finished being interviewed and is being escorted to another door on the left by a paunchy little man with close-cropped hair on a large round head that bulges out peculiarly at the back. At the far end, the little inspector sits alone at a table, examining the print-outs. He is still wearing his crumpled raincoat and smoking a small cigar.

Rita walks straight up to him and sits down.

Well Inspector? Kelly, get that chair and sit by me. How're you pitching?

Ma'am? I don't think I've had the pleasure.

Professor Rita Humboldt, I'm the head of the Central Committee and chief organiser of this Convention.

A real Professor! That's very interesting. My wife has a tremendous respect for −

This is Miss − er − McFadgeon, who spoke with the terrorists.

I've already seen her ma'am, Professor. Do you have any other recollections miss?

That's NOT the point Inspector, she's with me, I have news for you and she agrees. You might show a shade more professional curiosity, not to mention manners.

He raises both his arms above his head in a submissive handsup gesture, still holding his cigar.

I beg your pardon ma'am, we cops aren't always so refined on the job. As to curiosity, well − he sighs and brings down his arms − you're right, Professor, what is your information?

43

Have a cigarette, oh shucks, you're smoking a cigar. Were the bodies real?

If you'll excuse me Professor, that's a question.

It's preliminary to my info.

They were real enough.

Have you traced the White Knight? I know, that's another question.

You're on the ball, aren't you. No, we have not.

Not surprising, since he's non-existent.

So some of the witnesses maintain.

And they're dead right. The police are so illiterate.

But the result of his gesture was real enough, ma'am.

Sure. Fantasies worked out always are. Now my point is this. As you know, the order of the sessions is drawn by lot, and this has long been democratically agreed by all parties.

Sure, sure, ma'am, Professor, he doubly echoes.

That squares their first objection. As you also know, or should do, the oxblood in the chalice is not oxblood. Only the organisers know this. So, therefore, should the terrorists, who are always well-informed.

Are they, ma'am? He takes a puff at his cigar, but it has gone dead.

So that squares their second objection. As to the eye, it's always removed for the Islamic session. That squares –

Excuse me, Professor, but would you mind coming to the point. I do have –

All that was camouflage, hocus-pocus. For attention. Their real hang-up, clear as the light of day, was that the first session tomorrow is to be celebrated by Gibreel Farishta.

So I'm given to understand, ma'am.

Oh? Who by, may I ask? This morning's witnesses can't know a thing beyond what goes on in their own narrative.

But they meet here, ma'am, they talk to each other. And what do people do when they talk to each other? They exchange stories.

None of the characters from Islamic literature were here this morning.

If I may say so, Professor, how can you be so sure? They weren't at the prayer-session I'll allow, but all the guests are invited to the whole Convention, am I right? And some may well come to get their admission-cards early.

One-up to you, Lieutenant. But you've only been interviewing the witnesses of this morning's session. So how could they, as you put it, give you to understand?

We do have our methods, ma'am. And there's nothing to prevent anyone else from joining the line out there, isn't that so? Was that your, I beg your pardon, do you have any other information?

Well, it hardly matters how you came by this item. The important thing is to segue on it.

Segue on it, ma'am?

Get real, man. These terrorists are dead, but terrorists are like the widow's cruse.

I beg your pardon ma'am?

Illiterate, didn't I say? There are plenty more where that lot came from. Probably roaming the pandemonium in the lobby right now. Oh, not dressed up as imams, real terrorists never are, that was just the picturesque warning, even if it misfired, hardly the word perhaps, glitsched, I mean, in a kamikaz way. It sure didn't fail to warn. I guess they hoped for TV cameras, but those are never on tap when anything really happens.

It's funny you should say that, Professor. My wife would agree with you. She always says –

And Gibreel Farishta's almost certain to be around. Not that these people ever read what they condemn. They're not just non-readers but disreaders.

I thought you said, ma'am, that terrorists are well-informed?

They are that, sufficiently to carry out their orders. It's the top that disinforms. That was by way of an aside. From one who does read.

I'm sure. Thank you Professor, we'll give every attention to this, er, valuable lead.

You'll do more than give every consideration, Inspector, you'll give protection.

We'll give protection. We are giving protection. Now, if you don't mind, ma'am, I do have –

Thank you Inspector. You've been most kind.

This is said icily, loftily. And up she tinily swoops, out she tinily marches, using the exit door. Kelly can't help flashing an amused glance at the Inspector who, to her surprise, returns it as he relights his cigar, before bending his head very deliberately onto his printouts.

She walks unsteadily to the exit-door and out, but Rita Humboldt has vanished into the crowd. Despite her lunch Kelly feels weak, or because of it, nauseous, and wishes someone would show up with a litter, a calèche, a cabriolet, a chariot of fire. Where has Jack Knowles gotten to? He's been pursuing her and although she's not hyper-interested, a little attention of a more personal kind would be welcome right now.

The crowd, however, seems quieter, though much present and still thick. The noise is more of thousands yammering, like a hencoop, than of thousands roaring in protest and panicking, like a herd of elephants in stampede. The cops must have done their job, in fact are still dribbling around, or someone must have made another announce-ment. She keeps bumping into people and saying sorry. She bumps into a tall bronzed man in a check shirt and red sash, with wide black whiskers and white teeth, who disappears as soon as she's read his label, Nostromo. She bumps into the same Renaissance gentleman called Philip II, from Terra Nostra, by Carlos Fuentes. Another book she's heard of, should have read but hasn't. It took her a hundred years to get around to A Hundred Years of Solitude, not to mention Hopscotch, but Fuentes – how can she keep up with the twentieth century when, apart from Lispector, she's so plunged in the nineteenth? He's all in black with a white ruff, talking to an elderly man in a dark cloak with stand-up red-lined collar. Again she apologises.

No hay porque, señorita. ¡Ah, señorita! ¡Es Usted! Se ve muy cansada.

No, todo está bien, gracias.

¡Habla español! ¡Estupendo! I have been talking in bad Italian to Señor Goethe here as I do not speak German. His Italian is not better. But he does not like the branches of this machine in his ears. Señor Goethe is interested in hunting, but he talks about a lion, can you explain? I do not hunt lions, I hunt the stag. But where is Guzmán? he carries my pelerine of Biscay gabardine, which I always wear to hunt. Do you think there are lion-hunts here? Why does Señor Goethe hunt the lion?

I don't know, Your Majesty.

It escaped, from circus, says Goethe in English. It was only in a story I wrote.

46

¡Ah, bueno! But you understand Spanish? And you speak English! Natürlich. I understand Spanish durch Italian. And I love Shake-speare.

Why you not say? We are all in stories, are we not. Stories, histories, I feel not difference. I am history.

They start a philosophical discussion and Kelly slips away, straight into the arms of Jack Knowles.

Kelly, honey! Where'd you gotten to? I looked everywhere for you. Are you okay?

Get me out of here, Jack.

He guides her, his arm round her shoulder, gently parting the crowd like a sea. At last they step out of the hotel into the grey street and blue sky of San Francisco. The cold air hits her and she breathes it in, gratefully. They pitch into a colourful sect of singers on the corner among hurriers-by, and then past a couple of junkies lying freaked out and frozen against the wall, unattended. They find a bar and she climbs on a high stool, puts her elbows on the counter and cries into her hands, smudging her green eye-shadow. He is all focus, orders two whiskies.

And then she tells him, about the vote, about her lunch with Rita Humboldt, about the second interview with the Inspector, about the coca cola, about Gibreel Farishta. It all seems suddenly very funny now, reflected as it is by Jack's laughter and delight. She feels much better. He turns to catch the barman's eye for two more whiskies, and in the brief interruption she suddenly remembers the sharp look Rita had given her in the restaurant: Oh I shouldn't have said that, I hope I can trust you, keep it nicely tight. Rita was indiscreet on purpose. Rita knew she would talk. Rita intended her to talk. And now she has. Rita wanted the word to spread. And now it will.

What's bugging you, love?

Nothing. just reaction. I think I'd better go and lie down.

She gazes at his youthful face and his pudding cut of prematurely grey hair, and wonders whether she even likes him.

You do that. I'll take you to the hotel. We're not on duty this afternoon. Probably not at all any more. But I'll go and find out, and meet up with you later okay?

Their hotel is much less grand than the Hilton, but within walking distance. She is silent on the way, thanks him for his kindness and

47

understanding, is glad to be rid of him.

He walks back to the Hilton, elated. The streets are full of characters who have spilt out of the Convention, free of pray-ins, determined to live it up in the big city. Some go into bars, some are assailed by begging youths, some climb into Convention tourbuses to Chinatown, or the tower on the hill, or the buffalo park and the Bay road. Captain Ahab is being helped up into one by Odysseus and Leopold Bloom, followed by Vasco da Gama in plate armour over a green velvet skirt and high leather leggings, a young man all in white, and Captain Nemo in a stern dark uniform, all shouting, to the ocean! But the young man in white, from helmet to canvas leggings and pipeclayed shoes, hangs back at the words. His smooth tan- and-pink face, with its little blond moustache and a white line at the roots of his fair hair, is staring after the sea-going group, his youthful eyes, first darkened by excitement to a profound, unfathomable blue, are sud- denly dulled, as from a passing cloud, with an old, black, secret renunciation. Jack stops in his tracks at the poignancy of that look, knows and feels and loves the man before glancing at his label, Tuan Jim. Who turns away and walks off.

The hotel lobby has quietened to normal. The lectures and panel discussions have started and only a few characters stand around and talk. Some are making their way to the bar. Jack wants to follow them, but with two whiskies already on his stomach decides he'd better first go up to the office and find out what's happening. All seems routine. Several young women are sitting at their desks, typing or phoning or filling forms with items and time with natter. You heard, they say, business as usual, except no pray-ins. Academic stuff continues. You continue to be around and make yourself honeyfaced.

Jack feels deflated. He had quite expected to hear that Gibreel Farishta had been whisked away, which come to think of it wouldn't be a novelty for him. He spills his items of knowledge, feeling important. We know, they say airily, now scatter will you, we've work to do.

Crushed, he takes himself off and decides to go to the bar after all. But to the skyview restaurant-bar on the forty-sixth floor. The express elevator zooms him up in thirty seconds flat and he emerges into a small carpeted foyer that leads into the restaurant, at this hour not yet given over to diners. Few of the guests have discovered it and most of the tables are free. The view over the hill to the Golden Gate Bridge and the ocean sparkles in the sun, is reassuring, pacific. At a far table by the huge windows Emma Woodhouse, still in that slim gold dress and ivory mantle, is sipping tea with Emma Bovary, still in that profusion of peachy silk, Dorothea Brooke in a plain grey dress and shawl, and Mr Casaubon, who looks anguished at so much femininity. Sitting with them is also another woman, in modern dress, in her late thirties or so, unknown to him, nondescript. He walks towards them.

May I join you ladies, Mr Casaubon? My name is Jack Knowles, I'm an Interpreter.

Mr Casaubon nods, relieved at male company. Emma Woodhouse is being gracious all round. She seems to have taken Madame Bovary under her wing, which bodes ill.

Is this not a magnificent view Mr Knowles? says Emma affably. So very high. I have never seen the sea.

But Dorothea, visibly vexed at the interruption, wants to pursue the previous conversation.

We were discussing the religious event, Mr er -

Jack Knowles. I'm an Interpreter.

Ah then, perhaps you can interpret it for us. It all seems to me quite unacceptable. Why such unnecessary violence over the secondary importance of ecclesiastical forms and articles of belief? Compared, I mean, with spiritual religion, that submergence of self in communion with Divine perfection, which is expressed in the best Christian books of widely different ages. Do you not agree, dear?

Mr Casaubon gravely smiles approval.

But weren't you there this morning Mr Knowles? Dorothea continues, remembering her manners. You took over from that bold girl.

She was very brave, he corrects the nineteenth-century nuance. But they wouldn't negotiate with a woman. Very backward people you know.

Indeed. But why should they? Women, my uncle says — but she stops and ends lamely, it was all very distressing.

You know, they weren't protesting at all about the oxblood.

It would have been exceedingly foolish of them if they had been, says Mr Casaubon. It is a most ancient custom. It gave us all strength to live on. And living on is of course of primordial significance.

C'est odieux, Madame Bovary mutters. J'en étais malade.

49

But they knew it's not oxblood at all. It's coca cola.

I beg your pardon young man, says Mr Casaubon, but the sip I ingurgitated this morning did not in the least possess either the aroma or the flavour of cocoa.

Not cocoa sir, coca cola. The American national drink. With the gas taken out.

The ... gas? Do you mean ether? Dorothea looks puzzled.

No, the fizz. But of course there's still cocaine in it, whatever they say. That's why Americans are such easy victims.

Victims? Emma asks. To the English?

To the drug-pushers.

I see, says Dorothea. Mr Lydgate is rather against drugs I believe.

My dear Dorothea, pray do not meddle with elements that your fair sex must, in the nature of things, know nothing about.

The conversation lags. No one seems to grasp what he's saying, except, probably, the nondescript modern woman nobody bothered to introduce, who hasn't said a word but only looked on, listening and smiling. Still, it's important that the news get around.

What is this young man talking about? Emma asks. Do you understand, Miss Brooke?

Mrs Casaubon.

Oh, I beg your pardon. Your label –

Yes, I am afraid that she is better remembered, alas, under her maiden-name. I have come to count for nothing, despite my immense and important labours on the Key to All Mythology. I might as well be called Mr Brooke. It is a pity that they never reached the prayers for the dead.

Hush dear. Why don't we go down and hear the paper on you? It will do you good. It starts at four o'clock, in ten minutes.

Oh, all right dear, if you insist. But he looks pleased, as if he had been hoping all along she would remember. They rise to go, Dorothea supporting him as they slowly leave the restaurant-bar.

Four young men push past them and walk up to the centre-bar. One of them politely asks for mint tea, in fluent American with a very slight foreign accent. Jack perks up at the voice, turns round, looks across. They are well-dressed in Western suits, look vaguely oriental. In the mirror below the reredos of bottles he recognises this morning's spokesman, his dark fanatic eyes. But that's impossible! He looks away

50

at once, turns his chair around so as not to meet them. He knows his grey fringe and youthful face make him instantly recognisable. He even pushes his fringe violently to the left. No beards, no turbans, no broken English. How can it be? They were all killed. He turns his head again cautiously. Yes, it's him. One of the others carries a hold-all.

Jack mumbles excuses, rises, bows politely with his back to the bar, and then, in case they're looking at him, takes out his program and pencil, looks at his watch, marks a session and walks out towards the elevators. The express is free and open, he steps in and in thirty seconds emerges into the wide corridor between the downstairs bar and the long reception-desk, races to it and talks to a policeman on duty there. Within minutes the man has called up eight others and reached the elevator, with Jack behind them, curious to see if his hunch is right. Up in the restaurant-bar the four young men are surrounded without a struggle, in apparent astonishment, and taken off. Emma Bovary has screamed at the slight scuffle and fallen back in Emma Woodhouse's arms in a semi-faint. Emma shrinks, then controls herself and comforts her. What a tiresome woman. Worse than Mrs Elton. Does Madame Bovary faint? Jack finds himself absurdly thinking. Monsieur Homais says she never faints. Is it Monsieur Homais? Doesn't she faint at seeing Rodolphe pass by in the diligence? And in childbirth? The other people in the bar remain frozen in their places. Was für ein Land ist es? says a dishevelled woman in a torn Greek tunic and peplos, who sits on the other side with a glass of iced water, accompanied by a weeping girl who clings to her. Kassandra! Jack murmurs, wondering, as he did this morning, why a Trojan princess and priestess should always be represented in Greek clothes. And dishevelled. He has a theory that the Etruscans were really Trojans, who came to Italy from Asia Minor, and that therefore she should have complicated tresses, a wasp waist corsage and a tight skirt in horizontal pleats. He must ask her. But no, she'd only be confused. He walks across to her, addresses her in German.

Du bist Kassandra?

He notices that the weeping girl also wears a peplum, is labelled Simaitha, but he knows nothing of her and ignores her. Kassandra looks at him with glazed eyes.

Und wer bist du, junger Mann? Andron? Emmelos?

Ein Deuter.

Wie Panthoos, der Grieche, der Verräter. Er war eifersüchtig.

51

Kannst du denn auch meine Träume deuten?

Vielleicht. Wenn du sie mir erzählst.

Mit der Erzählung geh ich in den Tod.

Deine Erzählung aber lebt noch.

Wie auch ich. Nie war ich lebendiger als in der Stunde meines Todes. Jetzt.

So eben lieb' ich dich.

Ich, die schreckliche. Ich liebe niemanden. Oder, vielleicht, Aineas, Alle Männer sind ungezogene Kinder. Aineas? Unsinn. Aineas ist ein erwachsener Mensch.

Aineas, sagen Sie?

The trembling voice of the old man sitting in his litter at the next table interrupts them.

Kennen Sie ihn, mein Herr? Kassandra turns with relief from the weeping girl. Was ist mit ihm geschehen?

Ich kenne ihn. Ich kenne. Ich bin sein Schöpfer, Vergil. Doch ich bin aber sehr müde. Ich sterbe bald.

Vergil? Diesen Name kenne ich nicht.

Ach so. Also bin ich schon vergessen. Dann hat Cäsar mich angelogen. So muss ich also ganz vergessen sterben.

Auch bin ich sehr müde. Die Erde möge seine Asche ausspein. Jetzt nicht den Verstand verlieren, jetzt nicht. Sein Schöpfer sagen Sie? Wieso? Sind Sie der Heiliger Leser, den wir heute morgen angebeten haben?

But the little Inspector in the creased raincoat arrives, examines the bar, the four glasses with mint teabags in them, looks around, sees Jack and beckons him to the door with a sharp sideways nod. Jack takes Kassandra's hand and kisses it before she wrenches it free, and he whispers, Verzeihen Sie, ich muss mich auf den Weg machen, ich komme bald zurück, and leaves her with her melancholy new companion, as sad as the first, gazing at the ocean. Let them understand each other if they can.

6

You look kind of user-friendly sir, says the Inspector in the elevator, can you explain why terrorists should be compared to a sea-voyage for American widows?

A sea – ? No, Inspector, er –

Columbo. And your name is, yes, Mr Knowles?

Columbo! But then you're not a real inspector either?

What d'you mean, either? I'm just about as real as anyone in this case. A widows' cruise, she said.

Oh, I see. Jack remembers Kelly's hilarious account and giggles. It's cruse, c, r, u, s, e. A kind of pitcher. A biblical allusion, you know.

Ah yes. Illiterate cop, as she said. But what does it mean?

I forget who caused the miracle. A widow had no more oil, and suddenly it was endless. Like oilwells I guess. He laughs, pleased with his joke.

Hmmm. If they are. But tell me sir, what made you feel you recognised one of these men?

They emerge to walk the carpeted corridor on the way to the interrogation-room called Kennedy.

The eyes. I saw them in the bar-mirror. Happily they weren't looking at me, and I –

Mirrors can be deceptive. Especially in fiction I gather. I'd like you to come and identify him, would you mind? They deny everything of course, and they have papers as students. A deal too smart for students if you ask me. Materials for making explosives were found in the bag. Not yet planted, happily. The man carrying the bag also denies all knowledge, says the stuff was planted, but on him. Is your colleague around, Miss, er, McFadgeon?

53

She's resting at her hotel, I can call her.

You do that. Don't tell her why. My wife also likes to rest in the afternoon you know, she says it's very – But here's the desk, I'll wait here.

After the call they walk towards Kennedy.

Hell, the journalists. Always arrive when it's all over and there's nothing to film but afters. That's what my wife keeps complaining about, she says the news is always dead, they're never in on a real crash, nor, of course, on a murder. Though that's lucky for me, don't you agree, otherwise I'd be out of a job. Now sir, keep your cool, I'm gonna walk right through them saying no comment. But your picture'll be in the local papers and news. Just smile and keep mum.

Cameras on shoulders, flashes, an armoury of mikes held out like blunted swords, questions, jostlings, scufflings, hustlings. The two policeman at the door try to hold a passage for the inspector and his witness, who are prevented and pushed, push and prevent and reach the door at last as the cop holds the closest four journalists at strong arm's length. Columbo is experienced, opens the door, shoves Jack in, slips in himself and shuts the door. They're in.

The witnesses have gone. The four men in lounge-suits are each sitting at one of the interrogation tables. Columbo leads him to the first. He stares at the young man, who stares back, without batting an oriental eyelid.

No, I can't be too sure. This isn't the spokesman anyway.

Would you come and see the next one please.

He hesitates. Same scene. They all looked alike, he says, and the distance –

Okay okay, don't get nervous sir. Next.

The black eyes are wide-set, wide-whited, wide-pupilled, and look not into his own but just above, at his fringe.

That's him. The spokesman.

No doubts?

None at all.

Thank you sir. Would you be so kind as to go out through that other door and meet your colleague as she comes in to the hotel. Bring her here the same way, round the back.

He goes. His head is in turmoil. Kassandra, out of Christa Wolf, accompanied by a weeping girl out of some Greek complaint, cannot know Broch's Virgil or what happened to Aineas, Virgil's Aeneas. But he himself is real, he's supposed to know what's what and who's who. Yet he feels he doesn't. Twelve terrorists beheaded by the non-existent knight in one blow of his sword he could take, but four of them resuscitating the same afternoon as elegant students carrying explosives, interrogated by a TV actor who plays detective, that's way beyond him. Come to think of it the Ideal Reader must have recognised him long before he himself or anyone else did. But what's a TV actor doing here, in this Convention for characters made of text?

Ah, Kelly there you are. How d'you feel?

I'd have felt better for not being woken up. Hate sleeping in the afternoon. Have we time for a quick coffee? What's it all about?

No, sorry love, it's urgent. I can't tell you right now. I'll take you up to the panoramic bar afterwards. It won't take a minute.

And Kelly recognises the same man at once. Kahaba! he mutters quite audibly when she has done so.

As they go round the other end of the lobby they glance back across it. The journalists are still there. What did he say to you? Jack asks. It sounded like a guttural spit.

From the way he said it it probably means whore, like this morning. All men from everywhere have the same look when they utter that word. And yet they utilize the referent.

I wonder if we can find out. And whether it's Persian or Arabic and which Arabic, Palestinian or Libyan or Moroccan or whatever. To-morrow is Islam's day, there'll be experts around. Can you memorise it?

Could also be Classical Arabic, in which case it won't help.

What does it all mean, Kelly? he asks over coffee. The restaurant-bar is empty and they sit at a table near the huge window, facing the Ocean. And do you realise the inspector is Peter Falk?

Columbo! So that's where I'd seen him before! But that's ancient! This is crazy. Were all the cops actors? Oh! she suddenly exclaims.

What is it honey?

The other inspectors. When I went in with Rita Humboldt. I looked around. It's only just hit me. They were all fictional. Sherlock Holmes, Maigret, Poirot.

You mean as you imagined them?

No, I mean as acted in TV films. And there was Magnum, Steve

McGarrett, and others. And Dupin. I never noticed them when we were interrogated this morning.

Nor did I. We were too shaken. Why but you're right! Come to think of it Jabert was one of them, with his peculiar head bulging behind. And Porfyry Petrovich.

Who're they?

Oh, come on, Kelly, Les Misérables, and Porfyry who so gently harasses Raskolnikov into confessing. He's the direct source of Columbo. But surely nobody's ever played Dupin, that's Poe.

Oh well I dunno. Maybe he was Arsène Lupin, I saw him on TV last summer in France.

Arsène Lupin was a gentleman thief.

Lay off me Jack. Why didn't you support me at the meeting anyway?

But honey –

And what the heck is Peter Falk doing here?

What's anyone doing here? What are we doing here?

And so on.

But they are Interpreters. That is, they each see everything differently. Later, they're still quibbling, gazing miserably at the Ocean, oh not about terrorists or actors any more, not even about structures or significances or underlying themes, but about whether Emma Bovary has black or brown hair, is plump or slim, is over-dressed or elegant; about whether Dorothea Brooke is austere or frumpy, Casaubon decrepit or dignified, Felipe Segundo young and dark in embroidered doublet with a high collar or middle-aged and grey, all in black with a white ruff. C'mon Kelly, get real, what the hell does it matter? – It does matter, they've all been wrenched out of their contexts, so how do we recognise them except by their dress and appearance, apart from their labels? – Right, they're castration fantasies, they wander our minds like stray phalluses – Jack you don't have to be crude. – I didn't say pricks, did I, phallus is a psychosymbolic term, surely you – Oh, shut your face. – But not my mind, honey, it really is all in our minds anyway. – Not all, the text always – But the reader forgets, my love, he is extraordinarily inattentive to such details, since he's already constructed an image, not from descriptions, which he often skips, but from the way a character talks, feels, behaves. He may even identify and see himself, herself.

But the Reader, the Implied Reader, the Ideal Reader? She bows her head mechanically but slightly, as if impelled yet embarrassed.

Sordello, and my Sordello? Jack murmurs. Kelly doesn't understand.

And me, she goes on quickly, do you see me with red hair? Or black? Or green?

That's different. Red of course. My love.

He thinks of Kassandra and his declaration of love. But that was different too. I'm a Germanist, he says aloud.

What's that got to do with it?

At this moment three people come into the restaurant-bar, a young girl in blond plats and a white dress with pink bows, holding a little boy by the hand, both acccompanied by a tall dark-haired young man in black, wearing an embroidered waistcoat, holding a top hat. The group walks towards them as if seeking company, as if afraid of all that empty space in the sky. The boy is also in black, narrow trousers, short waisted swallowtail, grey waistcoat, white shirt and wide black cravat. He wears a high, narrow-rimmed grey stovepipe hat over untidy spikes of fair hair, and stares at the view, terrified by the height.

Lotte! says Jack, gets up and immediately rattles off in German, then translates for Kelly as they all sit down. This is Lotte, from Werther you know. She tells me she met an old lady, dressed exactly like her, who addressed her familiarly, as if they were acquainted, then excused herself. I explained that this was her older self, as imagined by Thomas Mann in a much later book. So on two counts she couldn't possibly know her. And now she says she's met this English gentleman, who's had exactly the same experience with this boy, David Copperfield. He knows the boy but the boy doesn't know him. And that's in the same book! So you see! How can the ordinary reader, or even the Ideal reader, imagine a character correctly at every stage? Felipe Segundo is both young and old. I saw him talking to Emma, who seemed to be treating him with much deference as elderly.

He's a king, Kelly objects. How can you tell what Emma's thinking?

That's what I mean, dearest, it's what we think they're thinking that matters, not what they look like.

In life it's both, she snaps. She stares at the boy, who stares up at his older self as if it were his never seen dead father, and shyly puts his small hand into the manly one. I want to go with Peggotty in the carrier's cart, he whines. David Copperfield Senior responds with a soft pressure and has tears in his eyes. He is about to speak when the restaurant-bar is suddenly invaded by a large mixed crowd, the men laughing loudly, the women shrieking, Here it is at last! Oh for a drink! What'll it be? and so forth. The boy lets go of his father's hand and hides his face in young Lotte's small bosom. She removes his tall hat and ruffles his spiky hair. A waiter appears through the noisy crowd and takes their order: grapejuice for Lotte, and then for the boy too, who doesn't know what he wants, tea for David Senior, whisky for Kelly and Jack, who are beginning to feel deeply fatigued and overwrought. The noise is too up-volumed for talk.

Kelly is amazed. These are all people she knows: JR and Bobby and the rest from Dallas, Santana, Kelly (not like her at all) and Eden and CC and Gina and Cruz and Mason from Santa Barbara, Gary, Abby, Jill, Val, Karen, Mack from whatsitscalled, Angela, Melissa, Cole, Chase, Kit from Falcon Crest, and many others. All soaps. She wonders why the old name soap hasn't been changed to chewing-gum, the multimini-episodes, though split every few seconds from one to another, are so long drawn out. She suddenly understands how the feminists can talk of both flow and fragmentation. Is that what they mean? Bubblegum endlessly chewed but blown up every minute or so into separate bubbles? And yet she has been addicted to every one of them, secretly, ashamedly. Perhaps she would have published more but for them. They are eternal.

And they're all shouting just that, we are eternal, we're real! We'll show'm! We are the ones people want and know and love! Down with all these dead people out of books nobody reads! We'll invade their seminars! In force! Plenty more where we come from! Everyone's been advised, they're all coming. We start tomorrow. Okay let's reconnoitre the ground now. Quietly, just a few of us, one in each session. Action tomorrow. Let's drink on it! Up yours!

At last they leave and Kelly, who has been gazing in both shame and horror from them to Jack, whispers in the sudden silence: Should we do something?

I guess so.

I'm sick of co-operating.

Yes, terrorists were bad enough, but this bunch is over the edge.

Oh come on, at least they're not planning to kill and lay bombs.
Was war das? Wer waren diese Leute?
Verzeihen Sie, Fräulein Charlotte, aber jetzt müssen wir arbeiten.
Arbeiten? Ach so. Gut. Auf Wiedersehen. Moment, bitte. Haben
Sie vielleicht den Werther gesehen?
Nein, noch nicht. Vielleicht wurde er auch gar nicht eingeladen.
Bis später dann, Fräulein Charlotte. Goodbye Mr Copperfield, Master
David, we'll see each other again soon. It was a real pleasure meeting
you. I'm real glad you've found each other.
A bad mistake of organisation, he says to Kelly on their way down.
We never invite same characters to the same Convention. Yet here are
two cases. Not to mention the two Virgils. I must report it.
Who to? Rita Humboldt? She's vanished into upper spheres.
Oh, in the office, it'll get to her. But now we'd better find the
Inspector. Oh, no! He's a TV actor too. Must be a conspiracy. D'you
think Bugs Bunny and all those round-eyed young knights and little
girls from Japanese lasarlike epics are in on it?
Quit ribbing, Jack. We'd better try and find Rita.
But her hotel isn't given in the list of convention-members. Up in
the office, the staff refuses to give it. We can't have her miseried by
young academics lobbying for jobs, they say. But we're not, we're the
chief witnesses of this morning's shindig! I lunched with her, Kelly
adds. After verification and a whispered consultation, the girl picks up
the phone and says, Zelda Ritchie here, Convention Office. Can you
get me Professor Humboldt please. And after a while: No reply, sorry.
Zelda Ritchie, a memorable name, says Jack on their way out. You
could try that trick later, when she's back.
You mean, pretend? Hell I couldn't do that.
Why not? Everyone's pretending here. You'd only have to assume
a lower voice and say 'a call for you', or no, better, 'will you accept a
call from Miss Kelly McFadgeon?' and if she says okay you wait a sec
and speak in your own voice. She'd never know.
Well, she's not in just now. Where can she be?
She's either at another committee meeting, and we know the room,
or at a panel-session, speaking or moderating. Let's look through the
program. Five-thirty. Jesus, there's at least a hundred.
There she is, look. 'Interpreting the soldier: From Achilles to Catch
22'. Let's go, I might learn something. Hell, it's in the Moscone

Center, miles away. Room D007.

We'll get the shuttle. What's the time? Christ, five forty-five already, and they only last forty minutes, let's go. At least it's in the basement. And we can catch her at the end, without interrupting.

When they get there, it's already six, and they get lost in the A, B,C,D corridors. At last they find it and slip into a row of chairs lined against the side-wall. Rita Humboldt stares at them angrily as they sit down. The three ten-minute papers are over and it's question-time.

Kelly notices that the audience seems to consist entirely of soldiers in varying types, ranks and period of uniform from ancient armour to coat of mail, from bright blue or red to lighter blue or grey, from various shades of khaki to spotted camouflage. All are wearing their talkmans. Nearest to her she can read the label The Good Soldier Schweik, but not the author, and, rather oddly, next to him, an Edwardian gentleman in mufti labelled The Good Soldier. And Woyzeck. And Baron Münchhausen in eighteenth-century gear. Belisarius, Gilgamesh, and what is it? Kalivipoeg is it? Strange name. And one lady warrior, Bradamante. In the front row sits Crane's youth in greyish-blue, with a bandage round his head and its badge of blood. Next to him sits a bright young captain in red – Henry Esmond, she saw him this morning. And mediaeval heroes with double names like Dietrich of Somewhere, and Greek ones. And Alexander the Great, looking mediaeval. An Arab called Antar. A Japanese labelled Something Benkei, a splendid-looking Slav called Jan Zagloba. And a dark man in a leopard skin: Tariel! She'd done him in her Georgian course. Someone called Corporal Trim. And then Fabrice del Dongo in his green uniform with white braid twisted all down the front and a high black hat, stolen by the jailer's wife from a dead hussar. And several Russian generals in fur caps, presumably from War and Peace, yes, there's Koutouzov. But also one labelled in French Le général Dourakine, very red in the face, who ever's he? And yes! Napoleon, quite small, in three different versions! But most of them she can't read or recognise. The modern ones all look the same, naked and dead from here to eternity. There is also a soldier in khaki at her end of the second row, with the numbers visibly missing from his cape, holding a shoebox-shaped parcel. His eyes are glazed and his talkman hangs unused round his collar like a stethoscope made of string. He is not listening.

60

The paper on Stephen Crane showed that a modern soldier does not fight singly and heroically as Beowulf or Roland or Achilles did.

This is interrupted by a few loud clappings from a group of warriors in the centre.

But surely we know that already, the questioner goes on. Fabrice del Dongo wasn't even sure whether he'd been in a battle at Waterloo. Fabrice smiles. That was perhaps the first example in modern –

Yes, we have your point. Professor Zieg?

If I may say so, that was only my opening gambit, a donnée as it were. In fact, if you followed it, my paper was a deconstruction – if a swift one in the time allowed – of the whole notion of heroism.

But here a man in coat of mail rises and blows his horn. The entire back row rises and starts shouting and fighting with huge steely swords and yelling in some incomprehensible language – sounds like Low Dutch, Jack mutters. This continues for at least two minutes while the rest of the audience and the panel seem paralysed. Then at last a tall grey-haired man in a grey robe draws a golden sword and holds it high above them, separating them as if by magic. Shame upon you, he says in more or less modern English. Without this human meeting, which has given you momentary life, you were all dead and forgot. You, Gunnar, and you, Earl Hakon, and you, Hrut, and you two, Flosi and Njál, and you, Havelock the Dane. Except mayhap for Roland here, and his namesake Orlando, who need not be so furioso. You were but references for the discussion. Wulf the Unwashed, go and wash. My name is Gandalf the Grey. I am truly alive, even in the bowels of the earth. Now sit down. And they do. Mumbling in what still sounds like Old Dutch.

Unhappily our allotted time has skedaddled. People are already entering for the next session. It remains for me to thank our three speakers, and to thank our audience for their kind attention.

A desultory clapping occurs, a scraping of chairs, a babble of voices. The heroes in the back row have vanished. Gone to Odin, Gandalf says to Jack near the door and sails away. The remaining soldiers stand to attention then march out in fairly orderly file formation.

Kelly sits on, dismayed. Yet no one else seems overly concerned. People are drifting out, others in. Come on, says Jack, and makes his way to the speakers' table, still surrounded by a few participants who couldn't ask their questions. She follows him in a daze. Jack signs to her to approach Rita Humboldt.

Please, Professor Humboldt, I apologise for –

Coming in at the end? Or did you come for the next session?

No, no. I'm sorry. But –

We have something important to tell you.

She looks sharply at him, then at Kelly.

Get this then, follow me out, I'll see you in the entrance hall. Come along you people, we must clear the room. Hi there, she says to the incoming performers, have a good pitch.

In the hall, she takes them to a circular grouping of upholstered seats.

Okay, spill it out.

Jack tells her about the planned invasion of characters from TV. She looks dubious. Can't be worse than invasions from old texts, she says.

But that's not all of it. The inspector investigating this morning's murder, he's not an inspector at all, he's Columbo.

Columbo? You mean Christopher Columbus?

No, says Kelly excitedly, Peter Falk.

My dear, I can't access a word you're saying. D'you mean Arvid Falk, from Strindberg's novel you know, what's it called now?

No, no, the TV detective Columbo. Played by Peter Falk.

I never watch the idiotbox.

And all the other inspectors, all the policemen are probably actors too. It's a conspiracy.

A conspiracy for what, honey? Simmer down. Have a cigarette.

Well, for – She shakes her head at the proffered case, looks wildly at Jack.

For undermining our whole Convention, he says. It's hard enough to keep all our textual characters alive, without these much, much –

Much more real ones invading our field? My dear young man, that occurred long ago. We fight a losing battle, I know. But we must continue to fight it. Heroically. To the death.

7

The Golden Gate Bridge is a pinky orange and endless, rising above them like an airy modern cathedral of curved metal as Mira Enketei is driven across by Orion Rigel. The December sun shines in a blue sky and the sharp winter light assaults their eyes, hearts, minds. Neither of them thought to bring dark glasses.

While you were about it you might have rented one with sunproof windows, she observes.

Almost twice the price.

At an M.I.T. salary? And travel expenses paid? By the way how come they invited both of us? Out of the same book.

They didn't. I came on my own. Because I saw on the program you'd be there.

Oho? Is it all over with Andromeda then?

You invented that.

I invented you too. Critics never seem to understand this, they keep writing about two couples, or even three, Mira and Willy, Cassandra and Orion, Andromeda and Orion. When in fact I am Cassandra and invent everyone, mostly out of constellations. It's perfectly clear in the text, but even serious critics don't read. Characters are constellations you know, constellations of semes.

Did you say semen?

Could be. In a spermissive society. You and I are situated at different narrative levels.

And yet we meet. Here for instance.

And there. How slow the traffic is. Everyone seems to be lunching in Sausalito.

I booked a table. By the window. Besides, you were invented by another.

63

Mira is amazed by the length of the bridge, so familiar from films it seems fictional, and of course is so now. How do they build bridges? she asks Orion the scientist. How do they plant those huge metal pillars in deep and often wild water?

Ah, you should read Kadaré's The Triple-arched Bridge, he describes just that, but in a fourteenth-century Albanian village, so it was very simple still. There they redirected the river.

You mean there's a novel simply about building a bridge?

More than that. The struggle between the ferry-owners and the bridge-builders, the playing on superstitions and old legends, quarrels of princely clans, sabotage, the coming of the Turks. A worker volunteers to be walled up in the bridge.

Human sacrifice for progress!

Hardly news. In fact he was the paid saboteur. And he was murdered first, not walled up alive.

Mira is silent, reflecting that there are other novels about bridges. As they slowly cross she thinks of Esteban and the four others who fall to their death into the chasm from the ropy bridge of San Luis Rey, and the bridge on the River Kwai, built by a crazy English colonel and his men for the Japanese. But then she thinks more pleasurably of Prince Rama, a devastatingly handsome Indian she met this morning in a golden dhoti and bejewelled red turban worn high over drawn black hair that curled under it, and enormous golden ear-rings. Through her talkman, he was telling her about the giant bridge, or maybe causeway, which he had built, or his architect Nala had built over the ocean to the island of Lanka (could that be Srilanka? but it all seemed to be happening on the West coast of India) to rescue his beloved Sita who'd been kidnapped and held prisoner by the demon-man Ravana. She gazes at the Golden Gate Bridge, lost in the tale, so that Prince Rama is sitting next to her, slowly driving the Buick and telling her of the battle as he exudes a rich scent of flower-oil and musk. She glances sideways at him and the olfactory hallucination zaps. What is smell, or sound for that matter, in words, except other words? The reader can't smell or hear. The only sense physically aroused by words is the visual, it forms images. Oh and sexual desire. But that's through visualising. The eyes have it every time, as Cicero said. It is Orion driving, handsome also, but in American clothes, and older, and blond, and Russian.

64

At last they arrive, and park near the restaurant that sticks out on stilts over the water, facing San Francisco and the Golden Gate, with the Bay Bridge stumpy and black much further away to the left. The place is already crowded but they are guided towards the huge glass panes and the scintillating Bay, and are handed a two-by-one-foot menu all in yellow and blue and orange with an infinity of seafoods and strangely named salads, sandwiches, steaks and sorbets.

I'm going to have a prawn salad, says Orion. And a glass of Californian wine.

Is that all? I'm ravenous.

You obviously don't know about American salads, they're big enough to feed for a week the Gulag prisoner I used to be. If you order more you'll have to leave half of it on your plate, as in fact they all do.

Okay, I'll have the same, I don't know what anything else is. This is lovely. I'm glad we came. Oh look, there's Odysseus, with Captain Ahab. He's put on a shepherd's coat since yesterday morning. I had a long talk with him you know, in Greek. As a reader. It felt strange to be both. And of course he had no idea I'm also a character, nor did I tell him. I played my role as reader to perfection. Readers are interpreters, and interpreters extrapolate. We're all spies from Extrapol.

Stop punning, Mira, it makes me mad.

But then Jude joined us and told us in halting nineteenth-century English Greek how he'd learnt it all by himself. He was a bit of a bore I'm afraid, and Odysseus couldn't understand him.

What did he say? Odysseus I mean.

Oh, lots of things. He was pleased they'd taken over the oxblood ritual for one. Was looking forward to the evening session, hoped to talk to Tiresias again, and Eurilochus and Anticlea and others. But they're not here. I didn't disillusion him. He must have been disappointed when the pray-ins were cancelled.

I guess so. Were you?

Well, I did attend the first, you know. When the hooha happened. Oh damn, that reminds me of another book.

Ah yes. The nuclear station you asked me about.

You helped me a lot with that one.

Anything to oblige. But you knew plenty about terrorists. From personal experience. What happened to that mad cousin of yours? Hans, was it?

I invented him too, silly, and his terrorists. But not this morning's lot. That would have been quite beyond me.

Oh I don't know. You invented Xorandor's little terrorist.

So you see I'm here on at least two counts, I mean I appear in two books, though I invented four. But I'm amazed anyone took any notice of them, enough for me to be here I mean. I wonder how these Balzac characters fare in this Convention, I mean those who reappear in several books. I didn't see any of them, I was so busy trying to meet the Greek and Latin ones. Those from epics and romances for instance, obviously those from drama aren't invited, and that's a pity, they're much more interesting. There was a whole procession of beautiful but crossed lovers in the lobby this morning, Anthia and Habercomas, Hero and Leander, Callimachus and Chrysorrhoe, Belthandros and Chrysantra. But also from Oriental sources, Laila and Mejnoun, and Karcha and Kadambari, Lybistros and Rhodamne, Vis and Ramin, Tariel and Nestan. Also Rama and Sita, she adds after a pause, then breathlessly continues: There's a book called Ocean of Rivers of Tales, isn't that beautiful? And of course Tristan and Iseult, Cligès and Fenice, Lancelot and Guinevere, Aucassin and Nicolette, Dante and Beatrice, Troilus and Criseyde. And many more. Renzo and Lucia, Edouard and Ottilie. Even Adolphe and Ellénore, of all people.

Oh yes?

She changes tack: I saw Aeneas incidentally, having a very difficult conversation with Kassandra, Christa Wolf's Kassandra I mean, who was in love with him in Troy, but clearly Virgil's Aeneas knew nothing about that. She was quite distraught. I allowed myself to explain it to him, in shaky Latin, which she couldn't understand. He was very astonished. Kept hoping to meet Dido. Though he treated her none too well. Oh, look Orion, there's Dorothea Brooke at that far table. Who on earth is she with? In that shabby grey suit. Can't be Ladislaw already. No, not young enough. She's in her widow's weeds today, how odd. So they do change times while here. According to the papers on them I suppose.

Stop gossiping Mira.

Sorry. Oh Zeus! She's with Pastor Oberlin, who was on the platform yesterday and tried to talk with the terrorists. What a serious couple. I wonder if they're talking theology. But does she know German? Casaubon didn't. They're not wearing talkmans. And all the

66

equipment she had to start with was a toybox history of the world adapted to young ladies. She is very handsome I must say.

Education isn't everything.

True. As she learnt.

Their food arrives, piled high as Dido's funeral pyre.

Lordy you were right.

What did you think of yesterday's business, he asks again.

The terrorists? Literary highjinks. They seem to have worried the congregation more than they did the organisers. But I suppose the police are continuing their inquiries. Pronounced ink-worries here, even ink-quarries, nice, no? Sorry. Yesterday I sat in the bar with Mr Casaubon, hoping to find out what he really knew of comparative mythology. He was both fabulously verbose and inarticulate with secrecy, takes some doing. But –

Oh come on, Mira, you know it wasn't him who knew or didn't know. You're pretty verbose yourself.

– but alas, he was surrounded with females, his wife of course, who was defending true religion as against what she called the secondary importance of ecclesiastical forms and articles of belief, but also the two Emmas, Woodhouse and Bovary. who seemed quite at a loss, especially when we were joined by that grey-haired young Interpreter who'd talked with the terrorists, and told us that the oxblood is only coca cola with the gas taken out. Gas? said Dorothea, you mean ether? I nearly collapsed. But he obviously hadn't a clue who I was, nor of course had the others. Nobody reads me, evidently.

Not surprising.

I don't mean that, but he clearly found me uninteresting. Nondescript, he seemed to be thinking. And of course, as narrator-character, I can hardly describe myself.

For that matter you don't describe me.

Orion whose doublesided sword so blunt so sharp will mar the memory of a menippean love.

That's not a description.

Which later becomes many-peon. Oh! She gasps. Look who's just come in.

Orion turns. At the entrance stands a small Japanese lady, startlingly beautiful in a black and blue and gold kimono, with large black and gold pins opening out symmetrically like fanbones from her massively piled black hair. She also holds, open in front of her, a huge black fan with golden cockerels and flying bluebirds on it, although the wintry weather hardly warrants this. Her face is deathly white, her eyelids painted black and downcast, her tiny lips the only red in the general apparition. Behind her, with her, is a strikingly handsome man like a darkfaced archangel, dark-haired, with low-slung lazy eyelids that seem almost purple with fatigue. There is something coarse about the nose, the mouth is too well-fleshed to be strong, the ears are long-lobed like young knurled jackfruit. How does this description enter her head? He has a glittering eye and he's wearing a golden dhoti and red turban. She has no doubt who he is, but murmurs to Orion: Who's he with? The Lady Murasaki?

But Mira, Murasaki Shikibu was an author. I read and reread The Tale of Genji in a tattered Russian translation I found hidden on top of a lavatory tank in my Siberian camp.

You did? The French call her cette ennuyeuse Scudéry japonaise.

They would.

But she also wrote a diary. Diary and Poetic Memoirs. And Poetic Memoirs are inevitably partly fictional. Anyway it's probably not her but Madame Chrysanthème or a cleisha-girl out of some postwar American novel. Unless she's Chinese. Ho Siao-yu for instance or the courtesan Li.

Stop showing off, Mira. And can't you distinguish traditional Japanese from traditional Chinese dress? Or for that matter, eleventh from twentieth century?

No, can you? Some change of horizon for him, anyway.

Why, who is he?

Orion, how can you not know?

I'm a scientist, that's how.

Prince Rama, from the Ramayana.

Never heard of him.

The exotic couple is shown to the table next to them, recently vacated. No one seems to take much notice of them, San Francisco being used to idiosyncrasies of outfit. Except Dorothea who stares at them in impolite amazement. A waiter hurries to their table, bearing the two huge menus. He too looks subcontinental, though less dark, and talks low and rapidly in an unknown tongue. Mira watches intently.

But the Prince is hidden behind the menu, only the top of his red turban showing. And then she gasps. For when he puts it down to address the waiter, she realises her mistake, and why that odd description had entered her head. He is Gibreel Farishta, in the role of Prince Rama. Was the Prince she'd met this morning not the Prince then? Is the waiter an Iranian? A Pakistani? An Algerian, a Libyan? Mira curses her ethnological ignorance. Is he threatening or warning?

Orion, she murmurs, don't turn round now, but it's not Prince Rama at all. It's Gibreel Farishta.

Oh, you mean the cause of all the highjinks?

Yes, and I think he's being threatened by the waiter, keep quiet, I want to hear what's happening.

Gibreel is listening with Olympian calm, well, that's hardly the word considering the filmparts of Hindu and other gods he used to play, elephant-headed gods, blue-skinned Krishna and all the rest. He is looking at the waiter with that quiet, unhurried gaze, as if he could see the future. Are characters aware of their future? Mira wonders. Does Emma Bovary know she will take arsenic? Does Dorothea Brooke at this moment know of Mr Casaubon's ungentlemanly codicil to his Will, that she is not to marry Ladislaw, of whom she has never consciously thought even as an admirer? Is she aware that Pfarrer Oberlin is out of another, earlier book? Does Gibreel know that he will shoot himself? Here they all are, caught in one temporal aspect of themselves and behaving like real people, ignorant of their destinies, and yet listening to papers on themselves that take a godlike overview, reveal structures and moral flaws, repetitions and balances and perfect circles and dramatic ironies. They have been doing this for years, for decades some of them. The Lady Murasaki, if it is she, has been a classic since the eleventh century. She sits with her back to them, apparently still plunged in the enormous menu, her tall hairdo with its fanlike horns bent almost into it. Is this because she only knows Japanese, and not Pakistani or Persian or whatever? Or is it because, with submissive feminine tact, she doesn't meddle in men's affairs?

Stop staring, Mira, and pay attention to me for a change.

But Orion, I must know. This is important.

How can you know by staring? They're talking another language, you can't even eavesdrop, let alone invent on the basis of a few words here and there. You're stumped, Mira.

He says this with satisfaction and goes on eating, his back to the exotic couple, unable to stare.

But the waiter has gone. Mira follows him with her eyes. Is he going to call up someone? He disappears into the kitchens. The Bay is still a scintillating blue, San Francisco still lies beyond the pale orange metal cathedral, its rectangular skyscrapers, and the pointed one, like an outsize steeple, shimmering white in the winter sun. The customers continue to eat, to drink, to talk, to order, to pay and leave, to enter. The waiter reappears with a tray bearing the exotic couple's Coca-Cola, sandwiches and salad piled high, delivers them with a glare and moves off.

Gibreel is behaving strangely. Like those of a carmaking robot, his glittering black eyes sweep slowly round the restaurant in a steady, circular stare, pausing slightly at each table. Everyone is absorbed in their food, no one is looking at him. Except Mira, whose stare meets his. She smiles, uncertainly, and even nods, as if they'd been introduced, which in a manner of reading they have. His gaze switches at once to vagueness, like that of a man who supposes this must be a past mistress − so he can't be Prince Rama − and moves on to the Bay outside. His eyebrows rise slightly, his heavy lids lift and an extra glint appears in his already glittering eyes, which widen to reveal the sharp whites around the black pupils. Has he just had an idea? Mira watches, deaf to Orion's talk. Then the eyes switch to where the waiters stand when unoccupied. Mira follows his look. The restaurant is much emptier. A few waiters are still serving or totting up checks. The oriental waiter is nowhere to be seen. Gibreel smiles to himself, then quietly slides the window slightly open, lifts his glass of Coca Cola and pours it quickly into the water below. As he slides the window shut, his eyes meet Mira's again and he smiles at her much more frankly. Then he guffaws and says, apparently to his partner but really across at her and loudly enough for her to hear: I don't drink oxblood. Isn't it, he adds for Indian idiom and bursts out laughing.

Madame Chrysanthème or the Lady Murasaki hasn't budged, seems immobile as a doll. Suddenly the oriental waiter is at their table again and stares at the empty glass. Everrything okké sirr? he asks. Anotherr kokka-kolla? Is good, yes madam? The lady bows her head.

Everything is delicious thank you, says Gibreel. No, no more coke thank you.

The waiter grimaces and moves off towards the other waiters who are now standing near the kitchen door, impatient for the last customers to leave. Mira watches him as he stares from a distance at Gibreel. Is he waiting for him to stand up in agony and die? She looks again at Gibreel who is now picking at his food, carefully, not eating. He looks up at her and she shakes her head, also her raised index finger at him. He gives her a thumbs-up sign, glances across at the waiter who is still staring at him across the room, slides the window open again and empties his plate carefully into the sea, pushing the food with his knife. Then he glances triumphantly at the waiter, who rushes up with a murderous scowl on his face.

What you doing mister, sirr? he asks angrily, I will report.

The flesh of wise fish is harder and more harmful than the flesh of foolish fish, Gibreel replies gnomically. So only the foolish eat both, while the wise eat only the foolish fish. Khazar proverb.

Shut your false wisdom sirr please, this is best seafood we serve.

Seafood, says Gibreel glibly. Best in the sea, no?

You, polluter of ocean, polluter of Eternal Truth, we have not ended with you, we –

Keep calm, old boy, says Gibreel, and kindly refrain from troubling the Lady Murasaki with your bad temper and bad words.

We have not ended with you, the waiter almost shouts. Get you out.

Orion turns round, the remaining customers turn round. But Dorothea and Oberlin have left, and Odysseus and Captain Ahab are laughing together at some sea joke. The manageress, a plump lady with a puffed-up blond hairdo and a puffed-up blond face, hastens to the table.

What's the ruckus, Abdel?

This man, who is not a gentleman, oh no sirr, he put all his food into the sea. Such manners I have not seen.

Now sir, that's no way to behave. If you had any complaint you could have just said.

Poisoned, says Gibreel. Not that I can prove it, now. I might have proved it earlier by dying. We'll see how the fishes fare. No damage done you know, I didn't throw the plate, and I shall pay for the food that didn't kill me. Consider yourself lucky, little memsahib, that the whole restaurant wasn't bombed to smitheroos, yes? Come on, Lady M.

71

He picks up the check on the table and marches out, rudely parting the manageress with the puffed hairdo from the scowling waiter. Lady Murasaki, leaving her food and glass only half consumed, rises meekly, kowtows to the manageress but not to the waiter, flicks her large black and blue fan open, flutters it, and trots out after him with short mincing steps.

The silence in the restaurant turns to a low murmur. Most of the customers have gone. Orion looks embarrassed and also picks up his check. Don't say a thing, Mira, he admonishes firmly as if she were about to protest, but on the contrary she follows him, less meekly, more with a quick stride to pass him and catch up with Gibreel Farishta at the cashdesk. But he has vanished. He usually does.

8

Dorothea stands on the sidewalk with Pfarrer Oberlin, wondering how they will get back to San Francisco, so far away and white on the distant hill. He brought her in one of those horseless carriages they call a cab, ordered from the hotel, and told her these can be hailed in the street. But none seems to be forthcoming, at least, there are plenty of carriages but they don't stop. How much more convenient it is to have one's own carriage and horses at beck and call. Even in Rome, where she was so lonely and so bitterly disappointed with Mr Casaubon, who spent his entire time in libraries, their hired carriage deposited her, with Tantripp, at this or that museum, and picked them up. And at home, at both the Grange and Lowick Manor, she can also ride, is known as a fine horsewoman, and loves long country walks. Here nobody seems to walk. She suggests it to Oberlin, who is used to his Alsace hills.

Meine liebe Frau Casaubon, we are not in the European landscape. It is a very long way, and full of danger.

She sighs. She was so pleased to have encountered him, by chance, in the hall of the hotel. She had seen him on the platform with all those romanic priests, and boldly addressed him, congratulating him on his courage. He answered in halting English, although he had refused to do so to the terrorists. She told him of her excitement when her neighbour Sir James Chettam had seen and approved of her drawings and plans for new cottages on his estate. Of course she didn't tell Oberlin she now knew that Sir James was courting her, while all the time she had thought him a perfect match for Celia. Indeed she'd been quite rude to him on that walk. But when he patiently ignored this and asked to see her plans she had exulted, and this she did tell Oberlin, and how she had thought, at the time, that it would be as if the spirit of

Oberlin had passed over the parishes to make the life of poverty beautiful.

But then, she reminds herself now, hadn't she thought of Mr Casaubon as a living Bossuet, whose work would reconcile complete knowledge with devoted piety, a modern Augustine who united the glories of doctor and saint? I should learn everything then, she'd said to herself, it would be my duty to study that I might help him the better in his great work. There would be nothing trivial about our lives. Everyday-things with us would mean the greatest things. It would be like marrying Pascal! Alas.

And yet, with Oberlin, they talked of reforms at luncheon. And of philanthropy in general, and of the Protestant Church. Until that strange Indian maharajah entered, with the little oriental doll, and behaved so oddly.

The Pfarrer is desperately hailing huge horseless carriages, some of them as large as cottages, purple, red, silver, but none stops. I think these are, wie sagt man, private landauern, he says, the cab-ones are different colour, but which I forget.

And then one does stop. It is just as enormous but a sober gleaming black. The darkened window at the back magically moves down.

Can I give you people a ride? You look stranded.

An apparently short young man with cropped black hair looks out and addresses them in a curiously high tenor voice.

Thank you sir, it is exceedingly kind of you.

Jump in then. Not sir. My name is Rita Humboldt. I'm the organiser of the Convention. Miss Brooke, isn't it? Come in here beside me, there's room for three. Your companion must sit in the front with my chauffeur.

Dorothea is bewildered and inwardly bewails her short sight. And what is a show-fur? But there are loud long coach horns bellowing behind.

Come on in honey. Our drivers are goddamn impatient in this country.

Dorothea gets in, shocked by the lady's language, but then, she looks like a man and seems to talk like one, very brusquely, yet slurred in that odd colonial nasal tone she's been hearing for two days. Oberlin goes round to sit by the driver, and off the carriage moves, smooth as a garden swing. The lady wears a scarlet costume like a riding habit, but with a very short skirt, like those Interpreters but bright red, as if she were in hunting pink. She is very small, indeed her feet barely touch the floor of the carriage. There is a man sitting next to her, almost as small, and they both move to make room for her. But the seat is immensely wide and comfortable.

This is Lieutenant Columbo, who's directing the inquiries. Miss Dorothea Brooke, from Middlemarch.

Well, not exactly, I'm from – How do you do Mr Columbo. She hasn't understood the gentleman's rank, Loo something, so plays safe. I trust you have enough room.

Sure, sure, thank you ma'am. I usually drive a much smaller vehicle, an old drophead Peugeot 403 that spits fire.

Dorothea ignores the incomprehensible last bit of sentence, and says merely, These carriages are certainly exceedingly spacious.

We've been lunching together, to discuss the case you know.

Oh, so have we. I mean, I beg your pardon, I quite forget my manners. This is Pastor Oberlin.

He turns round and bows his head.

Why, that's too bad, I should've recognised you. Especially with your label. You were officiating yesterday weren't you? So you'll have been grilled by the Inspector. Lieutenant, why didn't you recognise him and tell me?

I saw hundreds of witnesses, ma'am, and my inspectors –

But you should've remembered this one, he was on the platform, and parleyed.

Yes ma'am. Touché.

Well we're all connected up now, that's great.

Were you in the Gasthaus over the water? the pastor asks, turning his head again. It commands a beautiful vista.

No, never touch the place, too putrid. Doesn't exactly turn me on, you know, only assholes go there. Now honey you mustn't mind the way I talk, how could you know?

I see. There was indeed a curious incident. A tall Indian person, well, gentleman I suppose, richly and colourfully dressed, threw all his food out of the window into the sea, and then had an exceedingly loud dispute with the serving-man and the manager's wife. It was most disagreeable.

There you are, putrid, like I said.

75

Did you say an Indian, ma'am? What did he look like?

Oh balls, Inspector, there are hundreds of them around.

I hardly think so Mrs Humboldt, this was a public ordinary, and there was certainly no room for dancing.

Honey you're a wow! But come to think of it Inspector, maybe you're right on the ball again. Now why didn't I think of –

Can you describe him, ma'am?

They are sliding forward slowly on the endless orange bridge and Dorothea looks out anxiously.

I'm rather short-sighted you know and we were at a distance. But I recollect that he was tall and very dark, I mean dark-skinned as well as dark-haired, with extraordinary eyes, glittering under heavy eyelids, almost purple eyelids. I've never seen anyone like him.

That's him, Inspector.

What was he wearing, ma'am, can you remember?

Oh. A golden tunic I think, and a red turban. I thought he must be some sort of Indian king, maharajah don't they call them. Until he started to behave in this, well, outrageous way.

I don't get it, Inspector, that sounds like Prince Rama, one of our most honoured guests. Pre-Islamic you know, even proto-Hindu, not Farishta at all.

According to my information, ma'am, our man is a film-actor, who frequently plays such parts. My wife would be –

So he did, touchée Inspector.

What happened afterwards. Did he leave?

I don't know I'm afraid. We departed when it occurred. The Pastor wanted to go to them and smooth things out, but I do not like public disputes.

But you were standing on the kerb, ma'am, when –

The curb? To what, pray? A sudden premonition of danger fleets through her mind.

The sidewalk. Waiting for a cab. Didn't you see him come out?

Yes. At least I so did, the pastor says, wrenching his head round again. Frau Casaubon was looking away. He was by a Japanese lady accompanied.

Japanese?

Yes. Very beautiful she was. As in old oriental painting.

The Lady Murasaki. She's on our guest-list.

76

And where did they go sir? Did you see?

They entered a pferdlos er –

A what sir? I didn't catch what you said.

A carriage without horses.

I see, sir. A car. An automobile we used to call it.

Ah, that is most clever.

Do you remember the colour? Or the number-plate?

The colour was yellow. I not understand the other word.

Thank you sir. That was a cab. Not much help I'm afraid, Professor.

What d'you think of that, Inspector? D'you suppose he thought his food was poisoned?

Poisoned? But why should – Dorothea feels very tired and slightly ill. The driver hasn't ceased to raise his eyes at the little looking-glass fixed above him, as if he were examining her.

Does either of you remember the waiter? Rita asks sharply. Or maybe you don't know that word? The – er – serving-man.

Waiter is fine. No, I didn't notice him.

Did you, Mr Oberlin?

I think he was oriental also, but very paler. Perhaps, he continues, if you conduct the – er – search, you can us explain what the commotion yesterday about was? Is this Indian king with it connected?

Dead right he is. His name is Gibreel Farishta, he was going to officiate today, and the Moslems objected to him. THAT's what the commotion about was.

Both Columbo and Dorothea glance at her in astonishment at her rudeness, but the imitation has passed unnoticed by Oberlin.

With madmen am I very cognisant, he says. I had one madman in my house. Lenz, he adds as if all should acknowledge the name. But this too goes unnoticed.

You mean in your family, Mr Oberlin? How dreadful.

No, not in my family. Long hospitality I gave him. Yes, it was, very difficult. A great trial of Christian virtue. I wrote it day by day in my Tagebuch, this helped. And I prayed for strength. A poet.

You wrote it down in poetry? I didn't know you –

No. He was a poet. Many poets are mad.

Literature is full of madmen, look at Oedipa Maas, Tyrone Slothrop and all that crazy crew. Paranoid.

I don't see that merely being annoyed can lead to madness, observes

Dorothea. How very sad.

Rita chortles noisily. Annoyed, parannoyed, honey you're a scream.

This is followed by silence, puzzled for Dorothea, reminiscent for Oberlin, thoughtful for Columbo. Fortunately they have reached the Hilton, and emerge with thanks and thankfulness.

The huge lobby is full of caliphs and sultans and janissaries and oriental warriors of all sizes and colours, some totally black in garish robes. Dorothea feels bewildered, exhausted, and sits down suddenly on a miraculously empty high walnut and red sofa near the teak staircase, next to a thronelike dark wooden chair all in carved figurines. The stairs are now free of queuers. The short little lady in hunting pink has vanished into the crowd. Oberlin sits down on the tallbacked throne next to her, asks if she is feeling not well.

Not well at all Mr Oberlin. And I am very confused.

Perhaps you go to your room? Shall I give you escort?

Later, thank you, I will. At the moment I feel I can't take another step. Oh Mr Oberlin, I am quite distraught. I was so already before, I should not have approached you in the way I did. I thought –

I am very happy you so did, Frau Casaubon, please not to be distressed. But it is so noiseful here, can you not your strength gather, that we might go to a more quiet place to talk?

In a moment. Who are all these people Mr Oberlin? Mohammedans?

Yes. It is their day. They appear very angry.

Mr Oberlin I must tell you something. I am not distressed by my impolite approach to you, although no doubt I ought to be. I am not distressed by the events today, that strange Indian does not concern me, nor by the language of that extraordinary lady. I am distressed by something that occurred yesterday afternoon. May I tell you about it?

Yes, yes, natürlich. But you will have to shout almost.

He leans forward to hear her above the roar.

I had gone with my husband, Mr Casaubon, to hear a paper on him. He was so looking forward to it Mr Oberlin, there are not many you know, unfortunately. He is always so concerned with his posterity. The paper was called 'Casaubon and the Mystery Religions'. I felt so very sure it would give him a new lease of life. His great work, as I told you, is the Key to all Mythology. And if I may interrupt myself for one moment, I would like to ask you about this. Mr Ladislaw told me in Rome that Mr Casaubon's ignorance of German must throw grave discredit on the value of his work, since a great deal has been published on his subject in that language. I was quite disturbed about it I remember. It was the first time I began to, well, doubt. Is this the case Mr Oberlin?

I believe it is so, Frau Casaubon. But I am not authority in that domain. I also believe, if I may so say, that a pastor's work is first with his, how you say, his parish, his sheep, lost and found, and second, with interpreting the Bible to them. And third, if he is inclined so, with Christian theology.

Yes, says Dorothea, crushed but unable to disagree.

Please to continue with your story. Loud, if you please, it is difficult to hear in this great noise.

Dorothea is a little put out and feels she should have agreed to leave the hall. The crowd seems to churn around them, closer and closer, and she feels like souring milk at the centre of a huge butter-vat. But she prefers to shout than to move.

Well, we sat there and listened, and as we listened, I could see dismay, and a great anger, slowly spread over his pale features. He works much too hard you know, allows no time for rest or healthy walks, just a short turn in the shrubbery, that's all. I was watching him anxiously, not paying attention to the paper. But when it was over, and questions came, it became apparent to me that the paper was not about him at all, but about another Casaubon, a much younger man, who had even had, well, relationships with young ladies, and who was in some way connected with someone called Foucault, who invented a pendulum.

I have heard of a scientist in Paris called Foucault, but of his pendulum not. There however was a Renaissance historian called Casaubon, Isaac I believe. You know, Frau Casaubon, names are not a private property. I have been told that there is a town called Oberlin, in the State of Ohio. But that was named after me, he adds with a hesitant smile, so perhaps it is not, er, pertinent. Excuse me. Please to continue.

You are so modest Mr Oberlin. Well, it was this younger Casaubon who was the subject of this paper, not my husband at all. His face became even greyer than – I mean quite grey. He arose, with some difficulty, and with my help. We managed to get out before the end, which would have meant more pushing and scrambling you know, people seem to be so ill-mannered here – oh!

A dark Sultan in a robe of shimmering midnight blue and gold has just tripped over her feet, hidden under her black dress. He is exquisitely polite in excusing himself and she forces a gracious smile. He is with a Spanish Grandee in black, with a white ruff, whose label says in large letters even she can read, Philip II, but she can't catch the rest. Mr Oberlin gets up and insists they now move to a quieter place. She agrees and rises as Philip II bows and the Sultan joins his hands in an eastern inclination. They then sit on the high sofa and wooden throne just vacated. Dorothea accepts Oberlin's arm and they push their way through the crowd towards the bar.

Did you see? That was a King of Spain I believe. Mr Casaubon told me he had spoken with him. What is he doing here? Is he a character too?

He must be so. He sat in the front row yesterday morning and became very angry about the – er – perturbance. His companion looked as the Sultan from the Arabian Nights.

They reach the bar at last, which is empty, and order tea.

That is much better. Please to continue Frau Casaubon.

Mr Casaubon was also very angry, about this paper. I suppose he had secretly nursed too many hopes of being remembered, you know, alive again. We reached our room, and there he collapsed into an armchair and was speechless for a long time. I got him a glass of water and knelt beside him to give it to him. But then he looked at me, with a kind of deep hatred in his pale eyes. I have only once seen such hatred, Mr Oberlin, and that was in Rome, when – or perhaps no, several times, after we got back to Lowick Manor. This hatred is always connected with the visits of his young cousin, Mr Ladislaw, I've never understood why. But this time it was not. 'My love', he said – he never uses those terms except when very angry indeed, as if they were the deepest insult he can find. 'You win.' 'What do you mean, dearest?' I asked, completely at a loss. And then it all poured out, in a quiet fury, oh, so, evil, Mr Oberlin, I can think of no other word now, but at the time I was merely in deep dismay that once again I seemed to have done everything wrong and, well, annoyed him. That is why I made that remark about annoyance and madness in the carriage, which seemed to amuse the owner so much.

What poured out, as you say, Frau Casaubon? Please, do not so distress yourself.

What poured out was that I had stolen all his glory, with my youth, my energy, my good will, my passion. He uttered this word with utmost scorn Mr Oberlin, and yet, yes, with passion. But was my passion to learn enough to be of use to him such a terrible thing? And is not his deep interest in mythology also a passion, that consumes him to the exclusion of all spark of life, even of the passion with which I desired to help him?

She gives a little cry, a little sob, and Mr Oberlin puts his hand gently on hers.

The spirit of self-sacrifice in women is much known, he murmurs, but it is oft by men abused.

But what did he mean, Mr Oberlin, stolen all his glory?

He meant, dear Frau Casaubon, that you are better known, by posterity, you are more studied.

Oh, not at first. We were both quite forgot, for many years.

So was I. That is after all why we all come here, is it not? He perhaps is only studied as a great mistake that you made, that is, as part of your character.

Mistake! ... Yes. That is true. I discovered it too late.

He meant that you have survived. He has not.

So I have killed him!

My dear Frau Casaubon, you must not –

But I have, I have. My story is not ended. For after he had finished those terrible accusations, he waved the glass of water away, and me, and sat back in that yellow armchair, and, yes Mr Oberlin, he simply died. I had not said a word in answer. The silence in my husband's ear was never more to be broken. I looked for a bell-pull but found none. And then, quite suddenly, he wasn't there. And I found myself wearing these widow's weeds. I was free, yet distraught. That is why I should not have approached you Mr Oberlin, I was not myself.

But you were, you are, Frau Casaubon.

I shall never forgive myself.

You will, God will.

But how do you explain it, Mr Oberlin, how do you interpret it?

I do not, Frau Casaubon. Only God interprets. We exist only

because God thinks of us. If God would, no, should, efface Himself for one brief moment, the whole Universe, its past and all its futures, would be effaced also.

9

Felipe Segundo has tired of Goethe. Qué aburrido, un hombre fastidioso, at least in that version which, he has gathered from the label and from his presence at yesterday's session, belongs to the same century as his own, the twentieth. Perhaps the model was better. Whereas he feels in many ways more interesting than his model, insofar as he isn't it, though at times he also has the certainty of being his own model. The Nuevo Mundo, now that he is actually here, in it, seems very strange and very vulgar compared with what he had heard from the young castaway with the six toes. But then, stories!

Sultan Shahriar, King of India, has been telling him enchanting stories, or rather shouting them above the hubbub as he sits on the peculiar red sofa, shouting them across at him, Felipe, who has instinctively chosen the uncomfortable carved wooden throne. And inside the stories, begging monks called calenders, how odd, or dervishes, are threatened with beheading if they don't tell a good story. He likes that. But the Sultan has an odd habit of stopping at crucial moments to go to sleep, promising a stay of execution to someone.

He met the Sultan at a paper called The Art of Telling, much interrupted by a few people, oddly dressed, who insisted on talking about The Art of Tele, whatever that is. Tele means far in Greek, doesn't it? All about a Grand Vizier's daughter called Zejersade, or some such outlandish name. But then it got very confused with a certain Juan Báz, of whom he has never heard, who claims to be the real author of the tales. The Sultan explained to him afterwards that the Vizier's daughter is his favourite, because she tells him these stories every night. A strange way to spend nights with a favourite, he commented, and the Sultan smirked, or smiled in his big moustache, scratched an itch under his turban with a fine bone fork, and said love is always a story, a story is always making love. Curious, thinks Felipe, this instant sympathy he feels for an infidel, as opposed to his hatred for protestants and other heretics. The Sultan has just fallen asleep again, although he would drink no wine. Stories seem to be his wine.

Of course infidels don't drink wine. Or oxblood. Felipe hasn't altogether understood what all those caliphs yesterday were on about, or why everything stopped in the middle of the Mass for the Dead. He still feels indignant about that, though being in the front row he did get his royal sip. Someone explained to him what had happened, but he didn't witness it himself, he was praying and refused to turn for a mere popular tumult. And so he found it quite simply unbelievable. How could a knight – but no. Another fabulous story. He likes it, in the way he likes the Sultan's stories, however unfinished, but he can't relate it to his reality, anymore than he can relate to it the six-toed youth's story of the Nuevo Mundo, the initiation rites, the woman with the headdress of fluttering butterflies and all the rest. Initiation rites. He has passed through all the rituals, as king, as most Catholic King. But do stories have anything to do with ritual? Ritual is static, repetitive, a stage, another stage, like life, like nature, but is that a story? Stories are out of this world. Like the Sultan at the moment. Despite the huge din of the crowds in the vast hall.

Excuse me Your Majesty, says a voice in peculiar Spanish, but have you seen Goethe?

Felipe is vexed by this rude interruption of his meditations and looks blankly at the red-haired chiquita – who reminds him in a flash of irritation of his Queen Isabel, Isabel of England. But then he recognises the chica who had rushed up to the altar and caused all the commotion.

Shsh, he says with his finger on his black moustache, pointing the same finger at once to the Sultan on the pink sofa. He sleeps.

In this noise? says the girl, then I can hardly wake him. I'm looking for Goethe, or rather this lady, Mrs Charlotte Kestner, is looking for him.

Felipe looks with condescension at a plain elderly woman in a ridiculous white dress, unflattering to her figure, with pale red ribbons and bows scattered all over it.

El Señor Goethe has withdrawn from the tumult. I do not know where.

Oh, there you are, Kelly. I want you.

84

Felipe is shocked by the manly voice, short hair and brusque address, which ignores him, of the small dark lady in red. The Sultan jerks awake and beams at everyone.

There's to be a plenary pray-in for the dead tomorrow, the little lady goes on.

¡Ah! says Felipe. ¡Bueno!

Without ritual of any denomination, just a list, as long as all our arms put together end to end, damn it, to be read out, everyone free to pray inwardly as they like.

Ah, says Felipe again. That is good. All those people lying in books that are coffins.

Well put my dear sir. I'm agin it of course, but the pressure's been horrendous.

You mean, from the characters? asks Kelly, incredulous.

Hell no, what do they care, as long as they survive. I hope only few will come.

I care, I come, says Felipe, the dead are –

No, from colleagues. Those who can find nothing smarter to do than disinter what time and the canon have rightly forgotten.

The Canon? says Felipe. They did not finish it yesterday.

Didn't they, says Rita Humboldt, looking vague. Well I'm not surprised. I'm surprised by nothing at the present time. Goddamn assholes if you ask me.

Nobody does. Nobody but Kelly understands.

Come on, honey, you'll be needed. Where's Jack? I want all Interpreters in the Board-room by five. Will you sail up to the office and ask them from me to inform them by phone immediately. And tell any of them you see yourself. Gotta go now, so long.

Kelly leaves Lotte to the mercy of King and Sultan, who are courteously uninterested, and the Sultan starts another story, so that Kelly sees on turning round that Lotte is drifting off, disconsolate. But Kelly herself sails up, as Rita put it, to the office, unwilling to be of further help to the poor woman.

After leaving her message, with some insistence since no one would at first believe her, a mere junior Interpreter, Kelly starts for the lobby by the back stairs. She is beginning to know the topography of the hotel.

But suddenly she sits down on one of the concrete steps and takes a

85

cigarette from her purse. She feels angry with herself, with the office, with Rita, with all these guests. Why all this hierarchy? Why couldn't the office girls accept her message at once? Why do the guests gather in social groups, unwilling to talk to anyone out of their sphere? A king can talk to a sultan, even of another faith. Yesterday she saw him talking to Prince Ernest IV of Parma, surrounded by very aristocratic ladies, and she hovered among them all a long time to see their labels, smiling like an Interpreter on duty, saying a few gracious words to each while memorising their names and origins as if for an examination. A few she did know or at least had heard of, some never, and she had to make a great effort: la Princesse de Clèves, la Princesse de Guermantes, Prince Tancredi from Jerusalem Delivered, the Princess Casamassima, la Duchesse de Sanseverina-Taxis, Theodoric King of the Ostrogoths, Tsar Saltan, Charlemagne with his flowery beard, Prince Genji, Count Cagliostro, le Prince d' Agrigente, el Conde Alarcos, Prince Djalma, King Alkinoos, a Khazar Princess Ateh, King Alfonso VI, a gorgeous Indian Prince called Rama, who told her of his brother Laksmana and said how loyal friendship and brotherly love are much more important in his country than woman's love. Like Tariel and Avt'andil! Kelly exclaimed but he looked blank. And Prince Pururavas, and several Maharanis with unmemorisable names, an Egyptian Pharaoh in a loincloth and kalasyris, labelled Amen something, Amenhotep, that was it, King Arthur, Attila, Princess Bolkonskaia, a Chinese Empress.

And someone called Count Ferdinand Fathom, who looked a real fake. The Marquis Wilhelm von Eyrick, refined and coquettish, My Lord Edward, Geneviève de Brabant, Haroun el Rachid Caliph of Baghdad, la Reine Margot, someone called Marko Kralievich, was it, from some South Slav epic she couldn't remember, and a Prince Sadko from a Russian epic and a Prince Vladimir ditto, and a Mexican god-king-philopher Nezahualcoyotl, splendid in red and green and gold.

And Lady Audley – who on earth was she? And a Lady Metroland, and Lady Dedlock. And a Lady Dudley. And a Lady Brett Ashley, oh yes, out of Hemingway, she did remember that one. Now how could Brett, a kind of nympho, get on with all those people simply because she had a title by marriage? Does Emma Woodhouse feel more at ease with Dorothea Brooke or Mrs Dalloway than with Emma Bovary, a mere doctor's wife? And who can Jude talk to, bookish but poor? And Mr Verloc, can he only talk to anarchists out of The Possessed? And

Vasco da Gama, can he only talk to Captain Ahab or Capitaine Nemo or Odysseus? Or Babbitt to Frank Cowperwood or Gatsby or Gesualdo or Nucingen?

And what about the poor, someone like Lispector's Macabéa? Could she only talk to Oliver Twist asking for more or learning to be a pickpocket, or to Gavroche or Cosette? Or to Eugène Sue's La Maheux, misshapen, earning four francs a week? Or for that matter to Zola's Bonnemort or to Lem Something out of some novel about miners in the Thirties she read about in the Marxist barrel-scraping? Hadn't there been some sort of love-affair of intellectuals for workers, much unrequited, or at most like lords wooing poor sheepgirls or dairymaids, the way d'Urberville seduced Tess and left her? And all the dropouts of today, can they meet any but each other, Holden Caulfield and Lazarillo and Lucky Jim? Can Hiawatha only talk to Chingach-gook? Or Achebe's Onkonkwo to Huck's Jim or Toni Morrison's Paul D?

Can clerks only talk to clerks, Akakievich to Bartelby (if he talks), Devushkin to Uriah Heap or Sainthomme? Or priests to priests, the Reverend Collins to Gösta Berling or Don Abbondio or the curé de campagne or the curé de Cucugnan? Or Zola's l'abbé Fanjas to Jocelyn or Ernest Pontifex? Or the Buddhist monk Nagasena to Chaucer's Friar? She is astonished at the number of characters, with names and even details, that come crowding into her mind with this simple question. She must have read more than she thinks, forgotten less. She's not so illiterate after all. The very classification into ranks and social groups has brought them to life in her memory. Perhaps she should do comparative sociological analysis, golden-hearted prostitutes like Esther von Gobseck, melancholics, monks, traitors, scholars, thieves, musicians, poets, painters, servants, terrorists? She tries to think of musicians, Jean-Christophe, Vinteuil, but doesn't get very far. Poets, Demodokos, Tannhäuser, Malte Laurids Brigge? Painters, Frenhofer, Elstir? There must be others. Murderers, Meursault, and of course millions in thrillers and tecs.

And all the people in the lobby today, sheiks and houris, sultans and viziers, caliphs and emirs, maharajahs and memsahibs, Pakistani gen-erals, black palmwine drinkards and tribal leaders, they too seemed only to seek each other in small groups, isolated from innumerable other small groups. The only person alone seemed to be a Tibetan

87

ascetic labelled Milarepa, but even he was approached by a timeless looking man called the Wandering Jew. But whose Wandering Jew? This one had eyebrows that met in a long line across his brow. And all those Abrahams and Ibrahims, all those Moseses and Moshes, Joshuas and Jeshuas, all those Christs floating around in several versions! Even one in a short tunic! She remembers an old story of the Thirties her Irish grandmother used to tell her, about two English ladies in a drawing-room discussing the Jewish Question: Well you know dear, says one, Our Lord was a Jew. Oh no, says the other, not with that beautiful Italian face. She giggles. Then weeps briefly with fatigue.

Surely this gathering was supposed to be a grand carnival, all social rank and racial origin abolished, if only for seven days? Why has she abandoned Charlotte Kestner to her solitude? Who is Frau Kestner anyway, and why was she looking for Goethe?

Kelly puts out her cigarette on the concrete step and rises, tired and in a murderous mood, and makes her way down to the lobby, hoping to cross it somehow and get back to her hotel.

But outside Kennedy, now open and empty, she sees Jack, talking to a posse of journalists still hanging on in hope of a story, though most of yesterday's bunch have given up on that one. She delivers Rita's orders and the journalists at once surround her. Where? What time? Will the press be admitted? Do you expect any more shenanigans this time? What's going on?

When they manage to move away into a rare empty corner among the colourful crowds, Kelly asks him why there was a German journalist there, Werner Something. He must be German since there were two dots over his surname, which Americans rarely keep. Has the whole kaboosh spread?

An Umlaut, Jack corrects. That was Werner Tötges, the journalist killed by Katherina Blum. For her lost honour you know.

What d'you mean, killed? That's a helluva way to – Jack! You don't mean they're all fictional too?

Sure I do. There was Hemingway's Jake Barnes, you know him surely. And Huxley's Chelifer, I forget his first name. And Kolley Kibber from Brighton Rock. And Pernichon out of Bernanos, who's driven to suicide by the abbé Cénabre. And Boot you know, poor old Boot. But there were many more yesterday, Ian Scuffling from Gravity's Rainbow and Joe McCarthy Hynes out of Ulysses, and

Etienne Lousteau from Illusions perdues, and Rouletabille, who solves all the crimes the police can't. And Gedeon Spillett, and Jasper Milvain, and the journalist from L'Espoir, I forget his name. Even Miss Lonelyhearts was there, didn't you see him? And Justin Miller.

Never heard of any of them. Who's Justin Miller from?

Oh, Kelly, don't you read any modern novels?

The hell I do. I don't have time even to keep up with all the work done on my periods.

Absorbent Tampax all, if you ask me.

Oh shut it Jack, that's not funny.

If you're working on the novel you'd do best to read novels, all novels, not just those of your periods, as you call'm.

I'm not working on THE novel, I'm working on specific novels, Portuguese and Spanish, nineteenth-century. Who's Justin Thingummy from?

Coover. The Origin of the Brunists. I lent it to you. I guess you didn't read it. I'd like it back.

Sure I read it. I'd forgotten his name, that's all. Not a crime is it? Come to think of it he does have a central role.

Well done. There was also Jack Walser, from Angela Carter's Nights at the Circus. You know, cock-a-doodle-doo! He was sane, though.

You're just trying to put me down, Jack, why this downgrading treatment suddenly? I know you've read more than I have, so what, we're not having a reading competition. My point is –

I know: if even the journalists are fictional, where then are we?

No! I was going to ask, were ALL the journalists fictional? That huge crowd before I mean.

How should I know? I'm not Godalmighty.

Oh what the shit, Jack, what's gotten into you?

I've fallen in love, that's what.

Oh? … Good, then perhaps you'll stop hovering.

I was not hovering, as you put it.

The hell you weren't … . Who with?

So. You're interested enough to wanna know. With Kassandra.

This is a helluva dull conversation. Goodbye.

She stalks away, furious, both with him for no longer hovering and with herself for always revealing her ignorance.

89

At the meeting of Interpreters in the Board-room she sees him again, inevitably, and puts on a look of belle indifférence, lost on him however, since he's talking to another Interpreter in the dark red motley of about two dozen, some of them having to stand as the large board-room table isn't quite large enough. Rita Humboldt and Mansell Roberts sit together at the top. Rita raps the table with her lighter and the hum of quiet talk ceases. She has five tall piles of printout paper in front of her, still with the perforated margins.

These are the lists of dead characters they'll be praying for, she explains as she distributes them. We never had time to cut them so they're still in accordion but who cares. Goddamn long I'm afraid, but you might as well have them to follow the proceedings, as they're gonna be read out in their entirety. Just in the event there are any numskull objections you know. But you'll have to explain that they don't cover the whole field, they're just what scholars submitted this year damn their eyes. Or maybe you won't, that'll have bin said and hopefully accessed. Do you read me? I want you all there, in force, near the exits, and ready to act.

What kind of trouble do you expect, Professor? Jack asks.

My dear Mr Knowles, my horizons of expectation have been stretched to breaking-point. I can't answer that.

Who the devil do you suppose will come, Rita, I mean –

Mansell, don't you start on your line of scepticism. Nobody maybe. Everybody maybe. In which latter case they won't all get in.

The latter case is fundamentally unlikely. Not all religions have prayers for the dead, and even in ours there's –

That's barely relevant here. Everyone'll be anxious to see, or hear, whether they're dead or alive.

Most of the people here must know that, or they wouldn't have been invited to hear papers on themselves. Quit quibbling Mansell. We'll just have to see. I was against the whole thing myself as you know, but we're here to carry out a democratically voted decision. Any questions?

Yes, says Kelly. I'm totally confused about fictional status.

You mean, my dear, if they're all dead, can they still be fictions? That's a good question, isn't it Mansell? Bright gel. But you see, fictions function out of time, I mean characters operate in time and succession within a novel but are otherwise independent of those

90

elements. We tend to experience them as if history repeated itself in an aytairnelle retooah. Or disseminated, Osiris-like. After all the ego, or subject, is now recognised as not one at all, but dispersed. Characters aren't like hypotheses in science, are they, which are open to proof, or, well, disconfirmation. But if they come to lose their relevance, for some reason to do with changes of horizons, that is, cultural modifications, well, they're liable to neglect. They get dumped, if you prefer. By the canon. Which of course is institutional, and itself subject to change, but often conservative. Against chaos you know. So people are for ever trying to dig up characters from sepulture and show their relevance. As if their motto were post mod ergo propter mod, huh? They usually fail. Relevance is a protean concept. Okay?

Kelly is dumbfounded. This is the first time she has heard Rita use lecturer's language rather than bad language, though presumably she must do so as teacher. But also, none of this is what she'd meant, too clever by half, and she feels more at a loss than usual.

Okay, she says. Thank you.

What Kelly meant I think, says Jack, staring at her steadily as she stares back in horror and fear and mounting rage, is that she was confused to discover that not only are the detectives and policemen fictional but also the journalists. I was talking to some of them this afternoon. In fact one of them was dead in his fiction.

Oh that, says Rita. Is that what you meant honey?

N-no. I meant, what you said.

Goodoh. What were you saying to the journalists, Mr Knowles?

Oh nothing. Just chatting you know. About the coca cola and Gibreel Farishta and all that.

Were you? Hmm.

She looks pleased. So I was right, thinks Kelly, more confused than ever.

Any other questions? Do you all read where we're at?

There is a murmur of concurrence and movements are made to leave. Then Mansell Roberts says he doesn't understand why they have to go through with this nonsense. And what about this threat you mentioned to me from the TV lot? You're securing uptake aren't you, giving them the ideal pitch. I also heard, independently, that the I-narrators have formed an unofficial syndicate and are preparing a coup. It's just asking for a ruckus.

Wanna bet? Shove it along, Mansell, this isn't the place.

He shrugs and everyone files out. Kelly loiters to let Jack go out. Then, hugging her fat wad of dead souls, she escapes down the backstairs, and sits once again on the same concrete step, where her earlier cigarette stub still lies reproachfully, surrounded by sprinklings of ash. Kelly weeps. What am I doing here? I'm hopeless. I shouldn't even be in academia. I'm ignorant and naive and over-literal, and I don't understand the philosophy of fiction or whatever they call it. And so on until, after a while, she fumbles for her handkerchief and dabs her eyes, carefully so as not to smudge the green shadow, blows her tear-swollen nose, takes out a cigarette and lights it, inhaling deeply for many minutes, again using the concrete step as ashtray, her present ash rejoining her past ash.

She stares at the wad of paper on her lap. Maybe I'll recognise someone I know. All the characters are in alphabetical order, an Index of names Forbidden by the Canon, but independent of countries or periods – that unfortunate word. She snorts. Idly she lifts a fingerful of wad and looks for Braz Cubas, which takes a helluva long time, there are so many C's. He's not there. So he's still in the Canon, still a classic. But do modern characters get forgotten, even before they've been alive for a moment of reading? Is it just a question of time? She tries Macabéa. But long before she gets there her eye falls on the many names, later in the alphabet, that start with Mc, and she reads on fascinated. All registered as forgotten. Dumped. She hasn't heard of any. Until she comes upon – no, it's impossible. Yes: McFadgeon, Kelly. From Textermination, by Mira Enketei.

10

Mira has found a quiet café in the upper part of the old town, with tables laid out all over a pretty paved courtyard under trees still bare in the winter sunshine. The weather has turned warm overnight, and she has decided to sit out and enjoy it. No one is around, though a few people are having coffee inside. But it's early yet, for she left her hotel before breakfast to avoid other guests. Americans are so friendly, they will join her table and chat, addressing her at once as Hi Mira, and she has long given up all type of social activity in which she has to have breakfast with anyone. And now she's eating pancakes and maple syrup brought by a handsome black in a yellow shirt and flapping purple pants and hair separated and gelled up into blue, green and brown bananas. She has the Odyssey propped up against the coffeepot, open at Book VIII, when Odysseus, having heard his own story told by the bard at the court of Alkinoos, weeps and betrays himself, and then is begged to take it up himself and tell them WHAT HAPPENED NEXT and HOW HE GOT HERE.

Her peace, however, is soon disturbed by a large crowd of people, all to her dismay wearing Convention labels, who go into the café and then come out again, move all the tables together to form one long one and noisily sit down. Visibly they would like hers as well, for they are numerous, but she goes on staring at her book, though now unable to read. She can't help raising her eyes occasionally, wondering who they are. To her astonishment she sees Odysseus in person, facing her on the other side of the long table, between the backs of two unknowns. He recognises her and nods. She nods back. Their coffees arrive on two large trays carried by two waiters, hers with the blue brown and green hair, another more sober in black leather from top to toe with his balding greasy brown hair tied back in a black leather shoelace.

Odysseus stares at them.

Hey ma'am, calls the man at the end of the table nearest to her, who also has his hair tied back in a knot under a flat round hat and wears a ring in one ear, are you an I-narrator?

She sighs. I suppose so, in a way, at times, she answers and regrets her automatic truthfulness at once. She only had to shake her head.

Well, come over and splice the mainbrace with us on the bowsprit of this little sloop we've just constructed. We're having a meeting.

Aye aye sir. Her silly pun fortunately goes unnoticed. She closes her book and brings her coffee over, sits next to him, everyone pushing down.

Excellent, now we can appropriate your table. Here, shipmates, fetch it, will you please. Two men at the other end get up and move the table over, place it at the end, then bring her chair and the empty one. More scuffling as people shift down, some of them wearing talkmans already. There are three females at the other end, a Victorian young lady in brown, a little girl of the same period, and an Indian lady in a green and yellow sari with a green and yellow parrot on her shoulder.

That's better. You look to me like a pleasant New Bedford woman, what do they call thee?

Mira Enketei.

I fear I have never heard of you. No matter, you have more than likely never heard of me. That is what our meeting is about. Call me Ishmael.

I have heard of you. A whale-man. Or a whale of a man. He looks pleased. My name means inside the whale. How do you do.

English ey? Yes, I am fortunate, I freely assert, for most people have heard of me, although I disappear from most of the story. Even so, let me observe that I survive to tell it, which is a good deal more than Old Thunder does. We'll take a rollcall first, to see who is here, I mean, out of those so intended.

Even with that restriction to invited guests, the list seems endless: Bardamu, Ferdinand (absent), Barnes, Jake (present), Blas, Gil (absent), Cubas, Braz (present), Carraway, Nick (absent), Copperfield, David (present, with young Copperfield), Crusoe, Robinson (absent), des Grieux, Chevalier de (absent), Farange, Maisie (the little girl, present), the Figurines of King Bhoja (absent), Finn, Huckleberry (present),

Gbili (present, black and thin, crinkly grey hair, in blue and orange garb), Gjon, son of Gjorg Oukshama (present, an orthodox monk in black), the Governess (present, the one in brown), the Indian parrot (croak), Ishmael, that's me, Humbert, Humbert (present, nervously sitting next to Maisie), Lockwood (present), Malone (present), Marcel (present), Marlow, Captain (present), the Messenger Cloud –

Silence. Ishmael looks up at the blue sky, where a small cloud is sailing majestically North. That's him, doubtless, he says. From – he looks down again at his list, the Meghaduta. Everyone else has looked up, more dubiously. He can't tell no tale, says Huck. Well he does, young Finn, says Ishmael and continues the call:

Murasaki, The Lady (absent, pity), Odysseus (present), Santeuil, Jean (present), Shandy, Tristram (present), Sheppard, James (present), Strether (present) – now sir, you should not be here, and neither should the wench Maisie, you're both writ down as third person narrators.

I believe it comes to the same thing you know, says Strether, it is my viewpoint throughout.

Apoplexy! Better stop spinning that yarn to me. There must be someone telling the yarn if you don't do so yourself. I'm a good Christian born and bred in the bosom of the infallible Presbyterian Church and I tell thee, how can you be united in an impossible category? And what's this, Santeuil, writ down as sometimes I and sometimes he. This is where I ponder without fully comprehending. Ah well, no doubt the Lord knows best. You're here now, you may stay, but stash it. Watson, Dr (present), Westin, Lars Lennart (present), Zeitblom (absent). And now the anons: The I-narrator of The Aspern Papers (present), the I-narrator of The Custom-House (present), the – apoplexy! I'm not going to repeat that each time, just the title, agreed? Illusions pairdoos (absent), Invisible Man (present but invisible, says a handsome young black), The Library of Babel (present, very old), Louis Lambert (absent).

But here the list is so long, nearly all absent, that Mira zaps her attention, and picks up only at Voyage dang la Loon (present, with a nose like a peninsula).

Well, as I before hinted, the meeting is on behalf of anonymous I-narrators and none but four troubled to be present. You can tell pretty plainly, that is no genteel way to behave, leaving the main task to us shipmates, when it is their problem of Being. We exist, for goodness' sake.

Isn't it in the nature of nameless I-narrators to be more or less absent? David Copperfield Senior asks. His younger self is plunged in a book.

I hardly think so, says the governess. I have no name, yet I am as absolutely present as ... those dire presences. She stops.

I'm present all right, says the narrator of The Aspern Papers.

You, sir, are an unmitigated scoundrel, says Strether, and you don't even know it. Out and out flawed as a consciousness.

There's an exchange of angry glares.

Now, gentlemen –

For that matter, says James Sheppard, I'm the most flawed consciousness of all, you know, I tell of a murder and don't tell that I'm the murderer. Not till the end I mean, and I'm present throughout.

I only say I when I speak as character, Mira offers pointlessly, simply to join in. Not when I narrate.

Hey but you're not on the list.

No, you invited me over.

I'm present but impotent, says Jake Barnes. In every sense.

And I am dead at the beginning of my narrative, says Braz Cubas. I attend my own funeral.

I am dying during my whole narrative, says Lars Lennart Westin, ashen and thin, ignoring Cubas. I keep bees you know, and three different notebooks. I burnt the letter from the hospital, I preferred not to know. But I hadn't understood that only the possibility of a future enables us to feel like something united and well-ordered, something like a human self. The notion of self is wholly based on the certainty that tomorrow this self will still exist.

I wrote the story of the three-arched bridge over the Ouyane of Malediction, quavers the Orthodox monk in black. I had to, for nothing had been written about it in our language.

Mira carefully observes him. So that's the narrator of the story Orion was on about. But she cannot fathom any mystery in those dark and darting eyes, only cowardice and a mediator's willingness to please.

The grey-haired thin black man in blue and orange opposite her, labelled Gbili, Liberia, Guinea (Guerze) then claims to have invented writing. Oh, she says tactlessly, Plato says it was the god Thoth. No, me, guerze writing. Without no story, no lasting. Except by mouth.

But you all have names, gentlemen, says Ishmael, do kindly adhere to the main point.

I shall soon be quite dead despite of all, says Malone. And yet I have a name. Of sorts.

And I have none, says the very old man. Once dead, there will not be lacking pious hands to hurl me over the banister. May heaven exist, though my place be in hell. Let me be outraged and annihilated, but may Thy enormous Library be justified, for one instant, in one being. I repeat: it is enough that a book be possible for it to exist.

There is a silence.

Quite so sir, rejoins Dr Watson heartily. Some of us are more present than others. It's all a matter of degree. Absence is absolute, Mr Holmes once told me, but there are degrees of presence. I'm remarkably present, don't you know, he adds with a rosy glow over his blond moustache.

Moi aussi, says Marcel, dark and pale.

Stop whittling, all of you, counters Ishmael and addresses Marcel: Indeed, I heard a sermon around you yesterday. It didn't tell much about you, except how the real story of your whale of a book turns out to be Marcel becomes a writer. All on account of your being narrator. Well my book's even more a whale of a book, it's a book of the whale, a royal fish, yet nobody's said that of me, my being just a foremast hand. Ain't that right, Odysseus?

Odysseus looks lost. Then he declaims ancient Greek and everyone looks equally lost. Clearly the talkmans aren't up to that today. Mira translates.

He says he only tells part of his story. One bit of it is told by a bard, but in summary, and an immense chunk of it is told by an I-narrator who only once says I, or rather μοι, that is, me, I mean Homer, you know.

What's all this fuss you're making about, says Ishmael. There are all manner of defilements to this memorable occasion, depend on it. As I before hinted, the true question is, are we to take any action on behalf of these soaring and sinking pronouns or are we not? Some of them are as big as the white whale, for ever present, disappearing and reappearing and then engulfing us all. Except me of course.

Σειρῆνοϛ, says Odysseus.

There is nothing so foolish, says Tristram in a three-cornered hat, when you are at the expense of making an entertainment of this kind, as to order things so badly as to let your critics and gentry of refined taste run it down. Nor is there anything so likely to make them do it as that of leaving them out of the party, or, what is full as offensive, of bestowing your attention upon the rest of your guests in so particular a way, as if there was no such thing as a critic (by occupation), at table.

Huck gets up.

I don't care nothing about you, I don't take no stock in dead people. They're no kin to me and no use to nobody. Like Tom said, if I warn't so ignorant, and if I'd read a book called Don Quixote, I wouldn't be such a numskull. He said it was all done by enchantment. Well I reckon if we can't get some genies to help us we'll never lick them. Look at that boy, he can't even listen good. Hey boy, what's that blame book you're lost in?

The boy looks up.

David Copperfield, he says and plunges in again. Copperfield Senior looks alarmed and tries to take the book from him, in vain for the boy hugs it to himself.

I didn't ask your name boy. Why ain't you reading about Henry Eight and all his wives, Fair Rosamun and Jane Shore an' all of them, chop off her head, and he made every one of them tell him a tale every night, and he kept that up till he'd hogged a thousand and one tales that way, and then he put them all in a book and called it the Domesday Book. Now that'd be a heap better for you. But I got a raft, boy, come on the ocean with me.

But David Copperfield goes on reading. Huck stalks off. Copperfield Senior rises too, and as the boy regretfully closes the book he snatches it from him.

Where did you get that? he asks.

I found it. In the big palace place.

Come along, we must leave. This is too irksome.

In fact everyone gets up to go, the meeting is a flop. Humbert Humbert, who hasn't said a word, takes Maisie by the hand. Ishmael looks mighty downhearted. Mira stays put.

When they've gone, she gets up and drags her table back to where it was, carries her chair there, sits on it, orders fresh coffee and opens the Odyssey again.

The waiters are about to clean and rearrange the tables when there is another invasion, much quieter this time, of about ten people who tell the waiters to leave the tables as they are, order coffee and sit down. Far from inviting her to join them they take out Convention programs and murmur together over them, apparently marking off what each is going to attend. They're not wearing Convention labels, yet seem distantly familiar, not as literary characters she is free to recognise as imagined, but as real people. But surely real people don't attend the Convention, apart from the academic Interpreters? And they somehow don't look like academic Interpreters. Then she recognises JR. Not that she ever watches soaps, but she has seen his picture in TV journals and such. So they're actors. But drama-characters are not part of the Convention. She tries hard to hear what they're saying but can't. Oh well, not her business. She closes the Odyssey with a sigh, no real peace in this city, finishes her coffee, pays and leaves to enjoy the warm sunshine on a walkaround, then takes one of the colourful roller-coaster streetcars downtown, gets a bit lost, but is finally directed, with the usual American friendliness, back to the Hilton.

There she finds the big hall empty and eerily because unusually quiet and respectable. Even the police have vanished, though a few Convention officials are still sitting at the desks in the gallery. Presumably everyone is listening to panel-papers. Still, usually the lobby is full of stragglers chatting together. Only the grey-haired young man in the dark red uniform, the one who addressed the terrorists from the platform, is there, sitting on a Biedermayer-style red sofa near the teak steps that lead to the gallery, talking to a solid-looking man, iron-haired, iron-jawed, must be a professor. She approaches them.

Excuse me, but what's happening, or not happening? It all seems so peculiarly quiet.

They both rise politely. The Interpreter offers his place but she shakes her head and sits in a high-backed wooden chair with carved figurines bearing the arms. She sits thankfully, her feet aching.

I'm Jack Knowles, he says. This is Professor Mansell Roberts. There was trouble again yesterday at the Prayers for the Dead. We were just discussing it.

My name is Mira Enketei.

Mira what? Inkytie? says Mansell Roberts, rudely it seems to her, until she remembers that American insistance on getting a name right

99

is a form of politeness. What a strange name.

Enketei. I'm of Greek origin. Means inside the whale.

Ah. I see you're a classicist, he says more gently, taking the book from her and handling it like a bomb, then returning it to her unneutralised.

I used to be, she says carefully. But I didn't attend yesterday. Do please tell me. Where is everyone?

They've all been taken off on bus-trips. To Death Valley, to Silicon Valley –

I thought those were different names for the same thing.

Jesus, you really are a classicist, says Mansell Roberts.

It was a joke. Sorry.

Ah. Some went down to Monterey and Big Sur, others upcoast. Anyway we got rid of most of them. All papers were cancelled.

But why?

It's all Rita's fault. She would insist on having those goddamn Prayers for the Dead, giving in to minority groups you know. I told her –

But what happened?

In fact the attendance was pretty poor, as I'd said it would be. But hell, Gibreel Farishta came, like an asshole – forgive me – in a kind of off-white pajama outfit, showed up out of nowhere, when everyone including the police had been looking for him. And a character called Abu L-Fath Al Iskandari, an Imam, who'd been asked to sing the list of names, turned out to be one of the terrorists.

The very same I'd spoken to, Jack puts in, the one I'd identified later in the Interrogation room, by his eyes you know, that didn't quite look at you, with large black pupils and yet more white around than black somehow. How the police let him escape totally – he fumbles for a word and ends lamely, escapes me.

Our fault too, we should have known, he's a famous cheat from the Maganat, a money-extortioner who'd pretend to be a doctor resuscitating the dead or a pious imam directing prayers in the mosque. Anyway, he suddenly took out a gun and aimed at the front row, where Gibreel was sitting in full view. But Gibreel was faster on the draw and –

And shot him?

No, shot himself.

As in the book, says Jack.

So that's all right then? says Mira, classical in her taste for correct endings.

All right! Roberts exclaims. My dear young lady how can you say such a thing? There was pandemonium. Happily the attendance was poor, as I said, in contrast to the first day, but the panic was far greater, and the fury, due to the accumulated pressure on nerves you know, and the more primitive, well, let's say more passionate and uncontrolled audience, er, congregation. Hardly any Western characters came, as I'd warned Rita of course, and the Interpreters hadn't the least notion what to do.

That's not entirely –

Sorry Mr Knowles, but I was there. You hadn't been told what to do, that's what. The police, who were hovering, were equally incompetent, rushed in to control the people, to examine the body and all that, meanwhile Al-Iskandari had vanished through the side door he'd come in by. I tried to race after him but a damnfool cop barred my way and told me to keep calm.

So the White Knight wasn't there this time?

No, he's Non-Existent, besides, the situation was entirely different, wasn't it?

I don't see how. The same terrorist, threatening the crowd, or rather one person. For the same reason.

But the person, as you call him, shot himself.

Ye-es. Still, the Non-Existent Knight, had he been Existent and there, wouldn't have known that in advance, would he? He might have appeared from behind and sliced off the fake imam's head as soon as he pulled out his pistol.

That's a lot of conditionals, my dear Miss er – Inkytie, in the service of neat repetition. Too literary you know, life's not like that.

But we are literary.

Not literary characters though, we're Interpreters, we're real. The whole damned Convention is ridiculous, as I said –

As he goes off again about this person Rita and the idiocy of the enterprise, Mira is silent. She presented herself as a classicist, hence an Interpreter, and now feels on shaky ground. The grey-haired young man called Jack is trying to argue with the professor. She wonders why there was another prayer-meeting, when all had been cancelled. In a lull, she asks.

Well, as I was saying just now, it was Rita's fault. There was tremendous pressure from minority groups, who are now so numerous as to constitute a majority, those who want to alter the canon, you know, dig up forgotten works ignored by what they call white male warmongers – a lousy pun on canon-makers, hell – in favour, I guess, of black female peacemongers. Fine. Don't get me wrong, I'm for it, but the canon does change, has changed pretty drastically, in a natural way, and partly thanks to their efforts. We've always rewritten the past. But they're so aggressive. And their position is illogical. They ought to want to abolish the canon altogether, on their premisses that a canon is unconsciously a male preserve, a protection, like a club, a second matrix as Norman O. Brown used to say. So a female canon is a contradiction in terms. And deep down they know this, we can't work without some sort of institutional canon you know, to make some sort of sense, however changing, out of such a huge indiscriminate mass of literary facts. Well we could if we had unlimited memories, but we don't. Maybe with computers that'll come. But think of the chaos. It's already with us. There are far too many books in the world, the idea being I guess, that out of all that quantity some small quality will emerge.

Perhaps it's true. Qualantity, qualantiquity, she adds silently to herself and raps herself on imaginary knuckles in her head.

You're dead right it's true. I calculated yesterday that if you'd read one book a day from age fourteen to age eighty-four, you'd still only have read about point oh one percent of all that's available, isn't that scary? Just think of Chaucer, who was a learned man, and had forty books in his library. True, most of those are unread today, except by scholars. And if it isn't time that does the abolishing it's space. All those minority languages you know, so-called even when millions speak them, except us, the white West, too damned ignorant and arrogant, so that great works are only known to that one nation, except for those few that are translated, and most of us ignore those too. Not to mention all those states that exercise all their ingenuity to efface all cultural memory of books that don't suit their ideologies. This fortunately often has the opposite effect, so that characters from such books may even survive more vividly. But what are we to do? Still and all, that was a parenthesis. To return to our own so-called minority groups, though why women should be called a minority Godalmighty knows, they don't want time to do the abolishing, they think it's we the white males that do it, their attitude is we bind them, without maybe meaning to, they do give us that. What they want is to replace the existing canon with theirs. So they want power too, and warmongering. But the canon does change, has changed, a deal faster than they'll admit, like I said. They want it to change even faster. It's the old revolution/evolution thing, and look where it's gotten us.

I see, says Mira. She is silent. She has followed this diatribal little lecture attentively, but part of her mind asks, am I abolished? Another part tells her that on the contrary she is inventing all this, and has no idea how to go on. Someone should enter now.

Someone does. She sees Kassandra, tottering into the lobby, looking as usual distraught, on the arm of Philip II, who is trying to calm her.

Kassandra! Jack exclaims and runs towards her, brings them into the little sitting area. But they won't sit.

¿Por qué hay un tumulto cada vez que se celebra Misa para los Muertos? he asks.

Mansell Roberts raises his hands in a helpless gesture, clearly doesn't want to repeat his explanations. I thought you were all gone on a trip, he says, what is this? But Kassandra and Jack are talking in German, and Jack puts his arm around her, takes her away. Philip II shrugs violently, impatiently, and strides off, muttering escándalo. Mira is left with Mansell Roberts who doesn't know what to say and sits restlessly on the Biedermayer, as if trying to think of a way to end the conversation and leave, but more courteously than by just saying Well I gotta go.

Please, she says to help him, one more thing. How did these prayers for the dead get organised? I mean, which dead? Did these people, these majority-minorities, did they present specific names, of characters to be prayed for, as it were?

Relieved, he takes a fat wad of printout paper from his briefcase. The perforated margins haven't been ripped off and the sheets are visibly still in accordion, to be unfolded like parchment scroll. For a return to the codex culture one has to cut them up, align them, bind them.

Here, he says, that's the world-list for this year. Enormous, isn't it? They'd been having meetings for months and compiled it. Crazy crew.

What they don't realise, these numskulls, is that it functions like an Index, in the ecclesiastical sense you know, an Index of Forbidden Works. Forbidden by time and neglect, because unavailable to the general public, to the Reader in other words (he nods), except at best, to a small clique of scholars who ferret them out in libraries and persuade feminist and ethnic publishers to bring'm out. All these names of forgotten characters, which include, incidentally, characters from well-known books but whose names nobody remembers until they reread the book – after all we best remember those names that figure in titles don't we? – all these names, as I said, were to be read out at the pray-in, with one interdenom prayer before and after. They didn't get very far.

He chuckles as he hands it to her. It's quite heavy.

You may keep it. I can get another one. If I want to, which I don't. I'm afraid I gotta go. Glad to have met you.

The wad was evidently the courtesy he was looking for, and he gets up, gives a little bow and is off towards the bar.

Mira remains alone, as always, and stares at the wad. How to go on? she asks herself. That hasn't solved a thing. As she sits there in the tall wooden chair, which reminds her of the throne Greta Garbo sat on in Queen Christina, she fingers the figurines that support the arms like mini-caryatids. There are eight on each side. Eight? She remembers the Figurines of King Something that Ishmael had read out in the narrator rollcall. If parrots can tell stories to a human being, why not figurines? She turns round. The tall back of the wooden throne has more oriental figurines, in four rows of four. Thirty-two altogether with those on the arms. She strokes the lower left one. It comes to life as a small dark-haired Indian princess, steps down on the arm and starts talking in a language unknown to her. She sticks the stalks of her talkman into her ears and switches it on. Hail King Bhoja, it says hesitantly, evidently summarising a long string of greetings. Here is the thirteenth story of Prince Vikrama. She listens, fascinated, but dozes as the bad translation proceeds. Does each figurine tell a different story, thirty-two of them? She'll be here all day. But maybe they'll give her ideas. When the thirteenth story comes to an end she is about to rub a figurine under the right arm, but her sleepy eyes fall on the wad of paper still on her lap. Idly she lifts the zigzag scroll at an eighth or so of its thickness and her eye falls on a long list of forgotten names in alphabetical order. She can't resist, lifts another thickness, runs her finger down to EL, lifts another small thickness, finds EM, then EN, and moves down to ENK. Yes, she too figures in it: Enketei, Mira. She can't go on. She doesn't exist.

11

If she can't go on, I suppose I'll have to. I am not Mira of course, though many readers think I am. For one thing I have little Latin and less Greek. Curious how one can invent knowledgeable people without possessing their knowledge. One cheats, quite simply.

I didn't attend that I-narrator's little meeting – well, I wasn't even on the rollcall, any more than she was – because so far I haven't said I. As eye-narrator I've kept pretty quiet, effaced as they say, not a narrator at all, not fully-fledged, participating, not a character in my own right, *à part entière*, an expression which, as a child, I always heard as *à parent tiers*, a phrase that would mean, if it existed, 'with a third-party parent', and that too could have its ring of truth in this context. But then, as a child, I was perpetually mishearing what I was taught. I would sing 'Le belge sortant du tombeau', a line in the Belgian national anthem, as 'Le belge sortant du tambour'. A Protestant hymn learnt in Geneva went 'Avec allégresse, montons vers le ciel, Et chantons sans cesse notre Emmannuel'. But I sang 'Avec la négresse, montons vers le ciel'. Those were joyful visions. Clearly I do have that much in common with Mira, except that she does it on purpose.

I say not a narrator at all because, when came the fashion for the vanishing author, the silent author, the transparent text (not language at all but window on the world), the critics, always quick to adapt their vocabulary to the latest bandwagon, started calling narrator both the character who narrates and the producer of the text, that is, the author, not of course the real author, who misheard anthems as a child, who had marital troubles or who is undergoing a long and painful dental treatment of implants, but the Author, Implied, Ideal, or whatever, thus losing an important distinction: the character who narrates is limited to what he can know, the producer of the text can move among many knowledges. He used to be called Omniscient. Well, anti-God intellectuals (anti-author-ity) objected to that. Objected to the rigging, the fateful feel of divine providence. The author was out. All authority rested in the text. And later all authority rested in the Reader, Implied, Ideal or whatever. And so they passed imperceptibly from phrases such as 'the author's intention here is clearly' to 'the text clearly says', and then to 'the reader clearly infers'. But behind this lip-service to fads, what the author intends, what the text says, what the reader infers, is in every case what the one critic interprets. He too is Reader, he too is God.

Be that as it may, I am the author, take it how you will, and I am still alive and well, if not in Texas, at least here, and for a little while yet.

Not that I am omniscient. That term was always over-interpreted. Even in clear cases of the omniscient author, he was, as human being, omniscient only within the little (or large) world he created. And sometimes not even there. For apart from cases where he can be omniscient but not omnicommunicative, as they say, in other words holding back, he could also make mistakes of coherence, or errors in his research or observation, and many of our canonical authors re-searched and observed a great deal. And even very well. That was the big idea, to reproduce the world as it was. This was why people read them, to have reproduced for them the world as it was. But that world was reproduced as the authors saw it, and received as the readers then interpreted that vision. Otherwise there'd be no point, would there? But much confusion arose. Until a sort of consensus was formed, or a nonsensus as Mira would surely say, that omniscience merely meant that authors created their world, arranged it according to their vision of it. Which they do anyway, with or without a narrator.

Even within that restriction, however, I am not omniscient. On the research side, I have not read every tale that has ever been written everywhere, in Jewish Literature, in Islamic Literature, in early and late Greek literature, Persian, Peruvian, Japanese, Siamese, Indian, Amer-indian, African, Yugoslav, Polish, Finnish, Norwegian, Albanian (etc) Literatures. I have thus created a fiction too difficult for me to handle. So I omit what I don't know. A double absence. All authors omit, texts are full of double absences.

As to the arranging aspect, I too, like Mira, have no idea how to go on. I must go on, I can't go on, I'll go on (Beckett, The Unnameable).

107

Or: She was ended, the book could begin (Maggie Gee, Dying, in Other Words). I am a femme-récit, like Scheherezade, whose every tale means a stay of execution. Or as Muriel Spark says of vanishing Mrs Hogg: She had no private life whatsoever. God knows where she went in her privacy.

But does God know? If God exists, can He contain unontological moments? By God I mean of course, the Implied Reader. If He exists. Let's say He does, and can.

So I must bring them back. Oh, not all of them of course. Kelly and Mira are on the Index and gone for ever. But they were real, on their different levels, Kelly being on the staff, Mira having (she says) invented everything. Rewrite the last two sentences, keeping both versions, for both are true: But they were unreal, on their different levels, being invented by me, Kelly on the staff, Mira as inventor (she says) of everything. No, I meant the real fictional characters, those not (yet) on the Index. Back from their excursions. Upcoast, downcoast, inland to Silicon Valley, further inland to Death Valley, across the Mohave Desert not golden but black and purple and grey, bronze in the early winter sunset.

Touristic trips create brief links, if only from sitting in a bus-seat next to someone, strange conveyances like immensely long and narrow mail-coaches but without horses, only an abstraction called horse-power. On the trip out, Emma Woodhouse finds herself next to an exceedingly tiresome Frenchman called Valmont, who pours endless flowery phrases into her ear to seduce her at top speed. Very mortifying. Nor is he proposing marriage, as Mr Elton at least did, so unexpectedly in the carriage, oh dear, how aggravating that had been. But this is much worse, nor can she move away, she is transfixed to her seat, knees touching the seat in front as he keeps trying to caress her hand, her neck, her bosom, despite her admonishments. She manages to lose him as they emerge on Monterey Peninsula, so pretty with astonishing winter flowers everywhere, and walk towards the ocean. The ocean.

She has never seen the sea. Immense it is, to her right, all the way along that winding road, sometimes low and open, sometimes alarmingly high above steep rocks, with the waves crashing below. On the return journey she sits on the inland side and feels safer, next to a young Bohemian doctor called Tomas, who says strange things she can't quite follow, and talks a great deal about the cancellation of the Prayers for Being. Being seems to trouble him for some reason, and he calls it unbearably light. And to her astonishment she finds herself agreeing. She has never thought of it in that way, and it somehow relieves her of the oppressive feeling she has had ever since she arrived, that her certitudes are uncertain, that she no longer quite exists in them, no longer quite coincides with herself.

As for the other Emma, whom Emma Woodhouse has abandoned, she has phased out on a splendid trip, in every sense, finding herself next to Lancelot, a most attentive knight, not in armour, that would have been most unpractical, but in a kneelength tunic of blue and silver damask over close-fitting blue and red hose, one leg red and the other blue, the whole outfit under a long embroidered gown with tight bejewelled sleeves. Round his hips is a richly decorated belt from which, he tells her in quaint French, there normally hangs a sword and a dagger, but they had asked him to leave those behind, and now there is only his pouch. She sees all this when he stands to remove his mantle, and she is entirely overcome. Emma loves rich materials. He is equally amazed by her own clothes, so voluminous and in such a soft apple-green shade (yes, she has changed too). Our dyes and weaves are most delicate, he tells her, but I have never seen anything as subtle and fine as this. He fingers a fold in her skirt, and moves gently up to her corsage, murmuring urgently in a strange accent, Ma dame, m'amie, m'amor, mon cuer, ma druërie, m'esperance et tout quanques j'aim, sachiez que j'ai eü grant faim d'estres o vous, si comme ore i sui, trestoz jors puis que je n'i fui. She shudders in tremulous, nascent ecstasy, allows his roving touch over her breasts, closes her eyes, offers her lips. They see nothing of Fresno, Bakersfield, Mohave, Olancha or Townes Pass. Even earlier, in the plain, they were already so engrossed in each other that they saw nothing of the grotesque knight everyone pointed to and stood to watch, a knight in ancient armour with a pointed white beard sticking out from under his helmet, who was galloping on an old white horse towards a huge regiment of slim but immensely tall metallic wind-engines that stood in wide square formation with their wheelheads spinning slowly in the breeze, like the tall slim tuft-top palms that suddenly populate the desert in groups or line the streets of Californian towns. What a strange country America is, says Becky Sharp to her neighbour Friday, who grins and says island, very big.

When they at last reach Death Valley, Lancelot and Emma Bovary are in a state of high because as yet unassuaged passion from their heavy petting behind the high-backed seat in front of them. They get out with the others, still flushed with fantasy-fornicating, but he hands her down gallantly from the carriage, the large swelling in the scarlet side of his tight hose still slightly pushing out his tunic of blue and silver damask.

Behind them descends Herrera, also flushed but with happiness at having found a new courtisane to manoeuvre, called Criseyde, in a charming golden surcoat over a kirtle of crimson silk, très décolletée but with many buttons, and very tight sleeves. He finds her all the more attirante because she wears a creamy wimple of pleated linen that entirely surrounds her face, like a nun.

Dorothea, still in her widow's weeds, has been having a much more sober conversation in the long backseat with Jude Fawley, still about the difficulties of learning Greek, but much interrupted this time by someone called Ireneo Funes. Jude was telling her how, as a boy, when he first obtained a Greek and a Latin grammar from the schoolmaster Mr Phillotson, who later became a friend and then a rival, he'd been totally discouraged, disgusted, amazed to find, not one simple magical law of transmutation for the whole language, but that every word was to be indvidually committed to memory at the cost of years of plodding. Irineo Funes, however, could look at a grammar, or any other book, and commit it to memory in an hour. He could remember the shapes of clouds at dawn on the 30th of April 1882, or the shoots, clusters and grapes of every vine, or the marbled grain in the design of a leather-bound book he had only seen once. He told them he had several times reconstructed an entire day, second by second, each image linked to muscular or thermal or other sensations. I have more memories in myself alone, he announced, than all men have had since the world was a world. Dorothea looked at him in disbelief, almost in pity, but also with envy. Jude simply found him rather tiresome, monopolising an interesting conversation with wild statements that stood exactly opposite to his own: no key to knowledge painfully acquired for this peculiar person, no sense of system slowly and delightfully emerging.

They have arrived and everyone gets up. A young Jew who had been sitting beyond Funes joins in. This conversation is very interesting, he says as they cluster at the back of the centre aisle of the bus to make their way out towards the front, but you do not seem convinced of this young man's ability. My name is Zadok, and I learnt French by reading a Polish-French dictionary from A to Z three times. Then I remembered every word. I did the same with Hebrew. And German. And now I have done it with English. There are people like that.

They slowly reach the front. But Zadok goes on talking. Behind him is a tall incredibly thin man with pale blue eyes and no cheeks, a nose like a vertical fishbone plunging down towards two minute black nostrils like hidden insects. His mouth is a zip-fastener and two deep lines cross his face on either side from the temples, meeting at the chin. Dorothea contemplates him in dismay, he reminds her of Casaubon.

This gentleman, says Zadok, is Dr Kien, a famous sinologist. He has been telling me, in German, that he knows his entire library by heart, old Chinese, every dialect, and other books, in Latin, Greek und so weiter. He has his library in his head, and writes his articles without needing to consult it. And that is very fortunate, for when his wife turned him out, he had to wander from hotel to hotel, taking his books out of his head and arranging them on non-existent shelves for the night. So as to be able to sleep, you know.

They have alighted during this speech. Kien bows stiffly like a branch bending. But Jude and Dorothea, after a forced smile over cold horror, move on quickly. Dorothea wonders a little how three memory maniacs come to be sitting together in the last row of the bus, and why she has had to meet in quick succession three very different men whose relationship to books is so much more intense and all-consuming than their ability to face people. Perhaps when you marry one type of man he pursues you in other forms for the rest of your days. She tries to discuss this with Jude Fawley as they walk, but finds him morose now, and realises she has been tactless, his problem being apparently similar to theirs, if less extreme.

By now they have walked a long way, are told to admire Dante's View and its palette of pastel blues and greens and pinks in the rock. But Dante's Virgil stands near them and shakes his head, muttering non era così , and his bus-companion Frenhofer is equally scornful. Trop géométrique, he says, ce n'est pas la ligne qui compte mais la couleur. Et les couleurs sont trop pâles, elles n'ont aucune signification. Elstir murmurs his dissent and stands enraptured. Ulrich, the Man without

Qualities, who has been stuck with a young governess, quite pretty but extremely tense (almost neurotic he would judge, in the new jargon, for she has talked incessantly of death and dreadful presences), takes this opportunity to lose her and join the conversation, but against Frenhofer. Without line, he says, there can be no qualities in the colour.

Lazarillo, Oliver Twist, Gavroche, Mowgli, Janek Kowalksi and Huck Finn are scrambling up and down the rocks, having hilarious and noisy fun, watched in envy and disgust by the barone rampante, lost without his trees. But then he gets talking with Heidi, Alice and Peter Pan, who astonishes them all by flying above the rocks. Why that's better than trees/ mountains/ rabbit-holes, they exclaim together and clap. Goethe, in his dark wide coat with upstanding red-lined collar, is walking up a steep narrow path with Oedipa Maas, courteously listening to her as she insists on the existence of a secret and parallel postal system called Tristero. He wonders what would be the point, since only poets and princes, generals and officials, ladies and their daughters or lovers ever exchange letters, but he is open to the suggestion of spies and revolutionaries, finding in it vistas far more entertaining than Dante's view. As he walks, however, he gets lost in these thoughts and loses her voice, quite unaware that in his valiant old age he has climbed much too fast for her up an increasingly steep and narrow path, leaving her far behind. Oedipa is furious. She is out of training. Why do men on walks always do this? she asks herself. Must be some conspiracy. And now Pierce has left me this lunatic will of his to sort out, also leaving me far behind.

Frenhofer walks down in disgust from Dante's view and joins a group where a colourful lady well into maturity is surrounded by a small crowd, mostly priests and monks in varying degrees of fascination at her free and easy life-story, Herrera and Criseyde, Don Abbondio, l'Abbé Birotteau, Mr Dimmesdale, the Pardoner, but also Clarissa Harlowe who, together with l'Abbé Ovyde Faujas look libidinously shocked. Frenhofer notes the colourful lady's clothes: a red face amply wimpled in white, a blue hat as large as a shield, a thick green outer skirt over her wide hips, stockings of scarlet wool and yellow pointed spurs on her bright new blue poulaines strapped to wooden soles.

On the excursion upcoast, Lotte looks as ever for Goethe but finds herself instead with a Dublin Jew called Leopold Bloom, who talks a great deal but of things quite beyond her ken, except when he describes the preparation and eating of fried kidneys. Ugh! And the duchess of Sanseverina-Taxis, splendid but still blood-stained in her silken black and green dress, flirts outrageously with a hero in a leopard skin, called Tariel, who seems to come from somewhere in the Caucasus, Georgia he says, and from a long time ago, in the twelfth century. He is very ardent, and doesn't feel the crisp cold.

The trip to Silicon Valley is much less picturesque. Orion has been talking to the early Faust, who is fascinated by his explanations of computer science. Grobenius, a student in revolt against good education, is more scornful. Johannes Forföreren is furious at having chosen the wrong trip, no women to seduce. M. le professeur Brichet wonders aloud about the suitability of the word computer for a machine that evidently does so much more than compute. Belikov suggests a Greek word but is unheard. Wuz is telling Melmoth how he couldn't afford a library and so started copying books, and being carried away and adding bits of his own. These new machines would have considerably helped him. But Melmoth laughs his loud demoniac laugh and says he reached the summit of intelligence, and now only wants to discover the peace of ignorance.

Ernest Pontifex listens patiently to a tall young man whose waxy pallor is touched along the underside of his jaw with acne and whose sheepish eyes are of uncanny, unutterably cold pale blue, pale almost to colourlessness. He is wearing a peculiar brown and green jacket, army surplus camouflage, he says, which mystifies Pontifex. His name is Dale Kohler, he says sir all the time and makes interminable speeches about a computer program he has invented which will prove the existence of God. Who wants to? asks Pontifex. We need free thought, wisdom, not dogma and system. More especially, may I add, if you say that computers represent virtual reality, whatever that means. But Professor Diogenes Teufelsdröckh, overhearing them, disagrees. I may indeed have been disappointed by both love and science, almost to deep and total despair at their eternal negation, their everlasting no, but I have certain reservations, Mr Pontifex, I am partly on your side. Perhaps both these paths are equally chains of egoism, which may well prove to be insurmountable obstacles to the freedom of spirit that we need to see the essence of things.

So the buses return at last, to deposit their motley crowd couple by

113

disintegrating couple at the Hilton. But they can't pull in. Police cars and vans with their spinning blue lights are parked any old way in front of the hotel, and more arrive to a sick tootling sound few of the guests have ever heard before. The buses drive round the block to the hotel's other entrance. Same scene. Finally they pull up in the middle of the street, creating blockage of the evening traffic and more confusion for the police, who try to prevent the trippers from going in, but have to yield on seeing their badges and being told in no uncertain manner by some that they're guests here and have nowhere else to go.

Inside, the half-dreaded spectacle, from which they had been both relieved and regretful to be excluded for the day, awaits them, of another monstrously thick and variegated crowd in the lobby. A crowd from all over the enormous world, temporal and spatial, that most of them know so little about. They cringe. The unknown, the unfamiliar, the sheer foreignness of it all makes them cringe. People of every colour and costume, of every height and breadth, are massed in the hall, on the teak stairway, in the galleries, howling and cheering at more people of every colour and costume who are also howling, cheering and even fighting below, in every mode known to man save nuclear bombs and chemical warfare. But that might well come, judging by the ferocity and violence. The cops are there in huge numbers, in their black uniforms, arresting and dragging off this or that archer, this or that swordsman, this or that man with a bludgeon or Indian club, this or that man with a scimitar, crossbow, bazooka, bayonet, this or that gunman, this or that terrorist strapped with hand-grenades or holding one up and threatening to throw it. But the dragging is all to no avail, others materialise as soon as those are taken off.

Oedipa Maas is delighted. What did I tell you, she says to Goethe, here's proof of a parallel system, clashing at last with the existing order. But Goethe is calm. He has followed, if only on maps, all Napoleon's battles, and this is presumably what they looked like, except that they were outdoors. Fabrice is dashing around in his hussar's green uniform and the youth with the bandaged head plunges into the fray in search of the flag, while Gunnar, Haakon, Hrut, Njál, Wulf the Unwashed, Havelock the Dane, El Cid, Odysseus, Aeneas and the others slash right and left with their bright swords. Only the soldier with his shoebox and unnumbered cape stands in a far corner, looking on this Battle of Reichenfels and seeing snow, rain, sunshine on asphalt.

114

Roland is in the gallery, blowing his horn unheard in the din. Man Friday is doing a strange dance. The journalists are perched on the Biedermayer, on steps, in the gallery, filming and flashing. The crimson Interpreters are helpless, cowed.

The Emmas are mortified. Lancelot, Tariel and Mowgli join in. Frenhofer is sketching and Dante's Virgil is telling Jude and Dorothea that this is nothing compared to the Inferno. Lazarillo and Huck and Oliver Twist are hiding with Irineo Funes under the teak stairway and Herrera is protecting Criseyde as he tries to manoeuvre her around the lobby towards the elevators. Starets Zossima is sitting terrified on the wooden throne, trying to calm Vergil on his litter near the Biedermayer sofa, left there on the floor, abandoned by his black bearers who have rushed to join the fighting. Leopold Bloom is watching from a safe corner far away, talking to Ulrich about the Irish troubles while Ulrich listens politely and looks on, thinking of the Empire. He has managed to lose the governess for good, who has found Lotte and talks to her of evil presences. Valmont is flirting with the duchess Sanseverina as if they were in the Prince's reception-rooms, and indeed the Prince is nearby, observing the scene with Felipe Segundo, who daydreams the siege of Ghent. Next to him stands Kassandra, wailing of Troy but unwilling to listen to Simaitha's love-complaint in ancient Greek. Simaitha is being comforted, however, by Hadrian VII.

Three strident whistles are heard above the mêlée, but no one pays any attention except the cops, who suddenly stop struggling and quickly don their masks as more cops in black push in, already masked, and throw silently in all directions. In a second the entire lobby is filled with smoke and everyone is weeping, coughing, spluttering, sitting on the floor or writhing there, some with handkerchiefs to their eyes, or scarves, corners of mantles, wide sleeves, wrenched bonnets, raised skirts. The fighting has stopped.

A male voice comes over the system.

Ladies and gentlemen. Kindly switch on your translation gear ... We regret having had recourse to tear gas, but this was the only way to calm you all. Be assured, the effect will wear off soon. Meanwhile let me remind you that fighting never settled disputes, at least not permanently, and that in this day and age we prefer to negotiate, that is, to talk it over. May we advise those of you who feel unconcerned in this dispute to go up to your rooms. This will facilitate the discussion. Those of you who do feel concerned will form groups, not more than thirty in all, and name from each group a delegate, who will move towards Beverly in about fifteen minutes, when the doors will be opened after the effect of the gas has dispersed. Soft drinks will be brought to you to ease your throats. Thank you.

Gas? says Emma, dabbing her eyes, why do they keep talking about gas?

Je pleure, je pleure, c'est effroyable, sobs the other Emma as if she were the only one.

After a while the wailing and coughing and sniffing and sobbing give way to a rising murmur as groups choose their delegates. The hall slowly empties, the largest part of the crowd forming an interminable snuffling line at the elevators, though some have found the back stairs and prefer to walk than wait, not realising that nineteen or forty-five floors on foot feel very different from the swift swish of the lift. The big doors of the hotel have been opened, the air-conditioning has been cooled and pushed up to summer maximum to clear the air faster. The ladies start shivering and huddling in their shawls and mantles. Even Tariel in his leopard skin looks frozen, as he hadn't in the warm wintry sun upcoast, excited by the duchess.

At last the air is more or less breathable again, and the thirty or so delegates move towards Beverly, guided by the Interpreters. The delegates are all men, mostly powerful: Felipe Segundo, Hadrian VII, Herzog, Kirilov, Aeneas, Herrera, Goethe, the journalist Etienne Lousteau, Ivan Karamazov, Sultan Shahriar, Rodomont, Musa shi-Bo-Benkei, Tariel, Genji, Tristram Shandy, King Alkinoos, Professor Pnin, Rabbi Jochanan, Gilgamesh, Gandalf the Grey, Braz Cubas, Chingachgook, Li Kouei, Moses, Pan Tadeusz, K'ong Ming, Kalevipoeg, Pastor Oberlin, Rastem, Gibreel Farishta. In a black tuxedo. Yes. Why shouldn't he survive his own death? The terrorists did. Casaubon nearly did. So did Little Nell, Madame Bovary, Dido, Kassandra ... But no one knows him as such, except Mansell Roberts, who isn't there as yet, no one has seen him as anything else, except Dorothea, who has gone to her room, Pastor Oberlin, who only looked at his clothes, and Mira, who doesn't exist.

Behind them, however, surge and push a whole crowd of flat, filmy people, apparently determined not to send just one delegate but to appear there in force: JR in a ten-gallon hat, Mason and CC Capwell, Nicky Messiah, Dan Marshall, Klaus Brinkmann, Gary, Mack McKenzie, Gregory Sumner, Chase Gioberti Ridge, Cruz, Andy Kilvinski, MacGyver, John Steed, Columbo, Steve McGarrett, Rick Hunter, Magnum, Sherlock Holmes, Maigret, Mad Max, Jesse James, Spartacus, Adrian Cronauer, Dan Diamant, Valmont as Gérard Philippe, Julien Sorel as Gérard Philippe, Fabrice as Gérard Philippe, Heathcliffe as Laurence Olivier, Captain Ahab as Gregory Peck, Jean Valjean as Jean Gabin, John MacTeague as Gilson Howland, Superman as Christopher Reeve, Ewen Montagu as Clifton Webb, Philip Marlowe as Humphrey Bogart, Sam Spade as Humphrey Bogart, Aschenbach as Dirk Bogarde, Cal Trask as James Dean, Monsieur Klein as Alain Delon, Dr Jekyll as Spencer Tracy, Gatsby as Tom Ewell, Robin Hood as Douglas Fairbanks, Disraeli as John Gielgud, Maria Casares as the Duchess Sanseverini, Alphonse as Zbigniev Cybulski, Ishmael as Richard Basehart, David Copperfield as Freddie Bartholomew, Moses as Charlton Heston, Pinkie as Richard Attenborough, Mme Verdurin as Marie-Christine Barrault, Jo March as Katherine Hepburn, The Scarlet Pimpernel as Leslie Howard, Miss Faversham as Martita Hunt, Madame Bovary as Jennifer Jones, Delilah as Hedy Lamarr, Prince Fabrizio as Burt Lancaster, Pal as Lassie, Anna Karenina as Vivien Leigh, Esmeralda as Gina Lollobrigida, Sherlock Holmes as Raymond Massey, Humbert Humbert as James Mason, Dick Tracy as Warren Beatty, Odette as Ornella Mutti, Billy the Kid as Paul Newman, Sherlock Holmes as Basil Rathbone, Napoleon as Albert Dieudonné, Tom Joad as Henry Fonda, Kikuchijo as Toshiro Mifuno, Elmer Gantry as Burt Lancaster, Prince Myshkin as Gérard Philippe, Little Lord Fauntleroy as Mary Pickford, Tess as Natassja Kinski, Boule de Suif as Micheline Presle, O'Brien as Richard Burton, Gatsby as Robert Redford, Dr Fu Manchu as Peter Sellers, Little Lord Fauntleroy as Freddie Bartholomew, Dr Zhivago as Omar Sharif, Nicolas Stavroguin as Lambert Wilson, Sherlock Holmes as Christopher Lee, Napoleon as Rod Steiger, Pharoah Akhnaton as Michael Wilding, La Princesse de Clèves as Marina Vlady, Bonnie as Fay Dunnaway, Thérèse Raquin as Simone Signoret, Captain Edward Fairfax Vere as Peter Ustinov, Peter the Great as Nikolai Cherkassov, Rasputin as Conrad Veidt, Professor Stavroguin as Omar Sharif, Maria Chapdelaine as Madeleine Renaud, Countess Bathory as Delphine

Seyrig, The Prisoner of Zenda as Stewart Granger, Sherlock Holmes as Peter Cushing, Napoleon as Charles Boyer, Tootsie as Dustin Hoffman, Ivanhoe as Roger Moore, Capitaine Haddock as Georges Wilson, Heidi as Shirley Temple, Don Quixote as Nicolai Cherkassov, The Wandering Jew as Conrad Veidt, Lancelot as Robert Taylor, Zorba the Greek as Anthony Quinn, Zorro as Douglas Fairbanks, Lieutenant Pinkerton as Cary Grant, Dr Knock as Louis Jouvet, Moses as Burt Lancaster, Zorro as Alain Delon, the Youth as Audie Murphy, Armand Duval as Robert Taylor, Jean de Florette as Gérard Depardieu, and innumerable others. The whole TV and film crowd who were, it seems, at the origin of all the trouble.

Jack Knowles, who has been letting in the delegates in an orderly manner, who has so far not once allowed himself to be more than mildly surprised or failed to recognise anyone except Kassandra's weeping companion, who has not once, in other words, lost his cool, is completely taken aback and pushed aside by this modern form of fiction. Nor can his colleague on the other side of the door do a thing. They stream in, endlessly, and fill a good half of the huge room, behind the meagre delegation of thirty men sitting in front, who all turn round in amazement and full of fear at this unplanned new threat.

But now a tall man in grey, steely haired, walks in from the side door onto the platform and stands behind the long table, which is still draped in deep blood red. The eye on the wall and the diptych full of eyes have been removed. He looks alarmed at the film crowd behind the small group of evident delegates. But all are silent and he clears his throat.

My name is Mansell Roberts. I'm on the Organising Committee. It was my voice you heard on the intercomm just now. I wanna thank you for your co-operation. I guess we can settle this amicably, in a friendly way you know. You will now be addressed by the President of the Organising Committee.

Only Jack and Columbo know her and Columbo closes his eyes, while a murmur of astonishment goes up from the delegates and the film lobby as the tiny woman enters, manly, strong-jawed, short-cropped, in a black suit and bright yellow jabot like a host of golden daffodils. The thirty delegates, between her and the huge crowd of celluloid stars behind them, suddenly and unanimously feel lonely as a cloud.

118

12

Gentlemen, Rita says, for she sees at a glance that the delegates are all men. Then she notices a few women among the actors at the back. Ladies and gentlemen. I am sorry you were incommoded by the teargas. The situation had gotten so that this was the only way to stash it, as you'll appreciate. I trust the effects are over and done, and that we can now encounter each other in peace and have a full-bore attempt at a fruitful discussion.

This peculiar academish doesn't go down too well and a murmur arises, restless movements are seen, shuffles heard. But her voice has authority and she continues, a pitch louder.

This convention has been jinxed by several elements alien to it. The first seems to have been religious, but this has tinkled down, thanks to patience and understanding on both sides. Another element was the question of Prayers for the Dead, the ruckus being apparently about disagreements as to which characters are dead. This too was amicably settled. But it is more clearly linked to this third trouble today, namely, why we invite characters only from written narrative fiction, whether in prose or verse. I should like to say a couple of words on this, and hopefully you will hear me out without heaping shopworn miseries upon me right now, you'll have all the leeway to do so when I'm through.

Felipe Segundo looks puzzled and grave, despite his talkman. So do Aeneas, Goethe, Moses, Oberlin and Pan Tadeusz. Hadrian VII chuckles quietly, Herrera beams, Ivan Karamazov looks angry. Gandalf is abstracted into another world, Etienne Lousteau is taking notes, Rabbi Jochanan is praying into his white beard, Genji and Gilgamesh are whispering together, as are Benkei and Kalevipoeg, Herzog looks worried, Tristram Shandy amused. Sultan Shahriar is asleep, sitting

119

next to Felipe Segundo. Only Gibreel Farishta appears serenely unconcerned.

Rita goes on to explain the disillusionment of long and justly famous fictional characters at being no longer read, recreated and therefore alive. I give you that many dramas are equally dead and forgotten, but they can be regalvanised at any moment by an enterprising producer, with real people in the parts. It's seldom dialogues we remember from films, but images, stunning landscapes and gung-ho buildings and their innards in oddball framings, the whole permanently and subliminally intensified by lush or infernal or galactic symphony, not to mention hair-styles by X and all the panoply of people responsible for giving us the characters complete before us. The writer is alone. Mere language has its equivalents but they're not simultaneous, they need time and concentration to assimilate. So there's a helluva difference, a fundamental difference, between the reception of a character who's there in front of us on stage or screen, doing nicely for us with every look, gesture and bat of an eyelid as we watch and absorb, and a character who appears gradually out of the reading process, the letters on the page, mere words, not made flesh but creating phantoms in the very varied minds of each solitary reader. It is in this imaginative build-up that we're threatened, I mean that the characters of fictional narrative are threatened, in a way far more profound and more eroded by time than is possible with dramatic characters, at every moment made flesh before our eyes. I say flesh although film is also an image, but the actor, a real person, with immense talent, is there to do the realisation work for us. When we founded this Convention, many years ago, we all agreed, and ratified by democratic vote, that this peculiar threat to written characters did not affect drama, film and TV, at least not in the same way, least of all TV which is very much with us every leisure-hour of our lives. Nobody has ever questioned this decision before, and I have to say that I am surprised, since protest usually comes from those whose existence is threatened, rather than from those in power. However, I am willing, we are willing, to listen to any of you who feel they'd maybe like to make their contribution to the Convention, and maybe widen its field, why not, we'd be grateful I guess, at the present time, and you might well enrich us. Our statutes are not immutable. Thank you for listening.

There is a thunder of applause. Mansell Roberts looks amazed at this unexpectedly conciliatory proposition and its results, then scowls, but keeps quiet. A tall broad man with a smooth baby face under a ten-gallon hat rises. Yes? says Rita. Would each speaker mind giving the name of his character. For the benefit, she adds cautiously, of those from earlier epochs.

JR, from Dallas. Madam President, he drawls, I thank you for your generous offer. I'd only like to add, in answer to your – er – puzzlement, that we are indeed threatened, contrary to your – er – optimistic supposition. Serials come off the air and sometimes return. But more often they do not. Dallas, for instance, which ran for two decades or more, has been axed. And then we're deader in the short public memory than anyone in a book. Which can be picked up and read. At least by a few.

That's a very interesting point, JR, says Rita. You mean you're even deader than, say, characters in a Greek tragedy, which can at least be produced on stage by one enthusiastic director, whereas –

Whereas TV serials are big business ma'am, you're right on the ball. A drop in the ratings and you're a dead man. Or woman, he adds courteously. A gonner, either way.

Rita is equally courteous, has listened with a teacher's smile and sideways bend of the head to mark profound interest.

If I read you correctly though, this applies equally to films and plays, am I right? There's also big money behind them. Come to that there's big money behind publishing at the present time. Isn't it a problem of this or that serial, this or that film or play, being a failure after a while, as opposed to another which replaces it? But that used to be the case with books, when people had no films, no TV. And that is the problem the Convention addresses, we also pray for everyone, even the famous, classical characters, for very few people read, and those who do so read passively, whereas many more do watch TV and get totally involved. Yes, Mr – er?

CC Capwell, from Santa Barbara. I don't think JR has quite grasped the point, Madam President.

You bet he hasn't, a voice calls, he's a well-known boob.

Please gentlemen, says Rita after the outburst of laughter has subsided, kindly do not interrupt one another or we'll get nowhere real fast. Go on Mr – er – Capwell.

The point of our protest is this. We're all in competition with one another and we know it. There are too many of us. On the whole we cope well enough, with a fraction of solidarity and patience. One lot is out, another is in, that's the way the world goes. What we're protesting about is competition from the dead. Why, there are some nuts in California who pay vast sums for cryosis, having themselves frozen alive to be unfrozen in two hundred years. They're very optimistic that anyone would want to, if the world is to continue overpopulating as it does. Why the hell bring dead characters back to life? They've had their time, it's our turn now. Let the dead lie, if they've failed to survive, well, it's like life, the failures are left by the wayside.

The rich always did talk like that, shouts a young man with mousy tousled hair, then gets up. MacGyver, from MacGyver. I'm the decent American guy who always gets out of scrapes caused by the wicked and the greedy, with his knowhow, well, boyscout stuff updated with techknowhow. I don't belong to the Santa Barbara or the Dallas wealthy elite and the young love me. I'll never be dumped. And I say there's room for everyone, rich and poor, successes and failures, the survivors and the forgotten.

One loud cheer is heard, and some desultory clapping.

Perhaps we should hear what the delegates have to say at this present point, says Rita. Aeneas, what do you think?

Surprised, Aeneas gets up after a short moment to fix his talkman that has got entangled with the chlamys over his shoulders and short tunic. He spouts Latin. Nobody among the actors can understand, as they don't have talkmans, and there's an increasing murmur of protest. Hadrian VII rises, all in white. Perhaps I may offer my services as interpreter? And plunges in at once to catch up or at least summarise. He says your feuds are about a number of readers or spectators unimaginably vast, much vaster than the number who have read him, struggled over him at school, translated him, rehandled him parodically and so on over more than twenty centuries, on and off. He used to feel crushed under the weight and sheer longevity of that readership and identification. But now it has vanished almost to nothing, and this despite the fact that he is the hero of a recognised classic, translated and retranslated into many languages and published in cheap editions. He cannot understand, therefore, the complaints of modern characters, or the notion that the failures had best be forgotten. It is possible to be forgotten and yet not a failure, to come and go and return in different forms over the ages.

Aeneas has sat down. His voice has run parallel to his translator's, for there is no fade-out technique in reallife speech, nor would he have understood it if there had been. And as Hadrian VII didn't have time to explain to him in Latin what he was about to do, Aeneas thought he was being talked out and spoke louder and louder, as did Hadrian. Few of the audience were able to catch much of the speech, except for the last sentence in English, which trailed along after his own. This sentence, however, has a sobering effect, creating a silence followed by a rising volume of either appreciation or disagreement.

Yes, Rabbi? says Rita to Rabbi Jochanan who has shakily risen and tries to speak. He does so in Yiddish. Nobody understands. The Rabbi has said that the dead don't know everything, says Rita. How could Ecclesiastes say such a thing? he asks, and how is it that the immortality of the soul isn't mentioned in the Scriptures? He tells us also of an interesting passage in the Talmud, in which God is represented as poring over the Torah and studying it. The pre-Creation Torah if I've understood correctly. This has caused endless exegesis. Why should God study His own Work? One interpretation, which is also the Rabbi's, is that He is studying men's interpretations of His Work. Thank you, Rabbi, that is a most fascinating speculation, especially if for God we here read the Reader, she nods imperceptibly, the Implied Reader. Isn't it?

The audience is restless. Then a handsome dark man rises from the back, older than the boyish look he is evidently cultivating, for his serial has had a very long run. Steve McGarrett, from Hawai 5-0. What we are trying to face, he says brutally, is a population explosion. The planet is seriously threatened with this in real life, and so are the media, more and more entertainment having to fill the air between us to keep the people happy in their leisure, their unemployment, their misery and poverty, their longing for glamour and adventure. And what is the only way humanity has always dealt with population explosion? On the one hand it has tried, and mostly failed, to teach selection and control. On the other, it has fed violence by innumerable roundabout means, so that many happily exterminate each other in local wars, or just die off in famines, chemical warfare, nuclear catastrophes, brutal repression and other results of inefficiency, corruption and shortsighted greed. Of course we don't admit this, we protest in our assemblies, vote sanctions or send aid over and over. But we continue the violent practices, the selling of arms, the drug traffic, the spying, all reflected in our entertainment industry, even if there the good win. I suggest that this particular meeting is just another assembly of hypocritical lipservers and that we should face the facts. Inefficient characters do die, have died, always, and prayers have never stopped that process.

We all die, Moses as Charlton Heston calls out with a wide embracing gesture of his amply robed arms. What is at stake is spiritual survival. The delegate Moses looks back in surprise. So does Rabbi Jochanan.

Yes, and even threatened species can be saved. Sorry, Superman, from Superman. With care and a little consciousness of man's destructive depravity. I was out, a finished species, but I made a comeback, I'm more popular than ever.

As Mansell Roberts has expected, the meeting degenerates into a chaotic series of speeches by written or acted characters, each anxious to prove, with shaky analogies or blunt statements, that he has not died. Felipe Segundo says he is alive and well, even when dying in his coffin before the altarpiece which has itself curiously changed from what it was at the beginning of his story. Heathcliffe as Laurence Olivier declares that he continues to haunt the Yorkshire moors, Herzog that he is weary but still read, Ivan Karamazov that it's all a plot by the devil with whom he alone was able to hold out in a strong polemic. John Steed, in his bowler hat, says that his thirty-year-old series is still shown all over the world, with a new young lady as partner since women age more quickly whereas he. 007 as Seán Connery expresses pride in the fact that two other actors have incarnated him in new films that have nothing more to do with his author's books, and so on until the main purpose of the meeting, as so often happens, is lost in irrelevant self-assertions. Each story is greeted with whistles and shouts, who cares, let's get back to the point, but each speaker when given the floor returns obsessively to his own dwindling life-force. Many of those present, however, and more especially the delegates, keep quiet, Goethe, Oberlin, Tristram Shandy, Professor Pnin, Herrera, Gandalf and others, but also Columbo, Sherlock Holmes, Cruz Castillo, Klaus Brinkmann and most of the film crowd, all for different reasons from

124

wisdom to scorn to fear to fatigue to mockery, as does, out of caution or indifference, Gibreel Farishta in his black tuxedo.

Gentlemen, I thank you, says Rita Humboldt at last, having let this meandering self-indulgence indulge itself to boredom and pouncing on a brief moment of exhausted silence. Opinionwise this has been most illuminating. Maybe you're not all aware that many are in worse situations than yours. Some scholars for example devote their lives to what they call Lost Literature, that is, literature, or stories if you prefer, which haven't survived at all except from external evidence, references in other texts and that kind of stuff. This is perhaps the most extreme case. Be that as it may, two main views seem to have emerged, and hopefully you will forgive me if I seem to reduce them for the sake of clarity.

But she is cut off by a loud gasp and long murmur of admiration from the audience. Their eyes are not on her, and she follows their direction to her right. Four beautiful people are entering from the back of the raised platform, three women and a man, who slowly join her and her unwilling sidekick Mansell Roberts at the high table. The man, an ancient Egyptian, walks in profile with his elongated hands held up in front of him and flattened out as if holding an invisible and immensely precious urn. He moves to her left, followed by a dark Indian princess in yellow and green and gold, with a rich red jewel in her brow and a green and yellow parrot on her shoulder. Her body seems immobile but her eyes, her head, and her held out hands move rapidly upwards, downwards, sideways, with one or several fingers outstretched in mysterious mudras that tell a story as she glides into place next to the Egyptian. The other two women float in to the right of Mansell Roberts, the first pale and tall, with massive dark hair, clothed in a long white robe, the second an Arabian or Persian girl in blue and crimson veils, of ravishing grace. Rita is struck dumb, sits down, feels, perhaps, outclassed and small and irrelevant amid this astonishing beauty.

The young Egyptian speaks, to everyone's surprise, in perfect English: I am Prince Hordjedef, son of Kheops, great king of the Fourth Dynasty. None of you would be able to read me in hieroglyphs, and I am thus doing you the kindness of appearing to you in a translated version, bringing to you these three ladies, one of whom is American, the other two also in translation, who will address you.

My father liked to be told stories, endlessly stories. He believed that the fate of the kingdom depended on stories. Thus I used all my ingenuity and courtesy to persuade a well-known thaumaturge to come to the palace and distract him. I also believe that the fate of the world depends, has always depended, on our ability to tell and to listen to stories. To listen, to believe, to suspend our customs of thought and let ourselves be charmed by otherness. But I am a man. He was a man. You are mostly men here. Kings, princes, warriors, adventurers, policemen, aggression is your role. You distil violence, ambition and restlessness rather than beauty and serenity in your stories. Therefore I came with these three ladies, each very different, that you might hear of their traditions in story-telling. On my left is Princess Vidya, which means Wisdom. She will speak first.

Princess Vidya addresses the audience, also in perfect modern English, but with a singing Indian lilt. She tells them she is the daughter of the rajah Bardvan, and describes a great feast that was held to decide who should win her hand.

The audience is very quiet. After the description of the feast, the pretenders and their promises, she tells them of Prince Soundar, which means Beauty, who had disguised himself as a poor student, so that no one took any notice of him in the rich and powerful gathering of princes. And how he had sent her a vast bouquet of flowers, all arranged in a complex design of colour and shape that secretly spelt his feelings for her, which she deciphered with a sudden and rare delight. But of course I could only gaze at him as impartially as I could. She describes, in exquisite terms, the tremours of her nascent love, and how they must have been mysteriously transmitted through this impartial gaze, so that, for many days during the long feast, he dug a tunnel to her chamber and came to her, and possessed her in a sweet frenzy of gentle sensuality and slow but fiery passion that lasted many hours. She dwells on this gentleness with art and emotion, then skips and summarises. I hid him in a secret place. But I later discovered I was pregnant. My parents, the king and queen, were very angry and sent the police, disguised as women – for yes, women are sometimes more efficacious than men, and men sometimes admit this – to search him out. They found him and he was condemned to die. But at the moment of execution, my brave and loyal friend, here on my shoulder, informed the king, not only of the student's real identity, but that this

126

was truly love, with my full and happy consent, between Wisdom and Beauty, so that the king pardoned Soundar and consented to our marriage. And we are still happy, ever after.

There is a murmur in the assembly, partly of enchantment partly of scoffing impatience, while Rita mutters sheer allegory, allegorical characters are excluded, but no one hears her except Mansell Roberts.

Prince Hordjedef then introduces Ligea, who moves like a shadow but is silent. She prefers not to speak, he says. She guided her husband through the chaos of metaphysics, her knowledge is without limits. Her origins are mysterious, her will gigantic. She survives physical death. Some think she incarnates the perfection and triumph of all corruptions. I say she is the image of Woman, the mother and the lover, the guide and the inspiration, who may kill if wrongly and malely interpreted, but only with too much love. And now please listen to the best known, best loved woman narrator of all, defender of her predecessors' treacherous bid for equality of standards, symbol of both independence and submission in love as against the tyranny of man and state, who with her enchanting tales stayed her own execution, night after night. Scheherezade.

Felipe Segundo nudges Sultan Shahriar who wakes up and beams at his favourite. Scheherezade starts on the story of Giafar-al-Burmach, beloved vizier and adviser of Harun el Rachid, Caliph of Baghdad, but hated by Harun's wife. All are under her spell. But as she seems to be reaching the end she stops and listens to an invisible voice to the right of the platform. You are right, Dunayad, the dawn is breaking. Do you agree, oh my master, she addresses the Sultan in the first row who nods wearily, that I should resume this tale tomorrow night?

Silence follows, disappointed and estranged. Rita leaps into it, rises and continues her speech as if this had all been a dream.

May I thank the prince and princesses for their elevating contribution to this debate. As I was saying, two main attitudes have emerged, which I shall summarise with your permission. One, that this entire enterprise of prayer for being is bullshit and should be pitched out of existence. This view, I may add, depresses the hell out of me since I have devoted the clearest of my days and a large chunk of my professional life to its utilization and promotion, even, I humbly hope, to its success, since characters come here yearly from far and wide and from all epochs. Two, that this enterprise of prayer for being is on the contrary so successful, so interesting, so enriching, that many of you whom we maybe wrongly excluded, with the best of motives as I said, now want to join in. So how do you read where we're at? I shall of course put both these propositions to the Organising Committee, and I suggest that one representative of each view be elected by you, to attend this meeting of our Organising Committee on Saturday, Room 0127 at two p.m. This meeting occurs after the end of the Convention, so each delegate should be someone able and willing to stay on. His hotel expenses will of course be paid. Meanwhile the two main groups have time to meet and discuss their position, elect their delegate and instruct himorher, hopefully with utmost clarity, for the meeting will have, I'm afraid, other business, current business, to get through. Thank you for attending, for listening to each other, and for contributing. This assembly is now adjourned.

Before the eyes of the disbelieving audience, on either side of the president and her unwilling henchman, the four beautiful people have been slowly dissolving like vapour as this speech progressed. But Mansell Roberts is unaware of this. He is too amazed by Rita's efficiency, her clarity, her authority. So, apparently, is the audience. Out of noisy chaos has come some kind of peace, for a while, he thinks, and a promise of orderly, democratic solution. But he also wonders whether this has in fact come about through her efficiency, her clarity, her authority, or through what he calls the opium of the people, enchantment and mesmerization.

13

In the now empty lobby, a skeletal, bedraggled little man with a pigtail is sitting on the red Biedermayer, talking in Chinese to a large fat man, who is totally naked apart from a curved blackbone clasp holding his scraped up black hair, who sits imperially on the tall throne of wooden figurines. His belly protrudes in tyres over his private parts, but he seems unconcerned. The little man with the pigtail, used to being treated as the lowest of the low, even by the low, is trying to accommodate this evidently superior man, superior to all the superior men he has ever come across, but can't help glancing furtively at his vast nakedness.

I see you are admiring my p'ao, says the fat man, and I am delighted. Look at these immensely wide hanging sleeves, and these voluminous folds. The silk was specially woven for me by two foreign merchants, who came from exotic lands. It is so fine, so rarified, that only the very subtle can see it. You are very subtle I am glad to note, my friend, very perceptive. And the colours! Admire this incredibly soft orange, that shimmers into gold, and the exquisite chestnut shade of the wide rims. I am the most gratified, the most fulfilled, the most revered and respected, the most serene of serenities on this earth.

You are, a Serenity? the little man coils in terror and throws himself on the ground before him.

I am the Emperor, says the fat man modestly. Rise, my subject, and admire.

Trembling, the little man gets up and stands bowed before the Emperor.

Sit down, sit down. We must talk. What is your name?

AQ. Your Serenity.

What a strange name. Say it again.

AQ. That's what they call me, Your Serenity. Perhaps my name was Quei. But it got simplified by the foreign writing that came in recently. The English perhaps.

The English? What is that?

I don't know, Your Serenity. I am only an odd job man, the lowest of the low.

I see. Where do you come from?

Nobody knows. I live in the temple of the tutelary god of Weizhuang.

Never heard of it. But you do like my clothes?

Yes. Of course. Your Serenity.

But AQ has caught a note of anxiety in the Emperor's question, and is immediately transformed, at least to himself, resorting as he usually does to his thunderbolt glare, which has always enabled him to feel suddenly superior even to his cruellest mockers and tormentors, even to those in the tavern who seize him by his pigtail and swing him around and bash him against the wall. At any rate, he tries it. Perhaps not thunderingly enough, for the Emperor beams.

You have a sharp, appreciative look, my friend, obviously you are a man of exquisite taste. I must bring you to my palace, I shall rid you of these disgusting, smelly rags and dress you decently as one of my pages. Oh, not in these silks, rest assured, he adds as AQ looks suddenly horrified and hugs his smelly rags, these are only for the Emperor. But tell me, what did you think of the strange battle that occurred in this great hall a couple of hours ago? I have never seen anything like it.

You were there? Your Serenity! Like that? I mean, in those wonderful clothes?

Why yes, my little man. I was standing over in the corner. Unfortunately, the battle was so raging that nobody noticed my splendid apparel. Also, I admit, I became slightly nervous. About my clothes, you know, being possibly spoilt by swords, or blood, and I hid for a while under those wooden stairs. Not these here, the other ones, at the far end. I came out when everyone had gone, still choking from all that smoke I may say, highly unpleasant, and came to sit on this peculiar throne. And then you turned up, from under these stairs, looking terrified. I don't know why you need have been terrified, he adds, looking at AQ's rags with increasing distaste.

Well I was. Your Serenity. There were several foreign boys hiding

130

there with me, and a grown man who behaved like a boy, and they all pulled at my pigtail, mercilessly, although they were frightened too. What a noise. Your Serenity. But I'm only an ignorant man. Perhaps Your Serenity has views about it, more worthy than mine?

The Emperor opens his mouth to speak, but is stopped by a woman's scream.

Un homme nu! Quelle horreur!

Hush there, don't look dear.

Madame Bovary, still in her soft apple-green early crinoline, now half covered with a spreading ivory silk mantle, is standing with Hester Prynne, much more severely garbed in grey, but with a huge scarlet A richly embroidered over her breast.

Au secours!

Emma Bovary stands, repelled but fascinated, and continues to call Au secours! Au secours! Nobody comes. The lobby is empty, even the distant reception-desk in the wide corridor round the far corner of the lobby on the way to the elevators seems out of earshot.

Why is this foreign lady screaming? the Emperor asks AQ. She is strangely but beautifully dressed. Very voluminous. The silk, however, is not as exquisite as mine. He smiles affably to the lady, hoping she will be subtle and courteous enough to appreciate his soft orange and gold p'ao. He only gives a curt glance to the dull grey dress of the other woman with its messily drawn red sign for man.

At this moment the doors of Beverly open and the thirty delegates in various garbs come streaming out. But they move disconsolately towards the elevators at the back of the lobby, anxious to reach their rooms and recover from the dejection of the meeting where nothing has been decided, where they have felt helpless and unconsulted. They are soon followed out by the film and TV crowd, who have already divided, more or less, into two large groups, one staying behind in Beverly to elect their delegate, the other moving into the lobby to elect theirs, among them MacGyver, Maigret, Sherlock Holmes, most of the film classics. These are the joiners. The much larger group that remains in Beverly are the rivals, the would-be destroyers of the Convention, CC, JR, McGarrett and such. A few float indecisively at the door.

The joiners advance towards the teak stairway, perhaps aiming to sit on it, since the lobby offers no accommodation apart from the

Biedermayer and the wooden throne at its side. Then the apparent leader stops. At the foot of the stairs a woman in an ivory mantle is standing stockstill and whimpering, supported by a woman in grey with a vast embroidered A on her breast, upon which the other suddenly rests her head. Behind them, a skeletal little Chinese in rags sits on the Biedermayer, staring at the women, while, yes, a fat man is enthroned on the tall wooden chair, totally naked.

Hey folks, take a peek at that, says MacGyver with a happy grin. The Emperor's Clothes!

Everyone has read the tale and catches the reference. There is first a hushed silence. The Emperor beams at them and bows his head graciously right and left.

And that must be the little boy, though he sure looks old and decrepit. You know, the one who dared to shout, but the Emperor's naked!

The hushed silence turns into a burst of rude laughter. The Emperor, who doesn't even know what the English is and wears no talkman on his nakedness, looks offended, then scornful. These are unsubtle people. AQ, equally at a loss, tries his thunderbolt glare. In vain. The laughter turns to yells and shrieks, choking but endless guffaws and gasps. Heathcliffe as Laurence Olivier leaps about, delighted. Maigret as Jean Richard sucks his pipe, his eyes twinkling in his affably fat face. Valmont as Gérard Philippe has eyes only for Madame Bovary. 007 as Seán Connery grins and takes a picture of the Emperor through his wrist-watch. Sherlock Holmes as Peter Cushing looks through his eyeglass, quizzically of course. César as Raimu is shaking with uncontrollable laughter, the tears running down his cheeks. The general hysteria spreads to the two women, whose stony attitude melts into unreasoned mirth.

AQ looks thoroughly frightened now. His thunderbolt glare has failed. Nevertheless he feels as if it had succeeded. How foolish these people are, how unsubtle not to see the fine texture of His Serenity's p'ao robe. It's true he didn't see it himself at first, but he is exceptional, he grew into subtlety. Is one of those brutes going to swing him by the pigtail? But no one pays any attention to him. All eyes are on the Emperor, who seems to have decided that the mirth is one of delighted appreciation, and has resumed his dignified smiling nods all round.

Excuse me ma'am. Columbo steps forward in his creased raincoat and bows to Madame Bovary. Would you be kind enough to lend me your mantle? He can't be allowed to go around like that in his birthday suit.

She doesn't understand, has neglected to wear her talkman which looks too inelegant with her beautiful clothes.

Sherlock Holmes translates: Vottrey mantow, madame, seel voo play. Poor coovreer le mowsoiow.

Ah? Ce n'est pas un manteau, c'est un mantelet! Et pourquoi pas votre cape, monsieur? Ou la gabardine de Monsieur ici?

Il ne les mettrait pas, Madame, says Valmont, d'abord, il est trop gros, ensuite, il lui faut de la soie, très fine.

Ah! Bon. Mais rendez-le moi, après, n'est-ce pas? Il a coûté très cher.

She gracefully dismantles herself. There is a gasp of admiration as her full apple-green splendour is revealed.

L'intérieur de la pomme, tout blanc, se trouvait à l'extérieur, declaims Valmont, et maintenant nous avons la pomme, jeune et verte, c'est charmant. C'est à croquer.

She flashes him a flirtful, grateful glance of her big black eyes. Ah, l'amour existe, l'amour, l'amour.

Meanwhile Columbo is approaching the Emperor with the wide ivory mantle.

If you'd be so kind, Your Majesty, and put this on. He supplements his words with sign language.

The Emperor looks at him, furious. Such crude silk! He makes a scornful negative sign with his fat hands.

Have you seen his joystick? 007 asks. It's tinily concealed under the huge belly like a secret weapon. Can't do much with that.

Sherlock Holmes looks shocked. Sir, the ladies. Kindly keep such vulgar remarks to yourself.

But the Emperor refuses to cover his splendid clothes with the crude p'ao, a woman's p'ao moreover.

The laughter has died down into consternation. Someone should call the manager. The police. We need a strait-jacket. Never get one big enough. Sir, I am the police, keep calm. Etc.

By then, however, other characters, who had gone to their lonely rooms after the battle and the teargas, have become restless, are now straying down into the lobby again in search of companionship, drinks, reassurance. Dorothea comes first, with Oedipa Maas and Herrera. Goethe strolls in, and Jude Fawley, and the Duchess of Sanseverina. And Ernest Pontifex. All are irresistibly attracted towards the large group at the bottom of the teak stairway. Reactions are diverse, of shock, mockery, delight, puzzlement as the film people explain the situation to them. Some know the story, some can't. The babble rises but the status quo remains unchanged. The manager is nowhere to be seen. The staff, discreet at the invisible reception-desk round the distant corner, seem to have heard nothing, or have got used to the vagaries of this tiresome Convention.

Gee, look at that! MacGyver points up to the gallery where a Chinese lady in a crimson and peach p'ao is standing, has apparently been standing for quite a minute, her white face beautiful as an evening star above a flaming sunset. A murmur of admiration greets her as she slowly descends the teak stairs, tripping carefully and holding up her robe slightly to make sure her tiny bound feet don't tread between the wide steps. She is wearing her talkman in her ears and has taken in the whole scene.

Ho Siao-yu, she says when she reaches the bottom, and bows. I speak with him.

The crowd parts respectfully. She approaches the Emperor with innumerable kowtows and falls flat on her face. He looks pleased, but condescending. A courtesan! But at least, he seems to be thinking, she admires my clothes, and he caresses his long sleeves, preens himself, rearranges the folds of his p'ao. A long conversation in high-pitched noises ensues, amid total silence among the onlookers.

What's she saying? whispers Oedipa Maas to MacGyver. Shshsh.

The Duchess of Sanseverini has just spotted Julien Sorel as Gérard. Philippe. Is it Fabrice? No, it can't be, he really doesn't look − but there is a je-ne-sais-quoi. She sidles up to him, ignoring the ridiculous scene.

After a while the Emperor bows his head graciously. Ho Siao-yu gets up, takes the ivory mantle from Columbo, and gently, lovingly, sensually puts it over the Emperor's shoulders. Wide though it is, having covered a slight crinoline, it looks a bit skimpy over his great frame, but she arranges it carefully to cover his nudity, taking a clasp from her complicated coiffure to fix it so that it meets over his chest, and a brooch from her p'ao to fix it lower down.

Ma soie! Mon mantelet! Ne l'abîmez pas!

Taisez-vous chère amie, says Valmont next to her. Sois belle et tais-toi, he adds in a more sultry voice. And Emma simperingly obeys.

The crowd parts again to form a guard of honour for this strange couple, the naked Emperor in the tight ivory mantle, more like a nightdress now, on the arm of the beautiful courtesan in the crimson and peach p'ao.

What did she say to him? Oedipa Maas insists, and why the hell wasn't he wearing his talkman?

Everyone bursts out laughing. Where'd he put the gadgetry? someone shouts.

What d' *you* think he said? She turns to the man who'd got the coat from the woman.

Ma'am, I guess she said what any one of us would have said if we'd known the lingo. That his beautiful clothes might be spoilt by the crowd, that's us, the pollution, the remnants of teargas, you name it, and that he should protect them with the overmantle so kindly lent by this courteous lady. Or some such gob.

That's a helluva way to talk to a raving maniac. You're from the police aren't you? I don't trust you. You're not even bright enough to be aware of Tristero.

Tristero, ma'am?

There you are. Nor am I going to tell you, I've already said too much.

Well ma'am, it worked anyway, isn't that the main thing? Excuse me, we have work to do.

Columbo waves his cigar at her and goes to sit on the teak steps. The crowd looks up at him, surprised.

May I remind those of you who attended the meeting this afternoon that we have to elect a delegate. They might have given us a room, a boardroom or something, as we're so numerous. This'll hardly do, there are too many outsiders. I suggest we move into the other reception-room, called Kennedy, which was earlier put at my disposal for my investigations. I guess it's empty. And if it's locked I can get it unlocked.

He rises, without waiting for agreement, comes down the staircase and pushes his way again through the crowd towards the other end of the lobby. The film and TV characters follow him like sheep, all except

Julien Sorel as Gérard Philippe who looks so like Fabrice as Gérard Philippe and slides off with the Duchess; and Sherlock Holmes as Peter Cushing, who is examining the Biedermayer and its bedraggled little occupant through an eyeglass. AQ is left, bewildered on the sofa, surrounded by a desultory group of literary characters who haven't noticed him before and stare at this emaciated little man in dirty rags, with his dirty pigtail. He tries his thunderbolt glare, then whimpers in Chinese.

Madame Bovary wrenches herself away from Hester and Valmont and trips off in small mincing dignity towards the reception-desk to complain. Oedipa Maas has managed to interest Sherlock Holmes as Peter Cushing, to his apparent delight, in secret postal systems, and walks away with him. But he too, like Goethe in Death Valley, stalks ahead too fast for her and passes out of the hotel doors, apparently in a great hurry to get somewhere. Oedipa is left disgruntled and strolls towards the telephones. She wants to ring Mucho about Pierce's will, but a problem suddenly surges with far greater obsessiveness into her consciousness. She is half aware that this problem is atavistic, not part of her male-authored textuality, but it grips her uncontrollably. She strides forward out of the hotel.

Dorothea turns to Goethe and Jude. She is pale but smiles awkwardly, suggests perhaps tea in the bar, to recover from these emotions. They concur. Ernest Pontifex bows, introduces himself and asks if he may join them. I'm afraid I did not appreciate that incident, he says to Dorothea as they walk away. But then, I have to confess, I was once in holy orders.

And you abandoned them?

In a sense, yes.

But that must have been most distressing for you, Mr Pontifex.

It was, at the time. Not now. I suffered tortures over the Thirty-Nine Articles. And many other things. He looks shyly at her. Probably not what you think, Mrs Casaubon.

How do you know what I think, Mr Pontifex?

You're right, I don't, I can't. In fact you look too intelligent to think what I thought you'd be thinking. Forgive me.

You don't have to tell me anything, Mr Pontifex.

No. I'm simply a freethinker now, and much happier.

I hope so, Mr Pontifex, I hope so. But what were your feelings about that extraordinary scene?

It's only a fairy-tale, Mrs Casaubon. Haven't you read it? And a very moral one. About vanity you know.

As for Hester Prynne, she has hovered behind and stares, both compassionate and intrigued, at the small Oriental beggar on the Biedermayer, who sits in his filthy rags, whimpering and crabbed in upon himself. His label says AQ, and she longs to ask him what it means, but can't. AQ: Adulterer, Question-mark? But no, why should a man be convicted of adultery?

She touches him, with a slight repugnance, and he looks up, startled. She points to her much larger A embroidered on her breast, and then to the A on his label, smiling, repeating her gesture from one to another to encourage communication. He looks down at his label, astonished, but evidently cannot grasp the similarity between these typed letters and the rich red pattern on the lady's grey dress, which reminds him of written signs. He knows his name only orally. The label was handed to him on arrival. But he cannot read. He thinks she is inviting him to bed and grins hideously, tries to seize her hands, falls at her feet, clasps her grey dress, clambers up it, catches one hand, covers it with slobbering kisses. She withdraws it brusquely, flushes almost the colour of her A, and hastens away, straight into the arms of Hester Prynne as Lilian Gish, who has not followed the film-crowd as token woman but remained here to watch this grotesque mime with an amused smile of her small pursed mouth, absurdly lipsticked to look dark in the movies. Hester Prynne starts back with a cry. This creature wears a dainty white cap over soft blond hair, a shoulder-wide, breast-deep Puritan collar of luxurious lace, and an elegant lace apron over her well cut grey dress. Who is it? It can't be! But yes: just under her bosom is a small cursive but capital A, crimson and almost plain. Nothing like her own in such rich scarlet embroidery over her plain grey gown. Is this another adulteress? But the other smiles, holds out her hand and says, Your colours wouldn't have come out in black and white my dear. And the modern public has to be given a little frilling, you know. Come, we'll talk.

Hester doesn't understand this talk of black and white, but follows her meekly. The two women leave AQ grovelling at the foot of the Biedermayer, in a daze at this new apparition, more miserably in love than ever, and doubly so.

137

14

Jack Knowles is alone in the downstairs bar, which looks all the larger for being empty. No, not totally: Herzog sits at a distant table, slightly balding, pale, his face devastated about the eyes, busily writing letters, staring into the dark void. There is only one waiter. It is a bar for both breakfasts and drinks, discreetly lit, restful, only the coffee-machine making its occasional hideous noise, now quiet, and the bottles on the wall illuminated for easy recognition. The wall looks like a reredos. Someone said that before, who was it?

Kassandra has vanished from his ken, her room phone doesn't answer and he hasn't come across her anywhere for hours, for days it seems. Kelly has disappeared too. She has left her room at the hotel, without checking out they told him unperturbed since all Interpreters' rooms are paid for by the Convention. He feels useless, at a loss, doesn't understand. Since the day of trips and the great battle in the lobby, Interpreters are apparently not required any more. The lobby seems permanently empty except for a few guests who now don't ask their way or request information. Surely everyone can't be attending lectures and panels? The police have vanished, presumably pursuing their inquiries away from the scene, in their offices. Or back in their books.

The rebellion of the TV and film characters, which had promised such excitement, has evidently frazzled out, been quelled or recooped for the cause by the formidable Professor Humboldt, who is also never to be seen. But where, where is Kelly?

He even went up to the office again this morning, to find out, only to discover that all the Convention staff had been replaced by fictional clerks, Akaky Akakievich, Badin, Devushkin, Mr Guppy, Goliadkin, Sainthomme, Uriah Heap, who seemed to run the place, wringing his hands and smarmingly sending him away. Even Bartleby stood by the window, pale and staring, ignoring everyone. Furious, he stalked off, suddenly wanting Kelly's presence with passion, their complicity, their fun.

He regrets his dismissive words to her. Why does one say these things? How can he have opposed her to Kassandra in his affections, a mere paper character? Why is he always putting her down for her lack of reading? She's read plenty he hasn't, it's just different, that's all. A mutual enrichment, it could have been. Just as he loves Kassandra in a different way. But why couldn't she understand that? Why is she so sensitive? Women! Always so complicated. Slowly he lets this comforting thought engulf the glimmer of acknowledgment and feels better. Let her go, who cares? Nevertheless, he has a deep sense of loss, oh, not for Kelly, no, of course not, but for his own assurance, his total grasp of things, his enjoyment of the Convention, his excitement, his swift recognitions, his existential necessity.

Dorothea Brooke, accompanied by Oberlin, Jude Fawley and Butler's Pontifex stroll in, chattering of Church matters and paganism. What bores they are. He's not interested in nineteenth-century characters, they're all so earnest about things no longer relevant. Those of the twentieth century, especially of the latter half, are so much more alive, even as reenactments, Vergil or Kassandra for instance. Except for Thomas Mann's Goethe and Lotte, but then, Thomas Mann, he's antiquated too. Broch now, that's something else. Or those of the eighteenth century, now they had something, speak to us directly, just as earlier ones do, like Don Quixote. The nineteenth century is supposed to be the great century of the novel, but then, we always react against the century preceding, just like kids against their parents, preferring their grandparents. And that applies in a smaller way to shorter periods – he grins, thinking of Kelly – we can't really take the Modernists any more now. But what is survival? Derrida or someone said survival is a quality that starts at the beginning of life, sounds damn deterministic, a character or an author has it long before he actually dies and survives. So why are there so many false reputations, great names, great books hailed as modern classics that sink into oblivion after a generation, a decade even? And those ignored that are then later discovered to have had that survival quality? Perhaps they had it all the time, merely, it wasn't felt. So what's the difference? Contemporary success can lead to survival or not, it's the luck of the draw, while being ignored is not in itself a proof of unrecognised genius. Anybody can be ignored and no damn good too. Anybody usually is. What is survival? What use praying for it? What is the point of this Convention? Etc.

Hester Prynne enters with her scarlet letter, accompanied by, yes, Hester Prynne as Lilian Gish. They go and sit in a far corner, order tea. Hester Prynne is taller, much more imposing. Her letter A is larger, brighter, more complex, really scarlet, and contrasts in richness with her grey garb and plain white cap. The other seems altogether irrelevant, frivolous, dated. How strange. The power of the spirit over the permanence of celluloid. A fantasy, fixed in time yet fleeting. The spirit. He pauses and nods imperceptibly. The Spirit is the Reader. What the Reader constructs is the Other, and the Other is contained in his flight, the definition of the Other is flight. To fix the Other is to lose him, to let him flee and grow is to keep him.

The Hesters are quickly followed by Oedipa Maas with a handsome black girl and a dirty-looking white one, all three surrounded by three modern men he doesn't know, or at least doesn't recognise. Although there are plenty of free tables, Oedipa moves towards one near him, facing the reredos, away from the nineteenth-century characters. Perhaps his Interpreter's uniform makes her feel secure. Perhaps she likes his grey fringe over his youthful face.

The black girl is sturdy, wrapped in a brown shawl and a timeless present, her eyes are so expressionless he isn't sure they're looking at anything. Two crystal balls are fixed to her ears like pebbles. The white girl is small and thin, looks shabby and terrified. Their companions seem either scruffy or middle-aged. The young one is the scruffy one, tall, waxy pale, with acne on the underside of his jaw and almost colourlessly cold blue eyes in deep bony sockets. A woolknit navy-blue watch cap is stuffed into the pocket of his army-surplus camouflage jacket and he walks around the table awkwardly, his loafers flapping, waiting to be assigned a seat, looking around the bar as if he'd never been in such a swanky place before. The two middle-aged men are very different from each other. One is tall, but less tall than the young one, lanky, around fifty-five, with silvery hair and a disgruntled expression. The other is middle-height, in his forties, Jewish, self-assured. His label, Jack can just read – of course! Nathan Zuckerman. An author. A fictional author. This should be interesting. He smiles at him uncertainly, hopefully, as they sit down. Hi there, Interpreter, Zuckerman calls, come over and join us. Come over and Interpret us.

Oedipa looks pleased. Her pale hair is piled up, held with pins and magic, yearning to tumble down in a whispering avalanche for the adoration of the now four men to three women of whom one is black the other shabby, at her table. What luxury. What spendthrift folly.

Let me introduce you, she says affably. Though we're all labelled like official postal packages we must keep up our manners mustn't we. This is my friend Sethe Suggs. And here – she wrinkles her nose a little too perceptibly, as if the other smelt bad – is Macabéa. Jack is standing next to Macabéa and she does smell, looks as if she never washed. Nathan Zuckerman, Professor Roger Lambert, Dale Kohler. I'm Oedipa Maas. Ms, she adds dutifully.

My name is Jack Knowles.

We know, you're labelled too.

He sits down, away from Macabéa. Roger Lambert orders whiskies all round, Dale Kohler hesitant. Now Jack recognises everyone, Toni Morrison's Sethe, from Beloved, Roger and Dale from Updike, Roger's Version. But why two characters from the same book? Too many irregularities this year, Dorothea and Mr Casaubon, young and old Copperfield, young Lotte from one book, old Lotte from another, with Goethe, Dante's Virgil and Broch's Vergil, not to mention Aeneas.

You were the guy who spoke with the terrorists weren't you? says Zuckerman. Gutsy show you put on. What happened to them? I know all about terrorists, I was in Israel, up in the West Bank, Judea as they prefer to call it, to persuade my young brother away from a handful of Zionist fanatics. I failed of course. Then I found myself sitting in an El Al 747 next to a wild American boy who had a hand-grenade and wanted me to hold up the plane with him. We were pounced on in time, the first class section was cleared out and we were held there, stripped naked, handcuffed, manhandled, interrogated brutally while the plane turned back, on orders, to Tel Aviv.

You invented it, says Oedipa Maas. You invented your brother's death from a heart bypass operation, when you were the one who needed it, and had it, and died.

That's by no means as clear as you say, lady, but how come you read the book? Characters don't read other books.

Of course they do, you weirdo. You think because you're an author, also in a book, that your characters are just the way you depict them? But you of all people know they're not. You use your entire family, and your women, taking notes, then you tell your story as if it were theirs, using just enough truth to hurt them and piling up the distortions to hurt them more. Your brother was a conscientious dentist who wouldn't fuck his assistant for the world, yet you depict him having this bypass and risking his life, solely because he can't face the rest of his years without an erection ever. But you're the one made impotent by heartdrugs. Your brother never went to Israel.

Lady, if that's the way you read it then it's also there in the book. And who do you think writes those bits? But it doesn't answer my question. How come you read contemporary books? Any books?

And how do you think I occupy my time when I'm not doing what's described in the book? And why do you add any books, as if all women were illiterate? You male authors are so macho, and even more the socalled Postmoderns who think they're so avantgarde. You're with me aren't you?

She turns to Sethe who mutters, Baby Suggs used to say, a man ain't nothing but a man. But a son? Well now, that's somebody.

But Oedipa hardly pauses to hear.

Their women are all represented as boffable or no longer boffable. Intelligent, educated wives, brilliant even, yours – that's a helluva concession – but never shown being so, never shown using their intelligence or having a responsible profession. Or if she is then she's masculine and butch, who needs a good fuck. Even Rita Humboldt is a cliché.

Who? says Zuckerman, Well I'm damned, says Jack, each startled for different reasons.

Faithful or unfaithful, their main quality is to be bloody understanding, of you men and your putrid narcissistic torments. And everything would come right if you could give them a good fuck. Even a woman cramful of all you dislike, who tunes you right out, you say what she needs is a good fuck. As if that was the miracle substitute for integrating otherness. At best, your understanding is no more than measuring the space that divides us from one another, at worst a deliberate refusal to understand, preserving yourself from those little quakes that could disturb your precious peace founded on refusal.

142

That's one of the more current and subtle forms of cruelty. It's the history of man in the world, too, but you can't even cope with otherness in your little lives, as women have always had to. Polished callousness, Conrad called it, the polished callousness from which springs an easy tolerance for oneself and others, a tolerance wide as poles from true sympathy and human compassion. Nor do you ever admit this for a moment, even to yourselves. Oh, you easily acknowledge endearing weaknesses like clumsiness, or even selfishness, rarely in question, providing you can make that one mutual and keep it general. Never for one moment can you bring to consciousness a specific hurt inflicted, which would resolve all. It's in this way you can drive us women either to berserk behaviour and floods of trivial accusations – never the deep ones, we're too frightened to bring them up – by way of single examples of what you deny, in desperate attempts to get through, which of course achieves the opposite. Or to crawling submission and self-accusation, which gets you all affectionate again. I betcha the only thing you're wondering about this Convention is when's Emma going to get layed.

Which one? says Jack, When is she? says Roger Lambert at the same time, and adds, my wife's name is Esther.

Even there, in Israel, Zuckerman puts in, suddenly speaking, to Jack's amazed recognition, out of the book, in that Jewish hothouse, my brother Henry somehow managed to remain perfectly ordinary, while what I'd been hoping – perhaps why I'd even made the trip, was to find that, freed for the first time in his life from the protection of family responsibilities, he'd become something less explicable and more original – than Henry. But that was like expecting the woman next door, whom you suspect of cheating on her husband, to reveal herself to you as Emma Bovary, and, what's more, in Flaubert's French. People don't turn themselves over to writers as full-blown literary characters – generally they give you very little to go on and, after the impact of the initial impression, are barely any help at all.

And everything I've said, says Oedipa, furious at being interrupted in her diatribe – and by authorial musings of all damn crap – goes for you too Professor Lambert, Professor of Divinity, even though you're less directly responsible, not being an author but an I-narrator. You imagine in every detail the boffing of your wife, your favourite view of whom is the rearview, by your hypocritically supported protegé here.

143

Please, please, he protests. I agree with you. I don't like what my author does either. He not only gives pages of super-coherent speeches about physics and computers to this unutterable young man here, some of which I'm made to say I don't understand – so how come I narrate them? – but he makes me think, think, I ask you, pages of Tertullian's theology of the flesh – godporn I call it – with passages in Latin, translated for the benefit of the reader, as if I needed to translate it! Followed by *i.e.* explanations, as if I needed *i.e.* explanations! There are even footnotes! Might as well be in Eugène Sue on the Jesuit conspiracy!

Eugène who? asks Oedipa.

Sue. S,U,E.

Sounds like what we Interpreters call free indirect discourse, says Jack gently. But obviously ill-applied, as in so many modern neorealist novels. It used to be a most delicate technique for representing consciousness, but it's dead now, chiefly because modern writers have turned much more to direct discourse, but also because neorealists have gone on using it, or rather misusing it, as if its sentences were narrative sentences, to pass narrative information to the reader, which can't always be convincingly filtered through a character's consciousness.

Is that so? says Zuckerman ironically. You amaze me, young man. Are you telling us authors how to write?

Jack shrugs. Much of this book is free indirect discourse too, but in the present tense. Has to be.

Watcha mean, this book? Which book? Is there another author beyond me and mine? Hey, Sethe, say something.

Never did learn letters, says Sethe. Denver did. My daughter. For a nickel. Lady Jones taught her. Thought she'd stopped on count of the nickel but she gone deaf for a little while, wouldn't hear nothing. So she couldn't learn no more. Beloved could spell her name. She had no other name. Just, Beloved.

And all that, Roger Lambert continues as if uninterrupted, the supposed physics and biology and chemistry of Creation, I mean all that computer-program kludging connections and kranking out miraculous coincidences, all that to prove the existence of God. And my resistance to it – nice touch that, I admit. But as I said (I quote) 'what manner of God is He who has to be proved?' All that huge erection, if you'll excuse the term, to dress up a banal story of suburban adultery. You sure fucked my wife good – he turns to Dale Kohler – and she sure dropped you like the shit you are when she found you a bore.

This is very interesting, this revolt of characters against their authors, says Jack fervently, hoping for a new exciting turn to the Convention.

Nothing very novel in that, young man, says Oedipa, are you hoping for a new exciting turn to the Convention? Haven't you had enough shenanigans? Besides, this Convention's about the Reader (she nods), not the author. The author's just nowhere.

Still, Ms Maas, Dale Kohler stammers, speaking at last, you brought him up. You don't seem too happy about yours either.

Sure I brought him up. Because of ole Zuck here, the perfect and obviously intended representation of the irresponsible author, and macho author to boot.

Taboo, taboo, murmurs the macho author.

Yea, you're all female-deleting the lot of you. Ethnologists have shown that women in polygamous societies for instance, when accessed at all, and always in front of their husband, speak a wholly coded language in front of the man, which has to be decoded, by the ethnologist, rightly or wrongly, and most of them are men. Take my husband, Mucho Maas. He needs reassurance the whole damn time. You comfort them when they wake pouring sweat or crying out in the language of bad dreams, yes, you hold them, they calm down, one day they lose it. I know that. But when is he going to forget? And what a big non-help he is to me when I have to face Pierce's mad codicil and all the Tristero business. Pierce was an earlier lover but it was all over long before he crazily involved me in all that, from beyond the beyond. Did he think I didn't have enough to do with my life? Like read, for instance? What about me as a woman, as a human being, apart from, over and above, my being made to behave like a paranoiac? It happens to the best of us. But I am also other things. In there, I just don't, don't, coincide with myself.

But you're not a feminist in the story at all! exclaims Jack, astonished. And you're quite well treated by all those men around you. Besides, he adds gently, authors have to leave some things out, our daily lives would bore the reader.

Like hell they do. Not when they're writing of the central male character. Nothing, but nothing is left out. Women are still seen from the outside, as Jude permanently sees Sue.

She's shrieking hysterically now, and there is a movement at the far table. Jude gets up and walks over.

Did you mention my name? And Sue's? he asks, dark and threatening.

She looks flabbergasted and fearful, has a tight look. Then her hand goes up to her head, as if to express alarm, her fingers fiddle for a second, her hair tumbles down and she gives him a flashy smile.

Real hair, she says, not like Arabella's. No, Mr Fawley, I'm sorry, you must have misheard. We were discussing Eugène Sue. Weren't we Professor Lambert?

Who? says Jude.

You know, The Wandering Jew, says Lambert. Not about the Wandering Jew in fact, though he appears on and off in a supernatural way as a benign presence –

I'm glad to hear that, says Zuckerman.

Protecting this Protestant counter-conspiracy –

What? Zuckerman looks amazed.

– but about the scheming, murderous greed of the Jesuits.

I love conspiracies, says Oedipa, don't you Mr Fawley? Have you read Eugène Sue?

I don't have time to read any more, and when I do, it's the Classics. Or not even the Classics now, just the Bible is all I'm left with. The only conspiracy I know is that of society, the artificial system of things, to shut out people like me from their high institutions of learning. Excuse me. As you said, I must have misheard.

He wanders off, crushed and, Jack Knowles thinks, knowing he has not misheard. She was shouting too loudly for that. But she looks ravishing with her hair down.

When good people treat you good, you ought to try and be good back, says Sethe to Oedipa. You don't. You evil. There's no bad luck in the world but whitefolks.

She gets up, very straight, jerks her head upwards in a brusque farewell and is off. Oedipa stares at her as if she were staring at a nonperson, stares at her withdrawing back, almost seeing the tree of lashes under the shawl, under the callico dress. Stares at the otherness she was on about.

146

What's gotten into her? Hey, Macabéa, what d'you think's gotten into her, why don't you support me sister? You know dear, you have body odour, you should wash more often and use deodorant. That's meant as user-friendly. Women must be women, and human beings.

Macabéa, who hasn't said a word, goes whiter than white, seems white-washed into whiter silence.

Cos I'm not all that crazy about what some feminist authors do, Oedipa goes on inexorably, who create female utopias and segregations and want to abolish sex-difference as if it were class, or think that by rewriting male myths in parodic reversal and substituting female symbols for male ones they'll solve everything. Too late, too late, in a godless culture.

Is it? asks Roger Lambert.

At least in that line. I prefer revaluing bad female symbols. Like Medusa, that's quite something. But it's here and now that matters. In the old days women didn't even have the right to narrate except under the constraining eye of a man, who has the power of life and death over her. Look at Justine. Even lesbians had to be represented as shared by Restif de la Bretonne. Or else *to* a man, like Scheherezade, for his delectation, or like the governess, to convince him she's not mad. All by men of course. And all because of a primitive male fantasy of female-deletion, even in creativity, especially in creativity. It's the old myth that man isn't born of woman. Look at Plato, whose poet, tickled into creativity by a boy, is in fact already pregnant, fecundated through divine madness – God as prick in fact – but he also labours and gives birth. The myth of the self-engendered text.

The men are as whitened into whiter silence as Macabéa, sip their drinks embarrassed, wondering when this will stop, how to stop it.

Well, yes, I love conspiracies, Oedipa picks up as if none of her diatribes had occurred. I have to admit. Those Jesuits! Must read it. They sound worse than anything out of Foucault's Pendulum, don't they? Or SMERSH, or any of those villainous organisations against 007.

My, you do read, then. Strange books for a woman.

There you go again.

I mean, says Zuckerman, that I am more in admiration at your ex-libris reading of me, or of Roger here, than of your reading, in your spare time beyond your author's attention, all these books about secret organisations, which would merely confirm his diagnosis. Wouldn't it? he adds innocently.

Dale Kohler looks uncomfortable, tongue-tied, from the end of the book, Jack thinks, not the beginning, no long artificially coherent speeches now about physics and unexplained coincidences to prove the existence of God. He gave up on that one. Roger Lambert is quiet but grinning, pleased that his Version won in the end. After all, he had his fuck too. Nathan Zuckerman is looking quizzically, as novelists say, at Oedipa Maas, probably thinking pejoratively she's a honey, or this I may need, wondering if he can utilize her, or re-utilize her, as Jean Rhys reinvented Rochester's wife, another mad woman in the attic. Old hat paranoia, he mutters to Jack.

But Jack wishes Kelly were here, to share his enjoyment, his excitement. She'd be a good fuck too, he inadvertently zaps, better no doubt than Kassandra could be – even though she is fucked in the book, by Achil das Vieh – but that's no great shakes for him. And he zaps away again from this fleeting thought, now revealed as macho instinct. What he needs her for right now is to pass herself off as Zelda Ritchie on the phone and contact Rita Humboldt. A rebellion of characters! It may not be novel, as Oedipa crushingly said, but it would be a change from this emptiness, this long series of frazzled out crises, murders that aren't, terrorists that aren't, police that aren't, journalists that aren't, clerks that aren't, battles that aren't, film-characters' revolts that aren't, one helluva set of non-events and non-persons. Some will say nothing happens in this novel, in this, Convention, and they'd be dead right. It's not about events but about characters and their discourse. That's the way we read books or the world, thoroughly involved then nothing, a mist of shadowy figures, Dead Souls. Perhaps that's the way God sees us, if he exists. The Implied Reader. He nods imperceptibly. But these characters are real, here he is talking to them, fine-tuned, and they all hate their authors. That's something real rinky-dink. Rita'd be ape about all these sweet manoeuverings.

But he hasn't been able to contact Rita about anything, even the disappearance of Kelly, even the replacement of the staff by fictional clerks.

The group at the table has quietened down into polite small talk. Jack glances across at the others. Dorothea looks crumpled as a dish-rag, if she knows what that is. She hasn't or shouldn't have understood modern sex-jargon, but Oedipa has talked very loud, and she must have gotten the gist. Pontifex is visibly trying to engage her in a change of topic, but she's finding it hard to concentrate on whatever it is he's murmuring. Oberlin is courteous but evidently bored by Jude's earnestness and possibly repelled by his forgotten semi-education in the Greek classics. Or perhaps Jude is trying to interest him in the handicraft of stone-carving? The two Hesters are deep in conversation and seem to have heard nothing, or at least to have been impervious to the content, treating it as vulgar noise. Herzog has throughout been plunged in his interminable letter, staring at the source of the noise as if it didn't exist as noise but as a source of inspiration.

Into this hush walks Rita, looking transformed. Her face is made up, her short dark hair bobbed and tousle-fixed in a modern style out of Vogue, her dark eyes are extended by kohl and lusciously Oriental. She seems fresh from a beauty-parlour, perhaps the hotel hairdresser ominously called Delilah, and she's wearing an exquisitely cut crimson kaftan embroidered in gold down the front. Zuckerman whistles appreciatively, she looks at their table and smiles. Behind her, immensely tall compared to her small size, is a dark man with long straight earlobes. He is wearing a yellow sari-looking cloak over one shoulder, that covers a long-sleeved trouser outfit like a dhoti, its grey-blue merging into the grey-blue of his face and hands.

Rita advances towards Jack's table, after a courteous nod at Dorothea, barely returned with a puzzled, ladylike have-we-been-introduced composure.

Hi, Jack, she says.

Hijack? Zuckerman repeats facetiously. I was –

I was looking for you. But kindly introduce me to your friends. This is the God Krishna, our Ultimate Reader. Otherwise known as Gibreel Farishta.

15

They sit down, Rita orders more whiskies, except for Krishna who has water and quietly removes the ten icecubes from the glass with silver pincers out of a silken pocket. The group is silent, exhausted, relieved, embarrassed, afraid, reverent possibly, at least Dale Kohler's brain seems to frazzle in sudden ecstasy. But Jack notices that three anonymous yet evidently plainclothes men entered soon after them and now sit discreetly facing them in the low table area, where armchairs are distant enough from tables for them to leap up quickly. Bodyguards? Real or newsreel?

He tries to tell Rita about the fictional clerks, then about Kelly's disappearance. Fiction does that, she says and stares him into silence with her Oriental eyes.

These people, he then tries desperately, are all in open revolt against their authors. It's fabulously interesting, he adds to soften the unintended shape of accusation his syntax has assumed, which sounds, also, surprisingly oracular.

Aren't we all? says Rita. What do you say, Krishna?

Mankind is, and always has been, and always will be.

Personkind, you mean, says Oedipa.

Very kind, he replies blandly, putting his hands together and inclining slightly, his lowslung eyelids closing. Thank you. Mankind means well, yes? And you also, beautiful person, beautiful woman, is it? But not so much, if you excuse, as Radha. Or so much, but different, isn't it? I also like iceblond, Allelujah.

Roger Lambert, Professor of Divinity, is as stunned as Dale Kohler but for different reasons. Both seem to have forgotten, Jack wonders, or not heard, that this is an Indian actor playing his part. Zuckerman the unbeliever, Gentile among Jews and Jew among Gentiles, shrugs and watches, hoping for good copy, while at the same time trying to provoke it by gazing intently at Rita, with his own Oriental eyes suitably smouldering to convey admiration, hunger, desire.

Allelujah Cone, adds Krishna by way of explanation. But no one except Jack has read the book. Why cone? Roger asks. Do you mean icon?

The god looks offended. Then mildly turns away with a benign smile. Forgive, he says, and sips his de-iced water.

Is it an apology? A generalised commandment?

The Hesters have left. Herzog is still writing, tearing up and crumpling pages. Dorothea is now being monopolised by Jude again, but inattentively, gazing at Krishna's blue face with shortsighted creased eyes of disbelieving rememoration, while Pontifex has changed places and put on his talkman to discuss something or other with Oberlin, who looks relieved and interested, the plugs of his own talkman back in his ears so as to miss nothing.

I think I've come up with a solution, Rita announces to no one in particular, and no one in particular except Jack can even surmise to what, to which of the many problems. The terrorists? The battle of heroes? All forgotten apparently. The fictional detectives? The fictional journalists? The fictional clerks? They don't even know of them. The film rebellion? They seem unaware of it. The disappearance of Kelly? They've never heard of her. The way to run the Convention next year? They won't be here, others will come. The way to end this one? They're not interested. They're interested only in themselves, their own existence, inasmuch as they're willing to pray for it at all, and don't come just to escape from their books, for the highjinks of even brief contact with other lives. The recognition of desire is the desire of recognition, Lacan. No need for God-the-Reader at all. Zuckerman especially looks all kinky with pleasure, now that he knows he can be read by other characters, and has been. Jack feels disgusted, humiliated: what about him? He's a reader too, an Interpreter even. Hasn't his recognition of them given them any pleasure? A solution to what? he asks lamely to end the long silence.

Why to everything. To this whole –

But he is not to learn what this whole or everything means. A thunderous, endless, rhythmic roar is heard from the lobby, tonic-stressed one two three, huh-huh-huh in the demo-mode, irrespective

151

of the words shouted in any one instance. In one concerted movement the three plainclothes men are standing around Krishna muttering don't move sir, stay here, keep sitting and other such things, or more likely come along with us sir, act as if nothing, we're surrounding you, for in fact he rises majestically and is escorted out, presumably to the elevators between the bar and the reception-desk in the wide corridor leading to the lobby. At any rate he disappears. He usually does.

Rita gets up, furious. Her submissive Oriental beauty swiftly turns into her usual masculine authority, not all the perfumes of Arabia can sweeten this little lantern jaw, the sudden scowl, the scornful stare. Even her spraywork tousle-fix seems to have dropped back into a straight male cut. She glares at the other tables. Herzog writes on unperturbed, his table covered and surrounded with crumpled sheets of paper. You slob, why don't you use a word-processor, she shouts at him but he doesn't even look up, doesn't know he's being addressed. Dorothea meets her eyes, recognises her in astonishment as the lady in the horseless carriage and nods stiffly. Rita marches up to her table. You guys stay put, she orders, something's happening out there. I don't want anyone hurt. You too Jack, all of you, she turns back towards her own table, but it's empty.

Now what? she growls to Dorothea and her companions, and storms out of the bar, past the elevators, where she hesitates, then stalks on to the desk, where the one assistant is busy on the computer, the manager behind his glass pane on the phone. The huh-huh-huh from the lobby is deafening but, so far, she reassures herself, it's only vox humana, however multitudinous and disagreeable, no gunshots, no sword-clashes, no female screams. Call the police immediately, she raps out. We have ma'am, we're computer-linked. They're on their way. They'd better be on the ball this time, she replies, get me Professor Mansell Roberts at once. We've called him, ma'am, he's on his way too. We tried your room, he adds, but you weren't there. Of course I wasn't, you wimpy nerd, I'm here. Yes ma'am. She feels all the angrier for being outsmarted and helpless. She waits, drumming her fingers on the counter with impatience. Where will Mansell come from? If he was in his room, or on a panel, he'd be down on the elevator by now. If he was outside somewhere, or even in the lobby, he'd never get through to her. But how could he be outside or in the lobby? They couldn't have contacted him, he's not on a permanent

152

walky-talky. Even though that's all he can do, walky-talk.

But now great packets of people are streaming past her from the elevators, from the back entrance and back-lobby of the hotel, from the doors of the backstairs. It seems all the attenders of every panel-room and lecture-room have come pouring down in panic or thrill and are making their way towards the huge front lobby. Some carry wide banners held between two poles but bowed down or swaying illegibly as they're caught up in the race. She is swept along, tiny and crimson and Oriental, ignored. Her golden-sandaled bare toes are trodden on, her tousle-fix is limp, her mascara streaks down her face with sweat and angry tears. Gone is the Oriental beauty. Gone is the authoritative little President of the Convention in grey and plum, in hunting pink or in black with daffodil jabot.

The lobby is crammed like a Teheran street at the burial of Khomeini, like the mosque at Mecca, but not with praying Moslems – why do such comparisons cross her mind? It is crammed like a presidential primary, that's better, but no, she is president. Right across it and up in the gallery, young, old and middle-aged, black, pink, brown, yellow, bald, long-haired, straight-haired, afro-haired, green or orange, fur-hatted, Crocketted, baseball-capped in magenta green blue yellow, in Levi's knockoffs and logoed teeshirts, one white on black logo reading Innocent Bystander, in skintight fatigues, in leather, in three-piece city-suits, in sheepskin-lined jean jackets, in leotards and jogging-gear of all colours, in army-surplus. Women too, in much the same, or in silk, satin, muslin, rags. The shouting, the roaring is endless. She can't hear a thing. She's too small and trampled to see the banners waving aloft, one is very long, but she's at the back of it. Another is hanging all along the gallery balustrade and this she sees. It reads, in magenta pink on green: Fair deal for Gays.

Oh no! she groans. That's all I needed.

Rita is not Gay, despite her cliché butch look. She doesn't disap-prove, but neither has she fallen over backwards to fly that flag or support sexegregation, specificity and all the rest. I'm a humanist, not a sexologist, she'd say, and attract the ire of the supposedly female-deleted but more often self-deleted social groups. She has never been deleted, at least not to herself. Even as a child she'd get a little shudder of joy at being alone and alive, and still does, some ten times a day. She believes that this is the source of her strength, and of others' fear of her,

153

for although she has had three husbands, she remained throughout utterly self-sufficient. Too much so perhaps, men don't take to that. But she hates a mob. She can now see other banners waving and sinking. Hands off abortion. Black boffing is beautiful. Lizzies aloft. Which seem to her a mere reversal of male Grand Narratives that are contested as such by women.

Pushed and pressed and trodden on, she wildly stares around her, as far as she can see at all among the green magenta, yellow and blue clad bodies so much taller than herself. She looks for familiar characters, out of Proust, Thomas Mann, Radclyffe Hall, William Burroughs and all the rest. There would be, in any case, few overt ones until modern times, and that seems to be the complaint. But no, these are real tapettes, of every kind, gathered here in San Francisco, not for Gaylib Day which comes in June, but on a special December trip to invade the Convention of Prayer for Being. WE DO NOT EXIST! one shouts immediately near her. NOT REPRESENTED! yells another. WHERE ARE THE NOVELS ABOUT AIDS? Then one isolated, longer, unrhythmic shout in a fraction of a pause, just beside her ear: Blacks and women have it all their own way now!

Mingled among them are helpless Interpreters in dark red, as well as fictional characters who have rushed down from panel-rooms where teams of tapettes intervened, interrupted, ordered everyone down to the demo, in turbans, in bonnets, in top hats, in wimples and hennins, in mobcaps, in diadems, in kepis, in mitres, in long cloaks, djotis, kaftans, kimonos, p'aos, jellabas, cutaway coats, pinstripe trousers and bowler hats, silken tubes, paniered skirts, monks' habits black brown white saffron, black soutanes, archbishops' robes, royal ermine, coat of mail, breastplate, leopard skins, the lot. Moreover the film and TV crowd has rushed out of both Beverly and Kennedy where they were meeting, and squeezed their way into the masses. Seems like everyone, but everyone, is here, except for the five people she left in the bar.

The city-cops arrive at last in a gurgle of sirens. But they can't get in, the milling crowd is too dense. They have to push and scram and beat their way through, clapping handcuffs on here and there, dragging limp or struggling bodies away, set upon by strong groups of others, but they are soon outnumbered. Surely they're not going to use teargas again! Rita thinks, fumbling for a handkerchief and not finding one either in her pocketless crimson kaftan or in her tiny golden evening purse. It'd be no great shakes to use repetition, literarywise. But then the cops! Illiterate, the goddamn bunch. She feels pretty bad. Powerless.

Then she suddenly sees a tall man in the gallery, just above the long hanging banner. He's wearing a dark fur jacket and a fur bonnet over his long black hair. His black eyebrows join together to form a thick black line across his high pale brow. She gasps. The Wandering Jew! Not Ahasverus converted by Ananias from the old Volksbuch, nor Ahasverus from Chrysostomus Dudulaeus, nor Goethe's, nor Hamerling's, nor Chamisso's, nor Lenau's, nor even Apollinaire's, but Eugène Sue's, who tries to protect the scattered Protestant descendants of Marius de Rennepont from the evil and murderous machinations of the Jesuits, and fails; who like the others is condemned to walk for ever, century upon century. And who brings cholera over Europe and upon Paris with every step. Has he brought it here? And where is his sister in misfortune, Herodias?

At first he is unnoticed. The first hush comes from his immediate surroundings, and slowly reaches to the whole gallery, slightly lowering the decibels. The struggling groups below start looking up and stop struggling. The rhythmic roars quieten only gradually, the silence spreading like a contagion. Even the police cease their activities and stare.

He stretches out his hands. He starts speaking. In Russian, in Hebrew, in German, in Yiddish, in French. But everyone seems to hear him in English, as if he were dubbed, his lip-movements not quite corresponding to the words. Are there words? Rita can't hear any with her ears. But she absorbs immense and silent well-constructed phrases, interspersed with short sharp apostrophes, exclamations of love, proverbs, maxims, clichés of wisdom, brief prayers, blessings. Perhaps he is only pretending to speak, everyone hearing what they will. The effect is nevertheless electrical.

Herodias does appear, equally pale, equally clothed in dark fur, with equally black long hair. Then other figures in differently coloured robes, white, blue, purple, golden, lilac, crimson, orange, dark green. They fill a space around the man and the woman, having mysteriously or magnetically pushed the demonstrators up there beyond an invisible line. Some seem unfleshed-out, schematic abstractions, some on the contrary are outlined in black along every limb and shape, like

155

Botticelli's La Calumnia. Some appear to wear scarequotes round their heads. Rita groans. Not, oh not, allegories! Soon we'll be invaded by cartoons. And what the hell are they? Vices and Virtues? Chaos and Mutabilitie? Love, Truth, Beauty, Wisdom, Folly, Death? Or more concrete, like Langland's Seven Deadly Sins confessing themselves to inexistence or Hunger killed by being force-fed? Or are they modern allegories, Democracy, Hegemony, Utopia, Free Love, Free Economy, Freedom, Reality, Sovereignty, Cultural Imperialism, Consensus, the Unconscious, the Ego, the Superego, the Id? Or Aesthetics, Intertextuality, Infratextuality, Paratextuality, Hetero-textuality, Specificity, Metadiegesis, Semeiosis, Paradigm, Paradise, Paradismatics?

The hush that has accompanied the long silent speech becomes a rising murmur at the silent moment when the speech apparently ceases, but now the lights of the great lobby lower slightly, slowly, as when a curtain is about to rise. Then the lowering of light stops, and the murmur that has increased also stops, as in a theatre. But there is no curtain, no stage to look down on, the dense crowd is looking up. A unanimous cry of wonder arises, then is quenched like a flame. In the intervening instant between the light and the half-light, between the silence and the murmur, and in full view of the multitudinous blind stares of the multicoloured crowd upwards towards the gallery, the figures surrounding the furclad man and woman have vanished, leaving only the Gay protesters that were pushed beyond some invisible line around the space the figures were standing in. Within that space the man and woman stand alone, transfixed. Their black hair is totally white. Their youthful faces are aged as centuries. Their shoulders stoop, their bodies are diminished and fragile. They stare at each other. Their trembling hands grasp each other's long white hair, finger each others' wrinkled faces lovingly.

Oh my sister, the ancient old man calls out in a quavering voice that resounds this time for all to hear. For so many centuries has the hand of the Lord launched us over this earth, from one pole to another, so many times have we witnessed the awakening of nature with incurable pain, for ever separated, death for ever fleeing before us.

Glory to Him, oh my brother, for since yesterday that His Will has at last brought us together, I feel in my limbs the ineffable langour of approaching death. The anger of the Lord is at last satisfied.

156

At last. At last, my sister, my fellow-victim of this long persecution. Lord, if your mercy is great, so has your anger been great.

Courage and hope, my brother. Remember that after expiation comes forgiveness. The lord struck in each of us and in your posterity the artisan made wicked by misfortune and injustice. He said Walk! Walk! Without rest or respite, and your walking will be vain, and each evening of every century you will be no nearer the end than you were in the morning. My brother, a veil comes over my eyes. I can barely see that eastern glow which a moment ago was vermillion.

My sister, a confused vapour clouds the valley, the lake, the forest. My strength escapes me.

God be praised oh my brother. The moment of eternal rest is approaching.

The blessedness of everlasting sleep seizes all my senses.

My eyes are closing, sister. Forgiven. Forgiven. Die in peace, my sister, The dawn of this, great day, to him, the sun is rising. See.

Oh God, blessed art Thou.

Oh God, blessed art Thou.

The voices are silenced for ever, the figures slowly disintegrate in a radiant light that illuminates the entire valley of the Hilton lobby with its dazzling rays.

The crowd is shock still in its variegated costumes. Rita stands tinily within it, like a sardine crushed in a giant container. Is this another mass halloo? Or has she alone heard the words, because she knows the novel so well? Must all characters die, after all, exhausted by their timeless life, their timeless march through the minimising minds of mankind? Has this whole Convention come to just that? Has she too marched in vain?

What we need, my friends, says a curious high-pitched voice from the teak stairway leading up to the gallery – but evidently it has been speaking for some moments, quenching at first the murmur of mingled astonishment, anger, rebellion, mockery, wonderment or fear that had risen, without her hearing it through her small intemporal agony of permanent crisis but heard now in a brief retroactive flash. It's that young man Dale Kohler who was so tongue-tied in the bar. He has donned the woolknit navy-blue watch-cap which was stuffed into the pocket of his army surplus camouflage jacket. He is paler than ever and his acne seems to glow now from the underside of his jaw, his eyes in

157

their deep bony sockets are an uneasy, sheepish, unutterably cold pale blue.

What we need is computer-simulation programs. I have devised and kludged together hundreds, thousands, of connections and I don't know whatall, to prove the existence of Our Creator, the Implied Reader. Okay I failed. It all proved too much, and the scientists as well as the theologians were against me. I won't go into all that contingent crap now but you can believe me, it wasn't exactly straight-arrow. But if engineers, microengineers and designers can make up multidimensional models of buildings, automobiles, aircraft, spaceships, space telescopes and whatall, I can assure you it's just kidstuff to produce multidimensional models of ourselves, I done it, we are the models my models have kibbitzed, our deepest buried psychologies in microdetail, our sociologies, our chemical and atomic substances, our circulations, digestive systems, our thoughts, our impulses, our spoken and unspoken dialogue, our violences and hatreds, our passions, our growths and decays from chromosome to dust. We're really fleshed-out characters, as Interpreters say. You may feel you've come here wrenched out of your home-contexts, sometimes a mere name, trailing bits and pieces of your own world, but it's my program brought you, or at least will bring you next year, fully-fledged in a reconstruction as vast and deep as all existence, our own reality my friends, which we thereby prove, to ourselves. We don't need to prove the existence of the Implied Reader Our Creator. It may be beyond our technical capacities to prove Him, as yet, but we KNOW He exists. Our humble little existences, my friends, THAT's more within our power to prove. We can prove our survival too, our eternity. I suggest –

He goes on this way for some time. Everyone is transfixed. By hope, by disbelief, by the blank mesmerization of that hysterical voice. Rita is also transfixed, but by fury. And an unfamiliar helplessness. She can't move. She is held in by the crush of people that sways in ripples, in waves. Where is Mansell Roberts? What are the cops doing? Are they spellbound too? Well of course, if they're fictional. Mere celluloid, out of mere letters in a script.

Ruhe bitte!

A cracked voice yells, from several bodies behind her. Dale Kohler stops. Everyone looks back in her direction, but beyond her. She looks

158

back too. A tall old man, so incredibly gaunt his body barely seems to support his height, has spoken, and speaks still, in German. He is embracing a library ladder he has leant against one of the fat square pillars that mark the wide entrance out of the lobby into the reception-desk area. He is now climbing it, as if to find or arrange invisible books. On the fourth rung however he turns towards the crowd, his bony hand leaning against the ladder. His eyes are as icy-blue as Dale's but he has no cheeks. His brow is split like a rockwall, his nose is a vertical fishbone of vertiginous narrowness, at the base of which are hidden two minute black insects for nostrils. His mouth, now closed, is a zip-fastener. Two deep wrinkles like scars plunge from his temples to meet at the pointed chin, and, together with the nose, divide his already thin face into five vertical bands of fearful symmetry. His pale gaze rests nowhere, there is nowhere for it to rest. On the second rung of the ladder stands Jack Knowles, grey-fringed and baby-faced, incredibly with a microphone, simultranslating.

This is Professor Peter Kien, the famous sinologist. He knows many other languages but prefers to speak in German. I shall translate as he goes. Those of you who don't understand English too well and have your talkmans kindly use them.

16

I had a dream, my friends. A man was tied up on the terrace of a temple, defending himself against two jaguars on either side. I saw the feet of the jaguars. They were human feet. The jaguars were Mexican sacrificial priests, executing a sacred comedy.

Then the righthand jaguar brandished a heavy pointed stone and thrust it deep into the heart of the victim, whose breast tore open. Oh fearful spectacle. From the prisoner's open breast sprang a book, then another, then a third. A cascade of books escaped, by the dozen, by the hundreds. Fire licked the paper. Each book screamed for help, the strident shrieks flew up everywhere. I jump. Flames blind me. When I stretch my hand I seize human beings who yell, who grapple at me with all their strength. I push them back. They return. From below they crawl to me and embrace my knees. Let me go! I don't know you! What do you want? How can I save the books? They insult me, leap at my face, clutch my lips closed. An enormous book grows bigger and bigger, fills earth and sky, the fire slowly consumes it from the edges, it dies the death of martyrs. The humans scream, the book burns in silence.

Then I hear a voice – all-knowing, it is the voice of God – proclaiming: Here there are no books. All is vanity. I recognise the truth. In a few seconds I get rid of the scum being devoured by the flames and leap from the blaze. I am saved.

It is said that books have no life. But who has ever proved the insensibility of the inorganic world? Who knows if a book doesn't also aspire, in a strange way we cannot apprehend, to the company of other books in the society of which it has lived for a long time? We call them dead matter. But what is dead has lived. Books are more important than animals, more important than human beings.

Oh my books! I address you all, here listening to me, for you too are

160

books. I see that you are faithful to me and I shall now initiate you into our enemy's plan, as you deserve.

At this moment someone Rita can't see shakes the ladder and Kien comes tumbling down like a blown scarecrow, flattened out as a dead seascroll over the shoulders of the crowd immediately below him. Jack Knowles also falls, but from lower down, a mere stumble that makes him disappear down among the bodies of the crowd. Kien is carried like a corpse by six warriors in various garbs from coat of mail to leopard skin to a green hussar's uniform to camouflage battledress to the white armour of the non-existent knight. So he's back, goodoh, thinks Rita irrelevantly. A passage opens in the crowd to let them pass, slowly, as if to a ceremonious funeral march, towards the big glass doors of the hotel. Outside the escort can be seen throwing their thin burden onto the street like so much waste paper. It is picked up by the cops outside and bundled into a paddy wagon, which drives off in a flashing blue light and a giggle of siren.

Dale Kohler, observing the silence, is about to resume his speech, but the silence is not a listening one. It is a fatigued silence, Rita notes. The Gay crowd, by nature the most tolerant of aberration, has merely parted the colourful sea to let it out, but seems also cowed into shame at its own quiet exclusion of it. The innumerable others too, from all ages and areas, are suddenly tired of listening, tired of asserting their existence and being treated as dead matter, crushed into pointlessness. The police don't even have to push and clamp. Slowly the mass percolates through the various exits, towards the elevators, back into Beverly and Kennedy, up to their rooms, back to their panel-sessions, out of the gallery-doors marked NO EXIT, round the gallery towards other elevators, through to the backstairs, into the bar, out into the streets by the front and rear entrances. In fifteen minutes of quiet, of murmuring at most, the lobby is empty again.

Rita is left with Jack, who is sitting at the foot of the library ladder, still protecting his grey head with crimson arms resting on crimson knees. And with Mansell Roberts who comes hurrying over from the far end of the lobby.

Wow, Rita, you sure look terrific / Mansell what the hell d'you have to go and play hooky for? they say together and Rita adds, Don't be an ass I've been trampled out of existence while Mansell adds don't act so huffy.

Jack Knowles helps himself up with the lower rungs of the library ladder. He looks drawn, old suddenly and wonders if his hair too has turned white.

What do we do now? he asks.

My feet are killing me.

Rita is hobbling towards the Biedermayer sofa, supported by Roberts. Jack follows, though feeling tacitly excluded. They sit down, she bends to remove her golden sandals. Her feet are tiny, bruised and bloody. Jack sits on the wooden throne. Never has he felt less royal, less authoritative, less heroic.

You did well, Jack, damn good performance. He perks up. You should go in for it, sigh-multaneous interpreting. A deal better than interpreting. He feels excluded again, practically fired. Even crushed almost out of existence this little woman has what he has not, sheer méchanceté.

Why don't we go to the bar? says Roberts. You need a drink. I need a drink.

Can't move.

Shall I get you a double whisky?

Stay put, man. Even coke with the gas out won't do it. Shopworn idea. But Life, this I may need. Oh God, Oh Reader! Why don't You come riding nicely by?

Oh come on, Rita, you've been hassled a bit, we all have, but you're not shopworn.

Did I say I was? You spook.

I've been thinking, Professor Humboldt –

Really? What with?

Rita, have a little give.

Give? Give? I've done nothing but give to the Convention for years. It's never been like this. Why? Why?

Perhaps you gave too much.

Well, make up your tiny mind.

Mansell is silent, can't cope. Jack stares. She's like that with everyone, not just him.

Come on, let's have it, young man.

Only that – God, the Implied Reader, reads us, and forgets. I mean despite His infinite mind. He can't even remember a detail from page 172, let alone 935 in a blockbuster. And that's while He reads. He

162

punishes us with inattention. If He's transcendent He's far above and away, if He's immanent he's within, close to the weak. His world isn't accidental, but we have to finish it, achieve it, give mouth-to-mouth with the breath of God. And we don't.

For I the Lord thy God am a jealous God, visiting the iniquity of the fathers upon the children unto the third and fourth generation of them that hate me. Thousands of generations in fact. How's that for memory?

But that's the Real God, even absconding. God the Implied Reader does more than abscond. He's like the ordinary reader, like us. And fiction, I mean, well, Sartre said that to be is to be like a hero in a novel. Man's a kind of secondhand god, free man I mean, creating his own identity. But there are incoherences, gaps in the plot. It's just like a novel by Robbe-Grillet, people die several times. That's –

You read too much French theory young man, stick to American, we're pragmatists.

Are we? What about cartoon characters that get smashed to death over and over and recover without explanation for the next adventure? What about Barth? Resuscitating all the characters he ever created, in Letters? Isn't that exactly the process of reading?

You sound like that Professor of Divinity. He keeps quoting Karl Barth too. And Tertullian of all people. Why the shit do we all have to quote each other to live?

Love, puts in Mansell Roberts.

Jack is quenched to silence by Rita's ignorance of John Barth. How hard he was on Kelly. And he hasn't read Karl Barth after all, or Tertullian. Holes, gaps, lacunae, lakes of oblivian, Lethe. Death. Where is Kelly? Is she dead too? Not in his mind. It's Kassandra who's died there. Quite suddenly, wailing herself away. He can't even recall her eyes. Like Goethe with Lotte's eyes. Or her words. Only dishevelled hair and a white peplum. Kelly's hair is flaming red, her eyes green (are they? Or hazel?), her breasts small, handlable and freckled, her pubic hair soft orange, her thighs slim and white and strong, her words in his ear tender – but it flashes through his mind that he never got as far as that, only hovering as she put it. Her words of anger ring out in the lobby of his inner ear, Lay off me Jack. You're just trying to put me down. Why this downgrading treatment? This is a helluva dull conversation!

163

The exhausted silence between them is broken by a slim standing figure in a high-waisted Regency dress of fine gold-coloured muslin, with short puffed sleeves and a modest frill around the cutaway neck. Over her shoulders an ivory mantle hangs open and loose. Her dark hair is drawn up at the back into a frothy mass but curls short around her brow and temples.

Mansell Roberts rises, so does Jack.

Please sit down, Miss Woodhouse. You must be very tired after all that ... scene.

Oh, not at all. But thank you. I am happy to see you. I haven't seen anyone, it seems, for days.

She curtsies to Rita, taking her for some Indian princess, who doesn't move to make room for three, and sits down by her. Jack signs politely to Mansell to take the throne and goes to sit on the bottom step of the teak stairway.

You mean, you weren't down here in the ruckus?

The, er?

The huge crowd down here, Rita translates condescendingly. You must be the only one. And those few I left in the bar. Unless Oblomov couldn't be bothered to rise from his bed and Justine and Juliet were too engrossed in their doings.

I dislike crowds, Your Highness. This Convention has been particularly trying, and I have been in my room. A strange room, with very square furniture, but I have grown quite used to that. The heat, however, that comes out of the wall below the window is more than I can bear, nor does the window open. I suppose that is a precaution against falling out, from such a height. The heat made me exceedingly thirsty, and I did not like to drink the water from that spout you call faucet, which has a most disagreeable taste. There is no bell-pull. Only a strange box with a glass front and knobs, but nothing happened when I pulled them. But I discovered a button in the wall by the bed, marked Bell, and pushed it. A servant arrived, and told me, rather rudely I thought at first, that I could have all the drinks I wanted in the bar. I do not wish to go down to the bar, I said, a little primly I'm afraid. But she interrupted me and revealed that I had a bar of my own, and she walked to it and opened it for me. I was quite confused. She even served me a glass of a curious drink, fizzy as champagne but more like, well, a sour lemon drink. But it was so cold. I sputtered and couldn't drink it. Then she became very kind and thoughtful, and advised me to wait for the chill to wear off. It'll fizz itself out, she said, and you know, it did after a while. But we chatted in a friendly way. I asked her if she would drink with me, and she helped herself and sat by me. She is the only person I have talked to in twenty-four hours. Her name, she told me, was Jenny Gerhardt.

Jesus! Jack exclaims, even the staff is fictional now!

I beg your pardon?

No, nothing, sorry to interrupt.

Rita frowns. Mansell smiles.

Do please go on, Miss Woodhouse.

Oh, she was very charming, if a little, well, you know how servants are. She told me she is hoping to marry a, what is it you have here for the upper chamber, a senator. Now isn't that strange? Even Harriet could not aim so high, and she is hardly a servant. But you see, I was so glad of the company. There were no more papers on me in the programme and I was feeling a little lost, a little weak. I had been sitting in my room for so long, gazing at the ocean. I have never seen the sea you know. I have never found myself so high up in the sky, except, of course, in the aerobrain, but that view is somewhat different. This truly is a New-found-land, is it not? Nevertheless, I would very much like to return home, to Highbury.

Where you have not, of course, heard of the Napoleonic Wars?

The – ? Oh, well yes, of course, Your Highness, I must have done, distantly you know. But they did not truly concern us. Highbury is very, well, self-enclosed, self-sufficient. Perhaps we are too absorbed in ourselves and in each other. Still, I am very happy there, and my father is undoubtedly missing me. He is not well, you know, and depends upon me a great deal. Do you suppose it would be feasible to arrange some kind of conveyance?

Rita opens her smudged eyes wide at Emma's extraordinary, persistent egocentricity, but to her own mild astonishment says nothing, too tired even to be rude, let alone arrange a conveyance. Strange, she thinks wearily, how human faults dress up in the customs of their time, remain unbudgeable but adapt. Our own middle-class selfishness is far more blatant, less elegant, and yet I am shocked by this. As if I had time to arrange a conveyance!

But my dear Miss Woodhouse, Mansell is saying, you are free to leave whenever you like. The Convention is all but over anyway.

But, well, how?

You're not helpless, child, says Rita impatiently after all. You only have to get into your aerobrain. A womb of your own, you know.

A what? You mean, I can do it, by myself? But that journey, the Customs and Excise Officers, the change of vehicle in Atlanta City? All that is quite beyond me ma'am. Or do you mean the carriage, with that dreadful Mr Elton, who most provokingly vanished, much to my relief I may add, and I found myself speaking in German to a total stranger. It was exceedingly mortifying, I assure you. I would prefer –

But nobody hears what Miss Woodhouse would prefer, for Kien appears again, presumably let off, from the elevator corridor, waving his arms towards the high walls of the lobby and shouting in German. Jack leaps up and runs towards him. Herr Professor! Was ist los? Was tun Sie da? But he gets no reply and as he listens to Kien he realises the man is ordering down the imaginary books he has evidently been arranging every night along imaginary shelves, ordering them down, not back into his head but down into imaginary funeral pyres. But are the fires imaginary? A strident, continuous clanging suddenly overwhelms the lobby from all its edges, immediately echoed by others in the gallery, in Beverly, in Kennedy, in distant corridors, very faintly from other floors. Within seconds a so far invisible staff appears from nowhere, each running to different fire alarms and squirting foam on very real flames. One walks towards the group on the Biedermayer but Rita has already seized Emma by the arm and is dragging her out, helped by Mansell Roberts. Jack is still trying to calm Kien, who is shouting Seid bereit! to his imaginary books, Are you ready? Go! go! as they invisibly tumble down along the downward trajectory of his long lanky arms. Everywhere, he shouts in German, fire everywhere to the very top, on every floor, it took me five days to prepare. My whole library, the World, my Tibetan manuscripts, my Chinese scrolls and folios, quartos, octavos, go! Go away! He laughs, throws imaginary old newspapers crumpled up into balls, even a real one, The Los Angeles Times, onto the fires, getting nearer and nearer to the largest concentration of flames that lick the carpets, leap at the Biedermayer, creep up the teak stairway, reach the windows and the tall curtains. The firemen arrive in strength and put the fire out fairly soon, grab hold of Kien and take him out into the street to the ambulance men, then realise, looking up, that smoke and flames are pouring out from every single one of the nineteen or twenty-three or forty-six floors according to the different sections of the building, melting or breaking the unopenable windows, licking at the concrete façades.

17

Perhaps Miss Woodhouse would have preferred to travel with the King of Spain, who was so gracious to her on the way in. Or even with His Excellenz Goethe. Perhaps she would have preferred not to have come at all. Perhaps she would have preferred, like Bartleby, not to exist.

She is standing near a police-car on the other side of the street, with the little Oriental princess they call Rita and the iron-haired, iron-jawed man who both dragged her out of the hotel ground-floor at the beginning of the fire, and the young man with the grey fringe. They seem to have special permission to remain so near the police chief, whereas other people now pouring out of the hotel are being directed much further down the street, all choking as the enormous fumes spread. She can read some of their labels, Dorothea Brooke, Ernest Pontifex, Jude Fawley and, how odd, Excellenz Goethe, the man she talked to in the carriage. And many more, in the twentieth-century dress she has by now become familiar with. Why is she being allowed to stay? The little princess seems to have forgotten her and is now talking to the iron-haired man who is talking to the police chief. Huge insect-like air-vehicles are now hovering around the high building, spraying it with water, with white foam, then move away as others come in. The street is filled with the biggest fire-engines she has ever seen, that direct jets like cathedral spires up to the lower floors, and with policemen all in black and silver who keep away the gathering crowds and direct those still streaming out of the hotel down the street towards other police vans. Men rush into the building with masks on, bringing out the staff, some of whom bring out more guests. And more. The fat manager is wringing his hands, talking to the firechief who is too busy on a walkytalky to hear how many rooms, how many guests, what the insurance, or how he remembered to switch off the air-conditioning.

Thank God all those Gays got out earlier, says the little Indian princess in crimson. Emma doesn't understand. Where are the King of Spain, the Prince of Parma, Dr Casaubon? These are the only people she has met. Oh and her namesake Emma, the shameless one. And the little girl in white and blue who sat next to the White Knight so curiously reduced. But she hadn't really met them, only noticed them. And the handsome young romanic priest who read the Gospel in French. And that awful Frenchman who made love to her in that incredibly long mailcoach. And now, this Indian princess and her two strange followers. On reflection she has met more people here than in the whole of Highbury, how very peculiar.

The high building burns on. The camera crews are busy filming, the journalists busy at their microphones. Very few people can be saved, they announce in lugubrious but excited tones. The panic in there must be goddam wild, says Rita.

You never said an untruer word, Rita, says the iron-jawed man Roberts. For one thing most of the vast crowd in the lobby had exited through the doors, and have come wandering back, look, they're being held off by the police cordon. And all the film crowd who were in Beverly and Kennedy, they must have come out at once, followed us out.

The hotel holds far more than that, you prick.

I daresay. But the director of operations has just informed me that to his knowledge everyone is being safely brought out. Those who'd gone up to their rooms or to the restaurant-bar at the top were quickly called by loudspeaker and marshalled by the well-trained staff down the emergency stairs, even the elevators while they were still working, or through the back entrance of the hotel, and some, look, spluttering and coughing, are still pouring out through the front. There's Philip II, in black with his white ruff slightly ruffled, I'd pick him anywhere, and there's Odysseus, quite calm in his shepherd garb, he's been down to Hades after all.

There's Mr Sorel, says Emma, the one who –

So it is. As pale as ever, his hair a bit singed, and the white edges of his funny black split bib too.

Was he burnt, hurt? she cries anxiously.

169

Can't tell. Looks okay.

Oh and he's with that dreadful woman. He's holding her –

Emma Bovary. And the fake priest Herrera. Captain Nemo, why, Aeneas with his ridiculous branch, well, he went to Avernus too. And Captain Ahab, stumping on his wooden leg, lucky that didn't burn, Jesus! he's holding a parrot.

Two people are wounded! she cries.

No, it's Vergil on his litter, says the grey-haired young man. And Queen Isabella on hers.

Who?

The wife of Philip II. Who became Elizabeth of England.

Oh. Yes.

Only in Carlos Fuentes of course.

Who? Oh, there's the little white pope.

Mr Oberlin, cries Dorothea Brooke who has drawn back near them to look. She tries to run towards him but is held back firmly by the police chief. He rejoins them and she shakes both his hands in hers, with great emotion. Where did you vanish?

Many more come trooping out and past them to go further down the street, a colourful crew, Sultan Shahrian, Tariel in his leopard skin, musketeers, Roland with his horn, the two Copperfields, identified with complacency by the grey-haired young man to a journalist labelled Jake Barnes, the Princesse de Guermantes, a saffron-robed monk, the Lady Murasaki, Hester Prynne, old Starets Zossima, Oliver Twist, Pan Tadeusz, Dr Philifor, Kassandra. Emma hears the names the young man utters but knows none. Indian princes, Italian princes, Japanese warriors, French curates, English lords and squires, ragamuffins, well-dressed children, Norse warriors, soldiers of every colour and uniform, African chiefs, governesses, bankers, black women, workers, farmers, miners, a Chinese empress, a procession of young lovers in all kinds of costumes, gazing at each other in rapture. All forming queues further down the street to give their names at various police-vans further down still. Amazingly, there seem to be no wounded, although the ambulances still stand by and give first aid for shock or minor burns. Filing past Emma is a completely naked fat chinaman, and she looks away. He beams at her, at her friends, at the crowd, moving his upheld hand back and forth in majestic greeting. He doesn't seem to feel the coolness of the pale December day, but then, the heat of the fumes is rapidly warming that up. In the iceblue sky between the billows of smoke floats a little cloud, sailing North.

The last man to come out through the smoke-filled doors is another Indian prince, himself already on fire, who with all his remaining strength is dragging a heavy wooden throne from the lobby, also in flames. The firemen rush to beat the flames out of him but he shouts, My throne! My throne! They sign to a hoseman who directs his jet onto both the man and the wooden chair, flaying him to the ground with its power. Extinguished, he is put on a stretcher and carried to an ambulance, unconscious. The manager rushes to him. Thank you! Thank you! Your Majesty! It's immensely valuable. How could I have left it behind? It comes from India. It was fixed to the floor! How –

The fire chief calms him, moves him away authoritatively as he weeps. The ambulance drives off in a blue flashing. Get back there, shouts the fire chief through a megaphone. I want all of you off this street in one minute flat. The building has gotten dangerous. All of you off this street please.

The crowds look back up the three-level skyscraper as they walk away, start running and pushing as they see the sheets of flame and great panels of glass detaching themselves from the smoke and come crashing down, blocks of cement blackening and cracking. The helicopters keep buzzing around the building with their spray, but then suddenly move away all together as if giving up, or maybe to replenish.

Not to worry, it's pretty solid, says Mansell as he finally agrees to help the police by herding his little flock after the masses of people being pushed and pressed down a sidestreet. That must have been King Bhoja.

Mansell you sure surpassed yourself on the guest-list this year. Next time round I'll –

But she is almost thrown to the ground by Herzog in flight. Felipe Segundo and Mansell catch her and help her up, muttering to herself and gazing anxiously back at the flaming hotel.

Mansell looks at her. Small, sweaty, bedraggled, her mascara running down her cheeks, this is no longer Rita Humboldt, even in a crimson kaftan, especially in a crimson kaftan. He prefers her in black, or grey, or hunting pink.

Did you say if there is a next time? he asks.

It fucking grates me when you put words into my mouth, you slob.

171

I half expected the Slavic giant Sviatagor to come out of that asshole doorway, or Gulliver with a Houyhnhnm to give us Yahoos the downgrading works.

But it is not Sviatagor or any other giant, nor Gulliver with a horse that comes out. From the massive swell of smoke emerges, into the sudden silence and subsequent roar of terror and stampede of panic, twelve black-turbaned figures in white robes, holding machine-guns. Their robes are not even burning. Some twenty cops, to a man, draw. But the figures advance slowly, their machine-guns now pointing down. Behind them, four other figures, a knight in white armour, his sword held high above his head, a tall dark-faced man in saffron robes and a tonsure, a short man in a black cloak and a tall camelhair bucket-hat; and a bodhisattva all in gold, with an immensely high golden headdress made of golden faces one on top of the other, his golden hands joined upwards from horizontal forearms like an arum lily.

Rita stops in her tracks. The crowd in the sidestreet behind her, and those remaining still in the hotel street, have also halted their stampede. Even the cops shepherding them stand still for a moment and gape. Emma is caught between Felipe Segundo and Julien Sorel, much to her dismayed pleasure. She is standing just behind the little Oriental princess in crimson and sees her beckon to the iron-haired professor, who bends towards her.

Don't breathe a word, she hears her murmur in the generalised silence, but that is Gibreel Farishta.

Which one?

The bodhisattva.

Emma can't understand the last word, or even hear it properly. But the name, wasn't that the one who, according to the rumour, had caused all the trouble at the beginning? After which time she had effaced herself, except for that distressing excursion inland. She never did like excursions. Box Hill. She shudders, remembering her behaviour, so severely reprimanded by Mr Knightley, with Miss Bates.

But Rita is whispering to one of the policemen, who after a consultation with another, lets her walk back towards the burning hotel.

Get back there! shouts the fire chief through his megaphone, then stops at a sign from the policeman. Hey, you guys, he compensates to the strange group still in front of the hotel, get away from that building.

172

They don't move. No one seems to know what to do, except the firemen on their huge engines who continue to direct their jets from skyscraping ladders onto the lower floors while five helicopters are now back with their noisy hovering and silent spraying much further up. Rita's tiny crimson figure advances towards the fire chief, but ignores him and walks to the large police van and the chief of police in black and silver.

Hi princess, shouts the bodhisattva as if his very words were golden too. He has bellowed them very loud, and his voice carries over and above the whoosh of the jets and the roar of the flames, even to Emma who is shocked by this form of address.

I.D.E.M., he yells, pointing modestly to himself with his joint golden hands.

Sounds like a government department, says the iron-haired man still next to Emma, but to no one in particular.

More correctly, I should say, D.E.M. Deus Ex Machina.

Or the ghost in the machine, mutters the iron-haired man next to Emma, way back.

. Perhaps you all prefer the ghost in the machine, O Reader, O Implied Reader? loudly echoes the golden man at the hotel doors. Dear lady, aren't we all? Pray for us now and at the hour of our death. Here are other ghosts in the machine. The Non-existent Knight.

Who steps forward and waves his upheld sword.

And my friends the terrorists.

The dozen fake imams step forward to a man and bow their black turbans.

The calendar, or dervish, from the Arabian Nights.

The man in the black cloak and camelhair hat bows low, casts off his black cloak and reveals himself in his radiant white shroud of resurrection, consisting of a short destegül over a very white pleated tannur. Silently he begins to whirl, his huge skirt forming a cone. His eyes are closed under pale brown lids. He whirls and whirls round the space between the hotel doors and the ring of fire-engines and police cars. Nothing but the whoosh of jets and the rattle of helicopters is heard, forming a strange rhythmic music to his dance.

Buddhists, Moslems, Christians, all friends, shouts the bodhisattva hysterically. But here is the real D.E.M.: Milarepa. Tibetan ascetic, eighth century.

173

He steps aside and points to the saffron-robed monk, who moves forth as if on wheels, spreads his arms outwards and calls out a very long deep vowel to the universe, his bluish mouth pursed around it, his eyes closed under yellowish lids.

Suddenly there are yells and screams and shouts as the street below the feet of the crowd starts moving, tearing apart. The Hilton Hotel, although solidly built according to antiseismic regulations, is now thoroughly undermined by the raging fire and starts to sway on its foundations. Next to it on either side and all down the street, all around the packed crowd, lesser buildings rock and threaten to collapse. In five more seconds a smaller hotel on the corner does so. Then others. Clouds of dust fill the narrow street, adding to the billows of smoke. Ten more seconds later the Hilton Hotel falls, majestically, burying the entire quarter beneath its massive falling walls.

But there is no need to describe the long-expected final splitting off of coastal California from the mainland along the fatal flaw of San Andreas, it was on all the media, and is thus a historically attested fact. At least the results of it, since the media present at the time were all crushed to death, and were all fictional anyway.

San Francisco is engulfed, Santa Cruz and San Jose flung out into the ocean, which came roaring into the Bay, drowning the piled up cars, the broken girders of bridges, the high rocks and buildings that had collapsed into it. The Monterey Peninsula, the coast below it, Santa Barbara and Los Angeles are out at sea, forming a long curved island of rubble, crumbled skyscrapers, pulverised villas, universities, factories, condominiums, separated by the new inland ocean from the United States of America. Only a narrow causeway of newly leapt up rocks and giant pieces of wall at the extreme South joins this new isthmus to San Diego, left relatively unharmed – which isn't saying much.

Over this intermittent causeway engineers from all over the continent, from all over the world, have built an emergency pontoon bridge to try and save at least a few of the millions buried under the crashed buildings. The new sea further North is still too violent for emergency bridges, so that rescue by truck and ambulance has to take the long way round via San Diego, a way as long as Big Sur and Route 1, except that Big Sur and Route 1 are either in the ocean or on the new landstrip the other side. Planes cannot land on the high-piled rubble, helicopters

174

rotate back and forth endlessly for days, nights, weeks, in their own floodlights, doing what they can, lowering rescue-teams and flairhounds and doctors and nurses and emergency kits, raising the unburied dead that were flung there by the seismic force of the inner earth, and a few, very few, survivors.

18

Last night I dreamt of the Hilton Hotel in San Francisco. It was not in the centre of the city but on a small harbour, with low condominiums on each side of the European-sized bay, the one on the right made up of square black and white houses in stair-formation with slate roofs, the one on the left exactly similar but in red and white, with tiled roofs. They looked a bit like medium-sized battleships. The little bay was filled with pleasure-boats, like St Tropez. The hotel itself looked like a huge liner, but also like a cathedral, for it had a Viollet-le-Duc Gothic spire added to the flat roof of its lower portion. I wanted desperately to go in, to see what it was like inside, so as to describe things accurately, the lobby, the elevators, the downstairs bar, the restaurant-bar at the top. I wanted to count the storeys. I wanted to get it right. It seemed so different, at least outside, from the way I had imagined it. But I couldn't afford it. And yet, in the way of dreams, I found myself having a shower in one of the rooms, illegally. I needed it. Then, feeling clean and refreshed, I dried myself, dressed, came out, fortunately meeting no-one, and came down in the elevator. But it was a non-express one that only goes up to the nineteenth floor. So I couldn't count the storeys. It didn't seem high enough, in this tiny bay, to have as many as I thought, 46. Later I was with my ex-husband outside the hotel, by the toy harbour. He didn't want to stay there at all, but in a small Mexican posada on the other side of the harbour, near the red and white condominiums. I yielded of course. But that's when I woke up.

So do the rescue-teams. For after five weeks of non-stop work, long after it was officially concluded that no more victims could possibly be found alive, and the U.S. Government, and the State Government in Sacramento, barely touched, are still meeting to organise emergency housing and hospitals, to decide how to set about rebuilding, to resist or yield to speculators, and all the rest, the rescue-teams, social workers, doctors and other helpers are astonished to see innumerable people wandering the new long island of rubble. Who on earth are they? How have they got there? Why are they so strangely dressed? Why do they go around seeing only each other, as if what is left of the rescue-teams were invisible to them? Why are they all labelled? Why are they wearing walkmans in their ears?

They gather in little groups, large groups, couples. A young black woman in a callico dress and brown shawl with a thin white girl in a shabby black dress, hand in hand, like mother and daughter, happy to have found each other; a knight in shiny white armour, holding a little girl by the hand, with long fair hair held back by a blue ribbon, in a blue dress with a white pinafore; a skeletal little Chinese in rags, with a pigtail; a Mexican godlike figure in a high headdress, with a buddhist monk in a saffron robe; a lady in puritan grey with a mob-cap and a huge A embroidered in scarlet on her breast, together with a small replica, who has a smaller, darker A and more frills around her head and shoulders; a dark sallow man alone, in old-fashioned workman's clothes, sitting down in the rubble chiselling stones with great care; a small man in white like a pope; a man of heroic proportions, dressed only in a leopard skin, arm in arm with an Indian prince in a red turban and golden djoti; a tall Victorian gentleman in black and grey, with a grey top hat, holding by the hand a smaller replica in a grey stovepipe hat; a well-dressed but stern lady in grey silk, helping an old man along; a group of richly dressed princes and ladies chatting idly; an Indian girl dancer in green and yellow, her kohl-edged eyes moving right and left with her head, doing geometrical movements with her hands; an old man in a blue toga, carried on a litter by black slaves; a fat Chinese, totally naked and beatific; a dark-bearded Elizabethan all in black except for a white ruff and a golden chain; a Russian pope in black, very frail, with a thin pointed white beard; a lady in a huge peach crinoline, on the arm of a fair-haired knight in silver and blue and red, hanging on to him with upturned face and idolising eyes; a lost-looking grey-haired lady in a white dress too tight for her, with pink bows all over it; a young man with prematurely grey hair in a pudding-basin cut, wearing a crimson suit, walking between a red-haired girl in a similar suit and a dishevelled woman in a white robe; a man in a short tunic and long drape attached to one shoulder, holding a tinsel branch;

177

a large group of Viking warriors with horns; a Civil War soldier in greyish blue, with a bloody bandaged head; a mischievous youth who reminds them of Huck Finn, talking to a pretty but frightened Victorian young lady in brown, like a governess; a sickly but elegant Jewish gentleman from earlier in the century, with a black mustache, talking and taking notes as he scornfully observes a young black student who is shouting that he is not invisible; a Chinese lady in a crimson and peach robe; another Jewish fellow, with thinning hair, who sits on a boulder writing and tearing up what he writes; a middle-aged American holding a little girl by the hand and looking at her greedily; a Japanese girl in a black and blue kimono, mincing among the rubble and fanning herself violently; a little woman in hunting pink, dark and strong-jawed, talking to a young man in coat of mail, who is blowing a horn; a white-faced clerk, staring at the sea; a seaman with a wooden leg, also staring at the sea but holding on his arm a croaking parrot and apparently listening to it; an angry-looking young woman with blond hair precariously pinned up as if ready to tumble down in a cascade on her shoulders; a tall, incredibly thin man with a long nose that cuts his cadaverous face in half, waving his arms and raving at everyone; a handsome young man in a black cassock with two little white-edged bibs at the collar; a lady in a high-waisted golden dress and ivory mantle; Greek warriors, mediaeval knights, musketeers, adventurers, Japanese samurai, a tall black tribal chief; American soldiers, a young man in a hussar's green uniform, a soldier in a khaki cape with a shoebox-shaped parcel under his arm; a posse of journalists with notebooks, mikes and cameras; a sultan in midnight blue and gold, sitting on a wooden throne, listening in rapt attention to no one and falling asleep; a man in tweeds and a deerstalker, talking to an elderly eighteenth-century looking gentleman in a dark coat with upstanding red collar; an Egyptian walking in profile, holding up an invisible vase; and Laurence Olivier, dark and handsome and wild, Kirk Douglas half naked and swimming through the air with a rainbow chiffon scarf round his chest like a lifebuoy; Columbo in his creased raincoat, MacGyver young and tousled, keenly observing everyone from behind a rock, nineteenth-century doctors, curates, archbishops, ministering to all, humble clerks sitting on stones scratching at invisible documents, servants bobbing and bowing.

Innumerable they are, all over the long strip of land, talking to each

178

other, looking for each other, introducing each other as if nothing had happened.

Then vehicles appear from nowhere. Seán Connery shoots off in a super-automobile that takes wing. The little lady in hunting pink gets into a large limousine with Columbo, the well-dressed Victorian lady in grey but now in widow's weeds, and a youngish middle-aged man in a shabby nineteenth-century suit. They drive off bumpily towards San Diego. Phineas Fogg as David Niven slowly rises in a balloon. The man with a wooden leg, who looks like Gregory Peck, boards a small whaling-ship with the half-naked man who looks like Kirk Douglas and a French-looking sea-captain. A tall Indian in a purple bush-shirt and a white pajama outfit, his low-slung eyelids themselves purple with fatigue, his mouth too well-fleshed to be strong, his ears long-lobed like young knurled jackfruit, climbs up into a huge Indian Airlines jumbojet called Bostan, Flight AI420, followed slowly by an intermi-nable file of travellers. The journalists film and note everything but when the plane takes off they are caught in the air tremour and blur of its jet engines, gradually disintegrating into the rubble.

The rescue-teams, staring incredulously at these people one by one as they leave or vanish, have become readers.

Lotte gets into the landau and finds Goethe again at last. Guten Abend, meine Liebe, sagte er mit der Stimme, mit der er einst der Braut aus dem Ossian, dem Klopstock vorgelesen. Und so weiter.

Léon seizes Emma by the arm and drags her away from Lancelot, calling for a fiacre. Ah, Léon! … Vraiment … je ne sais … si je dois! … C'est très inconvenant, savez-vous? En quoi? It's done in Paris. And this phrase, like an irresistible argument, decides her.

I am not a traveller, says Lucien de Rubempré to l'Abbé Herrera, and I am too near the end of my course to take pleasure in smoking.

You are too severe on yourself. Although I am honorary canon of Toledo cathedral I allow myself a small cigar now and then.

The Gould carriage was the first to return from the harbour to the empty town. On the ancient pavement, laid out in patterns, sunk into ruts and holes, the portly Ignacio, mindful of the springs of the Parisian-built landau, had pulled up to a walk, and Decoud in his corner contemplated moodily the inner aspect of the gate.

A gloved hand appears between the curtain of a litter. Is it him? asks a woman. Show me his face. And later: Take him. But later also, on the

179

same spot near the Point of Disasters, a little black coach: Who is it? A castaway. No, a heretic. To hell with whether he is son of Allah or Moses. Kill him. That'll solve it. But they don't. They bring him into the coach, more dead than alive. Whoever you are, señor, keep still and show yourself grateful. And there begins the long monologue of Juana la Loca.

'I should like to walk a little,' says my Lady, still looking out of her window.

'Walk?' repeats Sir Leicester, in a tone of surprise.

'I should like to walk a little,' says my Lady with unmistakable distinctness. 'Please stop the carriage.'

The carriage is stopped, the affectionate man alights from the rumble, opens the door, and lets down the steps, obedient to an impatient motion of my Lady's hand. My Lady alights so quickly, and walks away so quickly, that Sir Leicester, for all his scrupulous politeness, is unable to assist her, and is left behind. A space of a minute or two has elapsed before he comes up with her. She smiles, looks very handsome, takes his arm, lounges with him for a quarter of a mile, is very much bored, and resumes her seat in the carriage.

The rattle and clatter continue through the greater part of three days, with more or less of bell-jingling and whip-cracking and more or less plunging of Centaurs and bare-backed horses. Their courtly politeness to each other, at the Hotels where they tarry, is the theme of general admiration.

The duchess lost her head completely on seeing Fabrice again; she was pressing him convulsively in her arms, and then was in despair at seeing herself covered with blood: it came from Fabrice's hands, she thought him dangerously wounded. Helped by her men, she was removing his clothes to bandage him when Ludovic, luckily nearby, forced the duchess and Fabrice into a small carriage hidden in a garden near the city-gate, and they left at full speed to cross the Po near Sacca.

Felipe Segundo gets into his coffin and watches the triptych behind the altar, which has strangely altered. Inside the diligence, the comfortable citizens all showed their contempt for Boule de Suif, clearly a girl of easy virtue. But as the heavy carriage, which had left occupied Rouen for Dieppe, advanced slowly through the snowy countryside, hunger began to nibble at them. Boule de Suif was the only one who had brought provisions. And when the carriage stopped, Augustin

Meaulnes woke from his trance to realise it had brought him into a strange domain, fairylike with festivity. But Clarissa Harlowe was horrified to find herself in a six-horse carriage with Lovelace, a man she did not love. She must write to Miss Howe about it.

The carriage continued gaily to climb the mountain road. It was a comfortable coupé with rubbered wheels, of the kind used as cabs in cities. The seats were upholstered in black velvet, but there was also something velvety about its pace, so that it moved more easily on this bad road than seemed possible, and perhaps it would have done so more silently without the panting of the horses and the clicketing of their hooves, which the velvet upholstery couldn't muffle.

Still holding his wife's hand in his, Bessian Vorpsi lent his head towards the windowpane, as if to make sure that the small town they had left half an hour earlier, the last at the foot of the Rrafsh, the high Northern plateau, had vanished from view ... It was an arid, almost uninhabited landscape they were crossing. Occasionally little drops of rain pearled upon the windows.

The Mountains of Malediction, he murmured in a slightly trembling voice, as if to salute a long-awaited apparition. He felt that the solemnity of this name impressed his wife, and was pleased.

She lent her face towards him and he breathed the scent of her neck.

Where are they?

Still very far.

She left her hand in her husband's and settled back against the velvet. The shakings of the carriage caused the newspaper that spoke of them to fall. They had bought it in the little town just before leaving. Neither of them moved to pick it up. With a little smile, she remembered the headline of the short article that announced their journey: the writer Bessian Vorpsi and his young bride to spend honeymoon on the Northern Plateau!

She herself, when her fiancé had told her of it two weeks before their marriage, had found the idea absolutely astounding. Don't be so surprised, her friends had said, if you marry an extraordinary man you must expect extraordinary things.

In fact, she felt happy. The last few days before their marriage, in the semi-artistic semi-elegant world of Tirana, their future honeymoon had been the talk of the town. Her friends envied her, saying: you will escape from the real world to the world of legends, the world of true

181

epic, so rarely found here. They evoked the oreads, the rhapsodes, the last Homeric hymns on earth, and the Kamun code of the mountaineers, ruthless but majestic ...

Much later, they saw their first mountaineers, and she was the first to catch sight of the black ribbon on the sleeve of one among them.

Yes, now I can say that we have truly entered the kingdom of death, said Bessian, without moving his eyes from the windowpane. Outside, the rain continued to fall, very fine, as if diluted in fog.

Diana tried to smile.

Yes, he went on, we have entered the kingdom of death, like Odysseus, except that Odysseus had to go down to reach it, whereas we are climbing towards it.

So that Emma found, on being escorted and followed into the second carriage by Mr Elton, that the door was to be lawfully shut on them, and that they were to have a tête-à-tête drive. It would not have been the awkwardness of a moment, it would have been rather a pleasure, previous to the suspicions of this very day; she could have talked to him of Harriet, and the three-quarters of a mile would have seemed but one. But now, she would rather it had not happened.